Small Corners in a Big City

by

Yoshimasa Ogawa

Gotham Books

30 N Gould St.
Ste. 20820, Sheridan, WY 82801
https://gothambooksinc.com/

Phone: 1 (307) 464-7800

© 2023 *Yoshimasa Ogawa*. All rights reserved.

No part of this book may be reproduced, stored in a retrieval system, or transmitted by any means without the written permission of the author.

Published by Gotham Books (October 6, 2023)

ISBN: 979-8-88775-586-1 (P)
ISBN: 979-8-88775-587-8 (E)

Because of the dynamic nature of the Internet, any web addresses or links contained in this book may have changed since publication and may no longer be valid.

The views expressed in this work are solely those of the author and do not necessarily reflect the views of the publisher, and the publisher hereby disclaims any responsibility for them.

This is a work of fiction. The names of the characters and the events in this book are fictitious. Thus, any association with an actual person or party should be regarded as a sheer coincidence.

Contents

Look Me in the Eyes   1

Coach   30

Quite a Few Cats   60

Breakup   71

Ordeal   81

See All Evil, Say No Evil   97

A Tent by the River   130

Top of the World   144

On the Sunny Side   170

Stick it Out   207

The Owner of a Castle   305

The glamorous residential towers, state-of-the-art suspension bridges, and the new Tokyo Tower—the visitors might associate the beautiful skyline with a futuristic utopia.

But in small corners of the big city, people are struggling to cope with real-life concerns and make ends meet.

Author

Look Me in the Eyes

The redevelopment of the area around Shimbashi Station was remarkable with a dozen thirty- to forty-story towers springing up in the past few years. But reminiscent of an earlier age, the space under the elevated railroad track was partitioned off into small bars and restaurants for salaried workers who needed to bridge hardworking days with a glass of beer or a cup of *sake*. At one of the drafty bars there, Masaru Kimura emptied his cup of unheated second-grade *sake* in one gulp, but a quick intake of alcohol did not lessen his misery and depression to any noticeable degree. At age thirty, he was now in possession of just enough money to order his last cup of *sake*; after that, he would be literally penniless. His pockets would be empty, and the wrinkled, stained jacket that he wore at the time was his entire wardrobe. He had not paid the rent for his one-bedroom apartment for three months and, earlier that day, had literally gotten an eviction note slapped in the face. The landlord had come to his door in person, accompanied by two heavyset men with an intimidating expression, so he knew that they meant business. His ties with his family had been morally and legally severed, so he had nothing else to lose and nobody to worry about. Neither did he have any home to return to.

A train rumbled past above his head, violently shaking the fragile structure of the bar where he was sitting. For a brief second, he imagined himself lying on the cold crossties, waiting for the heavy iron wheels of an oncoming train to run over and crush him like a tiny insect.

Masaru just did not understand why he, of all people, must be punished so cruelly and unjustly. A year before, he had lived happily with his wife and two children in a plush three-bedroom apartment in Meguro. He used to own a nice, profitable business—retailing bath and shower units or installing them in newly built houses and apartments. The sales had remained at a reasonably high level; although it did not make him a billionaire, contracts came in constantly, which enabled him to steadily expand his business and save money for his family. But then came the chance meeting with the wrong business client, and all hell broke loose. He knew that he no longer had any future at all, except for another cup of cheap, cold liquor.

"You want another *sake*?" the bartender asked in a detached tone.

"Sure," Masaru said, tossing his last coins on the counter. The bar policy required the customers to pay in cash for each cup, and he could now understand why it was important to the bar owner.

The bar was practically deserted at the time, but when he looked up, his peripheral vision caught a glimpse of the only other customer, sitting at the other end of the counter. The man was perhaps in his early or mid-thirties and had been drinking alone, picking at his baked mackerel. He had a dark skin with close-cropped hair, was about 165 centimeters tall, and looked skinny. But when he lifted his *sake* cup, his big muscular hand and thick forearm impressed Masaru as evidence of considerable physical strength.

He looks like a manual laborer, Masaru thought, whose major sport was to drink cheap sake after work at this shabby bar.

In fact, the dark-complexioned man wore a gray jacket and pants like a typical worker at a construction site, but even for a physical laborer, his big hands struck Masaru as something unusual. He twitched his narrow eyes from time to time, as if to drive off some nervous discomfort. He might have an early symptom of cataract despite his early age. Masaru felt more miserable when he had to admit that he belonged to the same socioeconomic group as people like him. To be a little more exact, he might be categorized below the man's position because he could not even afford a side order of baked fish.

The bartender tossed the cup of *sake* in front of him, spilling a little on impact. Masaru's fingers got wet when he tried to pick up the cup. *How rude*, he would have thought a year ago. But now, he was appreciative, instead, of the bartender's generosity to fill it up to the brim. He sipped it and stared into space when a whole series of unfortunate incidents flashed across his mind like a kaleidoscope—or a life review.

***

It happened a year after Masaru and Fumiko had a baby boy. It was their second child, and their daughter was already five years old. He had inherited a family business from his father, dealing in bath and shower units and their accessories. Kimura Inc. catered mostly to the well-off people who purchased plush apartments or houses in the inner city. Displayed in the front windows of his three-story office building were models of the latest products, which were, as he himself admitted, somewhat overpriced. Individual customers could walk in and purchase what they wanted, but the major source of revenue for his company was the contracts with a regular clientele, with which Masaru's father had established rapport and continued transactions in the past three decades. Of course, Masaru made his own efforts to find new regular customers, but owed his wealth and success mostly to the legacy of his father.

That morning, Masaru arrived at his office early and started skimming over a financial newspaper, killing time before his first business appointment. He heard the telephone ring, and his secretary, who had been typing some documents behind the glassed-in partition, lifted her receiver, put it on hold after speaking a few formulaic words of reception, and came around to his office.

"What is it?"

"Mr. Kimura! You have a call from a Mr. Hayakawa," she announced, poking her head around the door. "He says he wants to talk to you urgently."

"All right. I'll take it here."

The secretary transferred the call to his office, and he picked up the receiver. "Hello, Hayakawa-san. How's business?"

Hayakawa was a friendly man of about Masaru's age and the owner of a small construction company by the name of Kumatani Construction. He had himself inherited a family business from his father, who had identified his profession as a *carpenter*. Masaru had had several transactions with young Hayakawa, receiving an order of ten to twenty bath units at a time.

Hayakawa was rapidly expanding his business by capitalizing on the prosperity of the *bubble economy* and the public's tendency to buy larger houses and land areas. Moreover, with the aid of his younger brother, who had recently qualified as a first-class architect, he had just started constructing seven- or eight-story apartment buildings. When Masaru last met and talked with Hayakawa, he had hinted at the possibility of constructing a large apartment complex in the near future.

"Pretty good! We're doing very well. And I must say, today's your lucky day."

"I'm listening."

"We got a contract with a developer that wants us to build a full-scale apartment complex to the south of Ginza. It consists of five ten-story buildings and will house about four hundred families. So you know . . . ?"

"Four hundred bath and shower units?"

"Exactly. And we want them all from you."

"Oh, great! Hayakawa-san, it's just too good to be true!"

"It's nothing but the truth." Hayakawa seemed to be really excited about the new project. "And they are real luxury apartments, and we want to equip every apartment with a plush bath unit."

"I'll bring the catalogs right away."

"Please do that. The only problem is, we need them all very soon. They must be ready to be delivered and installed at once. There's another developer that is planning to make a similar housing complex in the same area, and my developer wants to have everything done very quickly."

"I understand there's been a lot of competition in that area."

"Right! And it's important for us to finish constructing the buildings, nicely furnish the rooms, and sell them on the double. The apartments will hopefully be sold out by September."

"That is, only ten months from now?"

"Exactly."

"All right. I need to make a special arrangement at once because it's a bulk order. If you tell me exactly what you need, we'll get all the fancy stuff in a week."

"Seems like we're having a deal. Can you come down to my office to discuss the details?"

"I'll be there in half an hour."

"Bring your company's seal, will you? We just cannot afford to lose a minute of time."

***

Masaru delegated his appointments to his second-in-command, named Yamada, and hurried to Hayakawa's office, where by the end of the day, the constructor and the bathunit dealer signed an official contract for four hundred bath-and-shower units plus fancy accessories.

The remaining problem was that in order to purchase the products from a manufacturer and hire extra workers to install them within the time frame, he had to loan a lump sum of money from a bank. But after all, the business climate was at the pinnacle of prosperity, and it just seemed like a reasonable risk for any entrepreneur to take. Masaru's father used to say, "Those who don't have the guts to stake their life and property on their business don't deserve the riches and more opportunities for business." Incidentally, his father, who had kept fighting as an aggressive entrepreneur, was already retired, leading a quiet life at a high-class sanatorium in the mountains.

Masaru mortgaged his new apartment—in spite of Fumiko's temporary protest—and applied for bank loans. He explained to his wife that he was not in debt in a true sense; his client was responsible for all the payments. And after the project was completed, the family would be moving into a much larger house in the suburbs.

***

Under the dim light of the bar, Masaru emptied his last cup of *sake* and bit his lips in anger and self-disgust. That moment, his eyes met the other drinker's. The man in the gray work clothes recognized it and, surprisingly, grabbed his own *sake* cup and moved over to where Masaru was sitting.

"Hey, young man! May I buy you a cup of *sake?*"

The word *young man* slightly annoyed the former president of a company. The laborer himself did not look that much older than he was. Yet in spite of his ragged appearance and abrupt introduction, the man sounded rather friendly and personable. For a brief second, Masaru even saw a bright sparkle in his eyes.

"That . . . that's very kind of you. But you know, I'm at this very moment literally penniless," the former business owner confessed to his financial destitution. "And I'm afraid I won't be able to buy you the next round."

"Oh, come on! You're broke, all right. But that doesn't mean I'm broke as you are." The laborer patted his back and laughed in good humor, baring his yellowed teeth. "My name is Sasuke."

Sasuke was a slightly unusual name for the contemporary generation of people, but it did not bother the fallen entrepreneur because he was, at the moment, preoccupied with his own personal predicament a hundred times more serious.

Masaru gave his name. Sasuke was missing two front teeth, but except for the dark vacuum where his missing teeth used to be, the alignment of his upper and lower teeth was quite regular, and there seemed to be no cavities or fillings, which was rather unusual for manual laborers who tended to be negligent in hygienic care such as brushing or flossing their teeth.

Sasuke took out a five-thousand-yen note and ordered two cups of unheated *sake*. The bartender put two filled cups on the counter at once, along with the change. Sasuke left the change on the counter instead of putting it back in his wallet, as if indicating that he would place another order soon.

"Hey," Sasuke lifted his cup and invited Masaru to clink it.

"Thanks."

"My pleasure." They both took a sip. "So, what's the matter? You look pretty bad."

It was no compliment when it came from someone whom he had just met. But Sasuke had bought him a beverage when he really needed one, and Masaru felt obligated to share part of his personal history with him. "I know I look bad. As a matter of fact, I don't think it can be any worse."

"Why don't you tell me? At least you seem to have plenty of time."

The fallen entrepreneur nodded to his new drinking buddy silently and began to recount his decline and downfall.

***

Masaru ordered four hundred bathtubs and shower units from a manufacturer and made arrangements for them to be installed in the new apartments. He hired extra contract workers to make sure that all the work was completed on time. During the period of several months that he was striving to make big time, however, the stock market crashed! At first, an economic slowdown was interpreted as a series of temporary setbacks, which would happen in any prosperous period of the nation's economy. Then, the media began to report more and more unsold houses and apartments, while the Nikkei Average took one major dip after another without any sign of an upward swing. Hayakawa called Masaru on the day that the payment for the bathtub units was due and requested an extension.

"I'm terribly sorry for all the inconveniences I'm causing you, Mr. Kimura, but the developer is having some trouble. They say some of the apartment units are still left unsold, and there have been a lot of cancellations, too. They haven't paid us the money they owe us yet."

Hayakawa explained apologetically how he was himself struggling to make ends meet. Normally, when a fancy apartment complex is put on the market in the heart of the city, the residential units would be sold out months before the construction was finished. A dozen people would apply for each unit on every floor, and only the luckiest applicants would win the lottery and move into the specific apartments that they liked. Even if the purchase of an apartment was canceled, a dozen other people were waiting to take any available unit.

"I understand your problem. But we are falling way behind on our own payment."

"Yes, I'm quite aware of that. But would you please wait for a few weeks?"

"Say, we'll wait for two weeks, but that's really all we can do."

In retrospect, Masaru realized that he should not have offered such an extension in the first place. He should have taken stricter measures to protect his own business instead of letting his silly compassion get the better of him.

"Oh, thank you so much. I really appreciate your understanding and thoughtful arrangement."

"It's all right. But please make sure to pay us in two weeks."

"We definitely will, and if the developer continues to do this unfair thing, we might hire a lawyer and pressure them to expedite their payment."

"Maybe you should, or I'd have to ask my lawyer to take action."

Again, several months later, Masaru retrospectively thought that he should have done so at that point.

Hayakawa, the constructor, never contacted him again in the next two weeks and stopped replying to Masaru's calls. It was always one of his secretaries that answered the phone, reporting in a reserved tone that Hayakawa had an urgent appointment to keep. Masaru perceived it as an ominously disturbing sign. The subcontractors had already installed the complete unit in every apartment, and it was no longer possible to take back the products or services.

"Please ask him to call me back at once, okay? He knows what it's all about."

"Yes, sir," the secretary answered in a deferential, and strangely controlled, tone.

Meanwhile, Masaru called on his high school classmate named Morita, who had studied economics at the University of Tokyo and was serving as a marketing consultant for a leading IT company. Masaru dropped by at his office and, without even inquiring about his friend's health and well-being or giving an update on his own life, asked for the expert's opinion on the recent economic climate.

"I have a serious concern. Will you help me understand how the present economic climate is likely to develop?" He recounted what had happened to him in the past few weeks.

Morita's comment was optimistic. "Well, you've got to be patient a while longer. I'm sure that the stocks will soon soar in value."

"Has the economy already bottomed out?"

"Hmm, not yet, but soon it will, and you know the principles of stock exchange, don't you?"

"Well, now, I'm not so sure if I do. You know, after all this . . ."

"It will bottom out eventually, and then the stock prices can skyrocket on the rebound. That's when you make profits. So be patient for just another month."

"All right, and thanks! Your words made me feel really relieved."

Later, Masaru was going to regret that he had not probed further or asked another expert's opinion. Besides, he was just so naive, not suspecting whether or not Hayakawa's predicament was solely derived from the developer's failure to pay for his company's service. There might have been a discrepancy between his descriptions and the construction company's real problems.

***

When Masaru returned to his office, a man from the bank from which he had borrowed money was waiting for him with a grim expression on his face. He appeared to be in his mid-thirties and was accompanied by another—somewhat older—man with weasel-like narrow eyes. The banker rebuked Masaru, the debtor, for his failure to complete the payment by reading out an officially phrased statement from his notebook, and his companion's eyes glinted behind his glasses every time Masaru responded apologetically. It seemed as if he was mentally recording every word, move, and expression as pieces of legal evidence.

"Mr. Kimura, your first installment was due thirty days ago."

"I know, but my client has been . . ."

"Your client is your problem, not ours. If you don't pay us by next week, we'll be forced to take legal action."

"Please listen. I'm supposed to collect money from my client in two weeks . . ."

"The due day has passed!"

The weasel-eyed man's presence as an observer scared Masaru more than the banker's harsh words of criticism.

"Yes, but would you please wait just two more weeks?"

"Next Monday—that's as long as we can wait, no more! If we don't find money deposited in our account by three o'clock, we'll just go ahead and do whatever we need to do." There was finality in the banker's voice.

Masaru could see that the banker was working under strict orders from his supervisor and that he would be sure to carry out what he implied as the last resort. Masaru had put his own apartment up as collateral, and if he failed to pay off the debt, the creditor would foreclose on it. If that happened, his wife, Fumiko, would be very disappointed. She would lose all her confidence in his abilities to support and protect the family and might never fully respect him again.

"I . . . I'll try."

"You'd better, Mr. Kimura. And though this is perhaps none of our business, your urgent problem is that you must pay *us* now," the banker said with a cynical smile on his lips. "And since you say you are owed a lot of money by someone else, why don't you just arrange another loan with a different monetary company?"

"But other banks wouldn't . . ."

"Well, there are different kinds of credit companies in town, too."

"You mean consumer credit companies?"

"Again, it's your problem, not ours."

***

The banker's snide remark shredded his pride to ribbons, but at the same time, Masaru had to admit that arranging another loan was the only way out of his predicament, and he was doomed to regret it as his second big mistake. The bank did not board up his private residence immediately for his failure to pay the first installment, but the next Monday, the same man with a weasel-eyed escort came back and issued the ultimatum that the bank was really going to take legal action. Masaru was ashamed of yielding to the money lender's heavy-handed tactics, but he seemed to have no alternative. For the first time in his life, he knocked on the door of an unregistered consumer-credit company, commonly known as *sarakin*, which catered to low-to-average-level salaried workers.

Until then, he had always perceived *sarakin* moneylenders simply as people who gave out small tissue packages for advertisement at the exit of a train station. He had often taken the compliments because he could use them, but he had never paid any attention to the inserted advertisement leaflet.

"What the hell! After all, it's not me who's in debt," he said aloud to himself.

He just had to bridge the span of time until Hayakawa would pay him, and there was no reason to upset his wife with his job-related problems. When he looked back afterward, it was the ultimate mistake, which he admitted was attributable to nothing but his vanity and ignorance. He was brought up in a wealthy family environment and had never had the experience of borrowing money from someone other than his parents.

Fumiko was a college beauty queen back in college. She and Masaru had various interests in common and spent a great deal of time together as university students. But he acknowledged that the Mercedes Benz that he had driven around as a student made her lean toward him as a marriage partner, as opposed to her other male friends. A woman would always seek a secure and comfortable life for herself and her children, a psychology professor had once said in class. Then, when they married, he bought a plush apartment with his parents' financial help, and they developed the habit of making two overseas sightseeing trips every year. They could still save a substantial amount of money for their children's education, and he knew that Fumiko was very proud of all the privileges. So, he just did not want to let a trivial obstacle in his business transactions tarnish his good image as a dependable wealthy husband.

***

However, as one month, two months, and three months passed, Hayakawa never showed up to pay the bills. And Masaru's own payment problems turned into a nightmare as his debt snowballed at a monthly rate of 13 percent. He started receiving a call from a dubious "contact agent" at five in the morning, who claimed that he was acting at the behest of the consumer-credit company.

"Are you playing on our patience?" the gruff, guttural voice said. "If you are, you'll be really sorry."

"No, it's not that. Please don't misunderstand! I'm really trying my best. In fact, I'm the victim of a delayed payment myself."

"It's your problem and none of ours!" The man exploded. "I'm warning you, we're really losing our patience. If you don't deposit money by three this afternoon, then we are going to come to your door and collect the money in person. You got that?"

"Y-y-yes. I'll call my client once again."

"You better do that. Huh, you have small kids, don't you?"

Shivers ran down Masaru's spine. He couldn't find a word to reply.

"I know your daughter attends Asahi Kindergarten in Shibuya."

Masaru froze at the implied message. "Please don't hurt the children."

"Then don't play on our patience. Okay?"

There was an abrupt click on the other side of the line, which scared him to death.

***

The moneylender's agent meant what he said. He actually came to Masaru's home later in the day. At nine in the evening, the time for joyous after-dinner conversations for families, the money collector banged on the door violently with his fist. "Hey, open up!"

Masaru had no choice but to obey the order when he sensed his neighbors peeping through cracked doors or pulling their curtains a few centimeters to catch a glimpse. The money collector, with a scar across his cheek, was accompanied by a young, big man of a heavyweight judo wrestler's physique, whose ears were disfigured like a cauliflower. These men were ten times more intimidating than the representatives of the bank and would not hesitate to physically hurt him and his family.

"Please understand. It's not my fault. It's my client's. I'm just waiting for him to deposit money in my account."

"I told you that it's your problem. We aren't here to hear you whine."

"Yes, I know it's my problem, but please don't raise your voice."

He knew that his wife was trembling in fear in the kitchen behind the wall. The children had just gone to bed, but they might be awakened by the belligerent voices.

Masaru tried to close the door, but the big young man—the money collector's henchman—wedged his foot under the door and kept it propped.

"Hey, what are you doing? Trying to close the door? We aren't even finished yet," the money collector raised his voice again.

"Please, don't."

"Don't what?"

"Don't torment us!" Masaru shouted, almost hysterical with a mixture of fear and anger. His earlier feeling of embarrassment that the neighbors might witness an ugly scene was now replaced with a secret desire that someone would recognize the crisis and telephone the police. "I know I owe you money, but the way you are trying to collect money is clearly a criminal offense. If you don't let go of the door, I'll call the police."

By miraculous coincidence, the wailing sound of a police vehicle was heard in the distance. The two tormentors exchanged glances with each other, and then the man with the scar turned back to Masaru once again and spat out his cursing words. "Don't ever think you can get away with this. We'll be back again unless we see the money deposited by three tomorrow afternoon. You got that? And remember that this is our last gentlemanly warning."

"Yes, I understand," Masaru replied sheepishly.

"And don't forget, you are the one who's breaking the law by not paying back the loans."

The *yakuza* gangsters left, but the moment Masaru entered the kitchen, his wife collapsed to the floor and burst into tears. "I just can't stand it anymore. Why do I have to be tortured like this? They may soon hurt the children."

"All right, all right! Just calm down! Okay? We'll soon find a solution."

"What do you mean *we*?"

"I mean, *I* will. I'll do something right away. Just trust me!"

Fumiko kept sobbing like a junior high girl despite his desperate efforts to calm her down. In fact, he had never imagined that the woman who he had thought was the most attractive and caring in the world would behave like a teenager in a crisis instead of being supportive. His own shock and disappointment were tremendous. But as far as the current situation was concerned, it was entirely his fault, and he needed to resolve the problems by himself. Then, after a few awkward moments, Fumiko suddenly stood up, went to the bedroom, and started opening her dresser and chest of drawers.

"What is it, Fumiko?" he asked, following her into the bedroom.

"What are you trying to do?"

She ignored him and started packing her suitcase.

"Come on, we've got to talk this out." He pleaded with her to sit at the dining table.

At least Fumiko agreed to sit face-to-face with him in the dining room. He struggled to talk her out of the hasty separation, putting forward a dozen different plans to ride out the crisis. But all his efforts resulted only in another uncomfortable long silence across the table. She was so upset and terrified that she just did not seem capable of any logical thinking at the moment. In fact, he was himself not sure if he could protect his family when the gangsters came back, let alone bear the humiliation of being shaken up in front of his wife and children.

Thus, he ended up resorting to the only practical way to deal with the present predicament. "All right. Let's finish packing your suitcases, and I'll drive you and the kids to your parents' place."

Masaru felt defeated and humiliated, but his sensible part dictated that the priority was to secure his wife and children's safety. Fumiko herself might come to her senses after settling down in a safe place with the children and would help him find the ultimate solution to the crisis. She might even mature through this ordeal and become more understanding.

In the meantime, he would have to deal with the debt and the gangsters on his own. Masaru dug out the handwritten leaflet from a stack of newspaper inserts:

Fixing a flooded toilet, gathering intelligence, quick transportation, or any other form of service you require.

He was in the habit of throwing mediocre ads into a trashcan without reading them, but he was now thankful that this crudely printed flyer had remained in his desk drawer—and in the back of his mind.

Quick transportation was exactly what he needed for his getaway. He must escape and go into hiding under the cover of darkness. Although he had seen such a midnight run in several TV dramas, until then, it had never occurred to him that he might turn into a fugitive himself. It was supposed to be a problem for people who belonged to some underprivileged socioeconomic groups. Now, he desperately needed to run himself using whatever means of transportation. All he wished to do was to hide in a safe and quiet place, compose himself, and work out a solution to his once-in-a-lifetime crisis. Fleeing into the night would not be a permanent solution, but it would at least enable him to buy time.

***

A month later, Masaru found himself in a small town in northern Kyushu. It was a peaceful and friendly community, which he had once visited with his university colleagues. He knew from his earlier trip that the town was fairly prosperous with fishing and timber industries, and he hoped that he would soon be able to find a job to support himself. The people in the rural area were generally kind and friendly, and the bucolic scenery and the warm and comfortable climate alleviated his fatigue, stress, and nervousness as a fugitive. He had also heard that one could even board a private ship at the local port and sail to Korea as a last resort. If worse came to worst, he might resort to the ultimate escape plan beyond the national boundary.

However, the fishermen's town was not the paradise that Masaru had perceived it to be ten years before as a sightseeing tourist. On his last trip, he had a large amount of cash in his pocket—an allowance from his father—and a Cannon camera hanging from his neck. This time, he was there to live. The first serious problem that he faced was housing. In fact, the going rate for a rental house or apartment was considerably lower there than in Tokyo, but the problem was that nobody was willing to rent an apartment to someone who had not updated his residency register, a legal obligation that he could not fulfill for safety reasons. If he registered himself as a new resident, the moneylender would track his whereabouts in no time and send the outlaw to catch him. Neither could he find full-time employment because he could not produce proper identification at a job interview.

After a few weeks of struggling, Masaru finally found a friendly local fisherman who would let him move into one of the small rooms in his detached building. The fisherman had a large house and had been using the annex as a warehouse. The same friendly fisherman also pulled strings and helped him find a temporary job at a local funeral parlor that needed an extra hand. Thus, cleaning dead bodies became Masaru's new career in the distant town of southern Japan. However, no sooner had he settled into his new home than he received a brief letter from his wife. She wanted an immediate divorce!

Masaru hurried back to Tokyo by the midnight train and visited her at her parents' home. Naturally, he made every effort to talk her out of legal separation, sitting with her until the small hours and discussing a dozen different plans to solve his financial problems. But after all, his wife was more successful in asserting her point that he should protect her and the children by severing their marital relationship at once. Otherwise, they would not only be burdened with legal obligations as the family of a bankrupt businessman but would also be exposed to the *yakuza*-affiliated debt collectors' pursuit and harassment. Originally, Masaru had hoped to return to Tokyo in a few years after saving up money to reunite with his family. Moving the family to Kyushu after finding a decent job and buying a reasonable house was another alternative. But his wife did not give him a chance to take any of the measures he had conceived. Her attitude had already irrevocably changed from that of a loving spouse to a detached person who wished to sever all relationships with the defeated man once and for all. Masaru could see that there was nothing he could do to remedy the situation.

Divorce was simply too humiliating for the former business owner, who had boasted a yearly income of thirty million yen per year. However, his last grain of pride was quickly diminishing, and he could not help but acknowledge that the best he could do to compensate for his inane mistake was to shield his wife and children from further mental anguish and physical threats. After all, it was entirely his fault and no one else's. On the other hand, now that he had lost his family as well, he was no longer sure if he had the willpower to return to his job at the funeral parlor in Kyushu. The mere thought of washing dead bodies and going home to a dark, empty apartment every night was enough to drive him insane.

With his small savings, Masaru rented a small apartment in an inconspicuous part of downtown Tokyo—the kind of residence that his former wife would never have approved as a healthy dwelling place. In despair, he frittered his remaining money away on liquor without trying hard to find a regular job, pawning his branded bags, watches, and other remaining valuables at a *shichiya* pawnshop. His small apartment was soon completely empty, except for a teakettle and his favorite coffee mug.

***

"So, you lost your wife and children, your money, and your home?"

"Yes, I lost everything. And though I hate to admit it, I didn't even have enough money to buy another cup of *sake* when you offered me one." He shrugged his shoulders and let out a long sigh of resignation.

His face was as lifeless as a wax doll, and his eyes looked like a dead fish's.

"Well, I'm so sorry to hear that. I know the economy is pretty bad, but even for that, your case has been awfully unfortunate. But you know something?"

"What?" Masaru looked up wearily.

"You've still got your healthy, strong body, and a man should never let himself look so depressed or defeated."

It was a harsh comment from a stranger—a hard straight punch in the face. Masaru was hurt and punished by the man's remark, but to his own surprise, he did not feel offended. First of all, it was nothing but the truth, and to his regret, he did not even have enough energy to blow up when insulted. He was weak and helpless. At the same time, he could calmly accept the man's candid advice when he had nothing to lose anymore.

"Hey, man, I'm telling you this because I know you're a good guy." Finding both of their cups empty, Sasuke ordered two more cups of *sake* and, then, turned back to the fallen man. "I can see you are down, but a man must uphold his dignity whatever the position he is in."

"Right," Masaru nodded obediently, although not completely clear at the moment about what his drinking buddy meant.

Another round of *sake* cups was placed in front of the two drinkers, and Sasuke motioned to his new friend to take a sip.

"Look me in the eyes," Sasuke said, leaning closer. Masaru followed his command and looked into his eyes.

"Now, do you know who I am?"

The glaring pair of eyes bore into Masaru's. The next moment, Masaru felt his eyes were going to pop out of their sockets. "You . . . you are the champion!"

Suddenly, a shabby-looking laborer in worn, gray work clothes was no longer there; sitting next to Masaru at the *sake* counter was a former featherweight boxing champion. Masaru used to watch his matches on TV when he was still active as a boxer.

Sasuke Nagata, or better known as Sasuke the Fireball, had retired after losing his sixth defending match. Masaru was not a big boxing fan, but he happened to have watched all of his six title matches, which, in itself, was a great coincidence. Sasuke was such a strong and gifted boxer that he was known to all the Japanese: young and old people, men and women, athletes or non-athletes. His sharp, strong punches and amazing ability attracted the attention of people who would not normally pay attention to contact sports. Masaru himself could not help being thrilled by the way he knocked out other strong boxers.

Masaru looked back on the former champion's past matches for a moment. If he remembered it correctly, Sasuke Nagata had lost his title some time before his own midnight run and disappeared from the media. The boxing champion not only disappeared from the boxing ring but retired from public life altogether. He never appeared on any of the variety TV shows that celebrities of his rank were often requested to participate in. Then, Masaru himself, who had turned into a fugitive after his bankruptcy, did not have much space for worrying about sports or entertainment.

"So, you are really the featherweight boxing champion?"

"I was." Sasuke corrected the tense with a mischievous grin.

"Gush! I don't believe it. I never dreamed of meeting a world champion in person."

The chance meeting with the former national hero at a small bar under the elevated tracks of a railroad was a mathematically miraculous coincidence. After a series of misfortunes and ordeals, Masaru felt that the dice that had kept showing an unfavorable number in the past several years had rewarded him with a combined score of twelve. He even felt that the spell of bad luck had finally run its course.

"Wow! Unbelievable! I always admired you as the greatest fighter." Masaru was thrilled and excited like a pre-school boy. Again, it had been his first happy surprise after his decline and downfall started.

"Thank you. But it's all in the past."

"Oh, no, no! Once a world champion, then a champion for the rest of his life. You're almost like a historical personage."

In fact, Sasuke's disappearance from public life did not entail any disgrace: he had been applauded as a legendary fighter even after losing his boxing title. The retired boxer had just secluded himself for some personal reasons and never again appeared on TV afterward.

"Thanks! It's nice of you to say so," he grinned again, showing his teeth and the dark vacuum where the two missing front teeth used to be. "But I just wanted to say something to you. It's okay to be mad and feel depressed when you are down, but you've got to uphold your pride. And more importantly, you've got to be honest with your own feelings. You aren't really *knocked out* yet, you know. You were just *knocked down* once—or maybe, twice—and can still get up and fight."

Masaru nodded silently.

"Did you happen to see my fifth defending match?" The former champion referred to the last match he had won.

"I did. It was a great match. We knew you'd gotten your back injured before the bout, and the odds were against you. But you put up a great fight and actually won it on a decision, overcoming all the disadvantages. I was really moved when the referee pronounced you the winner."

"I was lucky."

"Oh, I'm sure it was more than that."

"No, you got it wrong there," his voice was low-key but firm. "I was just very lucky. For the first time in my life, I had to admit I was simply lucky because I'd known before the match that Jose was absolutely superior. My endurance and muscle strength had considerably declined by then, and in fact, he was so good himself that I might not have beaten him even at the prime of my career. But this guy was totally out of shape that day and made several critical mistakes to wear himself out. I was kind of surprised that I ended up winning."

Masaru just nodded, trying not to take the risk of making an inappropriate comment.

"But the problem was, after that match, I did something I kept regretting and feeling ashamed of forever."

"What was that?"

"When I was interviewed after the match, I said I could take on a couple of more challengers instead of retiring. I said I was fit and confident to fight again."

Masaru remembered that there had been a rumor that the champion would most likely retire after the match. Sasuke had been injured in the previous matches and had clearly been past the prime of his career. He had himself declared to the media that he would decide whether or not he could continue to compete by carefully considering his condition, regardless of the results of the match.

"During the match, I realized I'd really reached my limits. My opponent was full of potential and far more gifted than fans and commentators might think. I was getting old, and it was time to step down and give young Japanese boxers a chance to experience big matches. I was losing my strength, and my back hurt pretty badly. I knew I was history. But when the reporter extended his microphone toward me, I was saying something I didn't mean at all." Sasuke cast his eyes down and, then, lifted and emptied his *sake* cup.

"Why . . . why do you think you did it?"

"Well, what can I say to the interviewer, after all? As a professional boxer who made a living by fighting in front of my fans, who were jubilant at my victory at the time, I really had no choice but to say I was confident that I could keep on fighting. I hated to lie, but I lied in public. I lied in front of tens of thousands of people who supported me. It was the saddest moment in my life and career."

Sasuke ordered another round of beverages for himself and his drinking mate and continued. "My manager arranged the next defending match with another boxer who was not half as good as the last one."

Masaru remembered that Sasuke had lost the next title match and retired without holding a full press conference.

"How . . . how did you feel?" Masaru ventured to ask a sensitive question.

"As a fighter, I was miserable. But as a retiring athlete, I felt good because that was the way it was," Sasuke said with a subtly sad expression, which made the fallen entrepreneur glimpse the complex and extremely difficult life that the former boxing champion had led. "But I just wanted to go away without making any excuses about my poor performance. I knew I was supposed to be gone several months before, that is, after that fifth defending match."

Then, Sasuke looked Masaru in the face and gave a wry smile. "But in your case, it's the opposite. You know, you're still very young as a businessman, if not as an athlete, and got enough strength to get up and start fighting again. You can fool others, but you can never fool yourself. I'm sure you know it." The failed businessman nodded.

"After retirement, I gave up boxing for good, and I decided to start a small business with my savings. Some TV producers invited me to appear on TV shows, but I hated the idea of being a stupid fighter-turned TV personality who clung to the past glory. I couldn't bear to expose my humiliated self. I was disgusted with myself and just wanted to do something on my own—steady and honest. I bought one two-ton truck, rented a small downtown office, and started helping people to move past midnight."

"Jesus!" Masaru was flabbergasted. "You know, I myself hired..."

"I know. The moment I saw you, you looked like one of my clients. The word *defeat* was stamped all over your face. No offense, but that was my honest impression. But anyway, ironically, I've been quite busy in the past few years since the bubble economy collapsed. You know what I mean, don't you?"

"Yes." Masaru blushed, reflecting on his own failure.

"A lot of companies and business owners went bankrupt, and they disappeared in the middle of the night, vanishing into the air. The more people run, the busier I get with new business appointments. Now, I own three trucks and was planning to buy another one soon and perhaps need someone to manage the office—someone who's more experienced than university kids I hire part-time. If you are available, I don't require any residency registration."

Masaru thought for a second and said in a low and steady tone, "Do you mind buying me another cup of *sake*?"

"I'd be glad to. Take your time and think carefully. At least you've got plenty of time to think."

Coach

"Oh, boy! It's Saturday, again!" The words popped out of our mouths at once when we stepped out of the school cafeteria. We were heading to the high school's judo studio, but our feet felt like iron clogs.

Saturday was supposed to be the best day of the week! There were class sessions only in the morning, and after that, we were all free to hang out with good friends, go to the movies, or just return home to relax. About half of the students voluntarily remained on campus after lunch and participated in extracurricular activities. In our case, we had our judo practice. Judo is a great form of physical education, and we were willing to spend a few hours every day practicing it. It was our favorite sport, after all—or had been, at least, until four months before, when Mr. Arai was appointed as our new coach. With his arrival, the high school dojo was suddenly turned into a place of torture and punishment.

Arai was a thirty-year-old *sempai* who had graduated from Asahi High twelve years before. He had a prestigious full-time job at a large insurance company, but when he was asked to be our coach last April, he made a special arrangement with his employer so that he would be excused from all duties at the company on Saturday afternoons and could coach his *kohais* at his alma mater. As it turned out, he not only had never missed a practice on Saturday but had come to dominate the judo club as the master of the dojo.

***

At one o'clock on the dot, the club members gathered in the two-hundred-mat judo studio—a rather spacious and well-equipped facility for a public high school. The participants sat in three rows: third-year students in the front row and the younger students behind them, lining up in descending order of year. The coach, or instructor, sat facing them. First, they ritualistically bowed to the altar in front and, then, toward the instructor to start the day's practice. The club's membership was also comparatively large, consisting of about thirty students. Considering the declining popularity of traditional martial arts at Japanese high schools and universities, the enrollment of about ten students in each year group was quite remarkable.

On Saturday, the practice session normally begins with twenty minutes of jogging. After a few minutes of stretching exercise inside the studio, they put on their sneakers and went out, running outside the campus. After that, in a little corner of the school playground, they went through the routine of two hundred push-ups, two hundred sit-ups, and two hundred squats, which was followed by a dozen fifty-meter dashes. Their hearts threatened to rapture time and again during the process. After this physical fitness training, they went back into the dojo to practice techniques on the mat.

The trainings that Coach Arai prescribed were modeled on an intensive plan for semiprofessional judo wrestlers. He had himself received very intensive trainings on a university judo team. The first training back in dojo included two hundred *uchikomi* (flipping one's body into the perfect position to apply his favorite throwing technique) and one hundred *nagekomi* (throwing the wrestling partner down on the mat). Then, the members proceeded to the *randori* practice. They sparred in the standing position for forty minutes and then practiced pinning techniques on the mat. All these series of trainings were carried out without a single break. When they were totally exhausted, Arai paired them up for practice matches. Those who lost the matches not only received harsh criticism from the coach but were also given dishonorable penalties such as two hundred more push-ups and the cleaning of the bathroom. Arai never failed to make the losers feel miserable and ashamed.

It was during the main *randori* practice that Arai treated the students most cruelly and savagely. Last Saturday afternoon, for example, they were engaged in a controlled form of sparring that he had devised. The wrestlers were allowed to use only leg trips or leg reaps against each other. Since the types of techniques that they could use were restricted, each move or technique had to be much sharper than in the free *randori*. Arai watched their movements with a kendo stick in his hand and yelled at anyone who either got off the mat or tried to rest behind his back.

"Move it, move it! Don't you ever stop your footwork or loosen your grip on the opponent's robe!"

A second-year student named Tanaka stumbled on his opponent's leg, losing his balance.

"Dammit! Don't you have any sense of balance or reflexes? How can you hope to win the prefectural tournament tottering like a ninety-year-old man on a cane?"

Arai never allowed students to rest or relax and demanded that they remain on the offensive all the time, even during the daily workout. He explained that the best wrestlers were able to employ sharp techniques when totally exhausted. He also proclaimed that, when he was in the dojo as the coach, his words should be taken as God's commands, and he warned students that his eyes would never miss any form of mistake or deviation. Nobody dared to protest against his policy. Under the *oni* (a legendary Japanese ogre with horns sticking out of its head) coach's supervision, they had no choice but to push themselves to their limits in every stage of the practice.

"Stick it out. Stick it out!"

Another student named Ishii made a little error and fell on the mat. I was the captain of the team, and he was one of the two sub-captains. Arai's bamboo stick whirled through the air, landing a merciless blow on his buttocks. "What are you doing, idiot?" His bamboo stick made a loud smacking sound on the fallen wrestler's back.

"Ouch!" Ishii squirmed in pain. I was sparring with a different student just a few meters away, but could clearly see his painful expression. I thought for a brief second that he might glare back or protest to the coach, but of course, he knew that it would invite another, much stronger smack of a kendo stick. He gritted his teeth and kept on wrestling.

"Keep on going! Faster!"

We fully acknowledged that it had always been our dream to win the prefectural tournament and participate in the prestigious national tournament. The Asahi High team had won second place three times (plus many third places) since its foundation thirty-five years ago. In fact, it was a tremendous achievement for a public high school that sent ten students to the University of Tokyo every year. Nobody had entered the high school on a sports scholarship. They had all studied very hard to pass the competitive entrance examination to get in Asahi and were currently studying very hard to gain admission to top-notch universities. Then, in addition to their serious academic work, the judo club members practiced judo two hours a day from Monday through Friday and three hours on Saturday. Winning second place three times in the past was evidence of the club members' serious efforts and determination.

On the other hand, Tenryu High School, the champion team in the same prefecture, was a private school that recruited gifted wrestlers from all over the country. Their judo club practiced ten times a week, and the members missed a number of class meetings every week and took it for granted because they were, after all, enrolled in the school as *judo students*. Thus, Asahi High's second place was, in a sense, as meaningful as Tenryu's predominant position in the prefectural judo league, although in a different way. However, Coach Arai perceived it differently! He aimed only for the best! From time to time, we could not help suspecting that our coach was obsessed by some demonic spirit.

"Give it all you've got and remain on the offensive! Don't give in at any moment in any position." Arai's kendo stick whirled in the air again, and somebody else screamed in pain. "What the hell! Can't you understand the simple logic I've repeated a hundred times? If you don't keep pushing, you won't gain anything."

"But, Mr. Arai," I had once attempted a protest after the practice, "we must do our mathematics and English homework and study for entrance examinations, too." As the captain, I had been receiving a great deal of peer pressure to explain to the coach that our top priority was academics, not judo.

"You know, Yoshida. It's your problem, not mine," he spat out his words. "I'm just here to teach you judo, and why should I worry about your homework? You just have to manage your time and figure out a coping strategy."

Then, he glared at me and several other teammates who stood by my side. "Tell you what, guys! Cowards always make up excuses to miss training, miss homework, or miss everything. The sissies blame their failure on something or somebody else. The first thing you need to do is to kick that bad habit!"

A few days later, however, two of the senior students who were really fed up with Arai's dictatorial behavior—and frustrated at my failure to negotiate a more reasonable club administration policy with him—confronted Arai in person. They declared that they would quit judo unless he reconsidered the way he supervised the club activities. Arai looked at them in the face for a long second and, without saying anything, made his way to the large nameplate holder on the back wall. He pulled out the two students' wooden membership plates and broke them in half before their eyes. He looked them in the eye again and said, "Now, get your asses out of this dojo. We've got some serious training to do." That was how our *oni* coach showed the club members that he meant what he said.

"Listen, kids! Yielding is the last thing to accept in dojo! You yield to hard practice, yield to a tough opponent, and yield to yourself, making up silly excuses to skip a practice or lose a match that you could actually win. Then, that's the end of your judo career or the end of your life. You've got a big goal, that is, to win the prefectural tournament, and you just keep fighting until you accomplish it."

"But, coach," I attempted another futile protest after the loss of two teammates. "I cannot help feeling it's more like your goal than ours..."

"Bullshit! That's why you keep losing. The one who looks for a way out is doomed to lose one way or another and to keep losing for life. Keep this simple logic in your head if you want to continue judo."

***

After practice, I summoned an emergency conference with the remaining senior students at a nearby McDonald's. Our school bags and the judo robes, neatly folded and tied with black belts, were tossed out on extra chairs, and we engaged in a heated discussion.

"Gee, this is just too much. I can't put up with it anymore," said Tomita, the other sub-captain.

"Me, either," Ishii agreed. "He really kicked my ass today, like the cattle on the farm. Even as a student, I want to be treated with some respect."

"What I really don't like is that he denies all our autonomous decisions. He doesn't allow us any latitude in the administration of the club. He's a coach, all right, but the club is supposed to be a student-run organization."

"Exactly! He's treating us all like preschool kids!" I concurred with my teammates on their logical analyses and apt analogies. At the same time, as captain of the team, I was frustrated at my own inability to resolve the problem on behalf of my colleagues.

"Or I feel he's using us like *shogi* pieces in order to win a game on the Japanese chessboard. It seems that he's trying to win the prefectural tournament for himself."

"Right!"

"He keeps saying that *we* will win. But he's using us to win himself a big trophy."

It had been four months since Arai was appointed as the new coach, and during that time, the team had participated in two prefectural tournaments. In the first tournament, Asahi High finished in third place and, in the second, inched up to second place, losing only to Tenryu High, the big powerhouse, three-to-zero. The fact that two Asahi students drew with Tenryu wrestlers—and the third one lost on points, not by *ippon*—surprised everybody present at the tournament because most of the other teams in the same prefecture lost five-to-zero. Many of them were slammed on the mat only a few seconds into the bout. We later found out that Tenryu did not enter the five best wrestlers, providing its alternates a chance to compete. Nonetheless, Asahi High was, in a way, gearing up for the fall tournament, which would determine the team to represent the prefecture in the national tournament. In the back of our minds, however, we all knew that it would never happen. Tenryu was indomitable; they were like professional athletes who devoted all their time and energy to judo practice, and all the members of that team had been learning judo since they were barely able to ride a bicycle. Furthermore, the more crucial point was that, even if our team won by some miracle, it would not compensate for the way our sadistic coach treated us.

"We've got to do something to stop his dictatorship."

"Right! This is our judo club, not his!"

High school students had their own values and ideas, and those who were aiming to win admission to prestigious universities might be, in a way, as opinionated as young politicians.

"I'd appreciate his trying to help the team win, but he doesn't have to hit us with a kendo stick every time we make a tiny mistake, as if we are slaves in the medieval times. It doesn't make any sense in this time and age, and it doesn't get us anywhere, except for making us humiliated and depressed."

"Right. Every time I make an error, he glares at me as if I've committed a federal crime or I'm a total imbecile. You see, I'm not a robot and can't make the perfect form with clocklike precision every time I move. Why does he have to get so mad about every little error?"

"Yeah, he gets almost hysterical during practice when we fail to follow his directions. And I hate it when he gives me a dirty look or blasts at me as if I'm a four- or five-year old who pulled stupid pranks. The other day, he pulled my ear and really slapped my forehead with his hand."

"I saw it! I couldn't believe he did it. Nowadays, even a father wouldn't do such a thing to his own son."

"Well," I hesitated, reflecting on the way my father treated me as a small child. He was a short-tempered, chauvinistic man and had often struck me with his fist when I did not behave myself. "Actually, my father did it when I was small. You know, he was like a typical farmer with no high education and didn't mind slapping his children."

"But, Yoshida, he's your real father who provides for you. Arai isn't. That's the big difference, isn't it?"

"I guess you're right!"

"Maybe we should talk to Mr. Gonda and explain how unfairly he's treating us."

Mr. Gonda, a fifty-year-old mathematics teacher, was the vice president, or head teacher, of the high school. He had himself been in the same judo club when he was a high school student a long time ago, but currently, he served as an advisor, mostly rubberstamping documents when the club participated in tournaments, black-belt-ranking promotion tests, and retreat training programs. Until a year before, he had occasionally showed up at the dojo and taught us techniques, but after appointing young Arai as the new coach, he delegated all responsibilities in dojo to him.

"Oh, I don't know. See, that's what's been bothering me. Strangely, he doesn't say anything critical about Arai. He sounds as if he's got full confidence in Arai."

"But he rarely sees him in dojo, and I think he's got a total misconception, believing Arai is a great, sensible man."

"It seems like it."

"By the way, when Coach Arai was a senior, how did the team do?"

"They finished in second place, losing in the final to Tenryu three-to-one. They didn't make it to the national tournament, but I heard they were pretty strong."

***

A few days later, two former judo-club members visited the high school dojo. It was Thursday. The two graduates, named Togawa and

Kayano, said that they happened to have a day off and decided to visit the club for the first time in three years. They were not among the *sempai*s who regularly showed up at the Saturday practice but were still fit and strong enough to spar with high school students. They taught their *kohai*s a number of effective techniques and strategies for winning a game. After practice, they took the senior students to a nearby *ramen* restaurant.

"So did you graduate from high school in the same year?" Tanaka asked the *sempai*s.

"Yes. We practiced in the same dojo every day," Togawa answered. "The practice was very hard, but now that I look back, judo practice was the greatest experience that I'd had in my high school days. I'm really glad I joined the judo club and stayed until graduation."

"Yeah, besides, we still have an excuse to come back to the school," Kayano added. "Many of my former classmates complain that they find it hard to step into the campus. They want to visit, but they feel like strangers in a strange land. They don't have a good excuse to visit the alma mater."

"Right, right. In our case, we even have our own dojo where we can either practice or sit and talk. I'm telling you, guys, you should never quit judo, no matter how hard the practice might be."

"When exactly did you graduate, sir?" I asked.

"Ten years ago."

"So, do you know Mr. Arai?"

"Yeah, He was a senior when we joined the club as freshmen. Oh, he was such a great *sempai!*" Togawa said.

"Right!" Kayano concurred. "He often treated us to *ramen* at this same restaurant, and he always took good care of us."

"But what was he like in dojo during practice?"

"Well, he was a really dedicated judo practitioner and practiced very hard. He never missed a practice, and he often remained in dojo after regular practice, training by himself or sparring with whoever he could retain."

"But what was he like as your *sempai*? Was he tough on younger members, like wielding a kendo stick or yelling at you when you performed poorly?"

"Oh, no! There was one scary *sempai* who sometimes yelled at us, but not Mr. Arai. He was a strong disciplinarian himself, but he was always kind and nice to others—particularly to us *kohais!*"

"Didn't he ever," Tomita dared to ask for confirmation after a moment's hesitation, "use any abusive language during practice?"

"Absolutely not!"

My same-year colleagues and I exchanged glances, still puzzled at the rather unexpected side of our coach that the visiting graduates described. We even suspected for a moment that the two *sempais* were mistaking someone else for our coach. Had there been another person named Aari? If not, how had he turned into such a savage man over the past decade? Suddenly, it was a big mystery to us, the current club members.

***

The end of the spring term was near. The first Saturday of July was a special day marked in the judo club's calendar. It was the last practice day for the spring semester. Although the members would resume their training soon after the final examinations to prepare for fall tournaments, they had a two-week break from practice to concentrate on their final exams. After all, Asahi High School's priority was to help its students enter prestigious universities, and the school dictated that no extracurricular activities be allowed until the final examinations were over. As was customary, the club held a little ceremonial gathering to mark the official end of the spring term, inviting its graduates to visit their alma mater and practice with their *kohai*s. After the practice, the students and graduates all sat in a circle for a little discussion session; snacks and drinks were served. Even Mr. Gonda, who was usually tied up with administrative work, managed to attend this particular meeting.

Coach Arai barked commands and guided students through the usual practice session. He dispensed with the auxiliary trainings, such as jogging and push-ups, in order to extend the practice time in dojo so that young to middle-aged graduates could participate in the *randori* sparring. As usual, he was acting extremely politely to the graduates and guests, and even in his interactions with the students, he refrained from using abusive language. But as far as the practice was concerned, he was even tougher than usual, as if trying to demonstrate his Spartan training system to the visiting graduates. Then, at the end of the practice session, he lined up students for practice matches. The students of comparable ranks and weight were matched and were ordered to face each other in the middle of the mat.

"Hey, why don't we make it students versus graduates? Just for the fun of it, you know!" Takuma, a forty-year-old graduate, suggested.

All the graduates who kept coming back to the dojo used to be strong and dedicated wrestlers back in high school. After graduation, some joined university teams to train at a semi-professional level. But for most working people, judo was now more of a means of physical fitness or a diversion from work, and a white-versus-red team competition was just like a Sunday baseball game.

"Hey, Arai-kun, will you match us up with comparable *shiai* partners?" Takuma was a father of three children and was already beginning to lose his hair on the forehead, but he still loved having a bout whenever he had a chance. It did not matter whether he would win or lose. He no longer had big muscles or quick reflexes that he had boasted of as a young man, but he was the type of man who needed to keep competing in order to demonstrate his remaining energy, strength, and masculinity.

"Well," Arai hesitated for a second. In fact, he had lined up the best students so that he could demonstrate their recent improvement in techniques. But as a typical martial arts practitioner, he would never contradict his seniors' suggestions, respecting the hierarchical order for the sake of overall organization and harmony. "I'll see what I can do, sir."

In his hand was a writing pad with a prescribed line-up printed on it; he had written it based upon his personal statistics and notes about each individual student's characteristics. But he began to consider an alternative plan. When he turned to the graduates and asked how many people were willing to compete, six volunteered, including Takuma and another man in his forties named Ishikawa. Arai took a few minutes and, on the reverse side of his line-up sheet, wrote a new set of matchups between high school students and older judo practitioners, considering their weight, experience, and current conditions. Then, he called out the contestants' names one by one, asking them to line up in a different order.

The two oldest men found themselves standing in front of freshmen who had started learning judo four months before and still wore white belts. Two men who were in their early thirties and still practiced regularly at a downtown dojo faced second-year students, and two young and strong men who had been on university teams until a few years before stood in front of two of the originally chosen contestants: Tomita and Ishii. They were the sub-captains of Asahi High and were among the best judo wrestlers of the present high school team. For them, the matches would be a serious challenge because the university graduates were far more muscular and experienced, having mastered more advanced techniques and experienced hundreds of bouts. It would be a really precious experience for Tomita and Ishii, and at the same time, the sub-captains would not be embarrassed even if they lost to such experts. Then, I was called out to fill the last slot on the students' team.

Serving as *taisho*, or the last and major contestant, was the captain's responsibility, and I was not surprised at all when called on to assume this position. What caught me unawares was that Arai put down the writing pad and asked another young graduate to take over for him as the referee. He stepped forward without an expression and joined the end of the graduates' team, standing right in front of me. Naturally, all the students were stunned at his unexpected move. If the graduates were surprised in any way, they gave no evidence.

***

The matches started in a good, festive atmosphere. The old wrestlers struggled to trip the young, white belts with their rusty leg techniques, and the latter resisted desperately and tried to counterattack, making up for their imperfect techniques with greater energy and agility. There were some comical scenes as well, such as a student's judo robe being ripped off while he was struggling to remain on the mat. All the spectators cheered for both competitors as at a Sunday baseball game. But the freshman students excelled in endurance, and the two old men burned out before the end of the game. Takuma somehow won his bout on a minor decision, but Ishikawa lost his concentration and got himself flipped out toward the end of the game. However, both graduates fully enjoyed their bouts and joked about their poor shape and lack of stamina while celebrating the new members' potential. They were just happy about having a great time and the fact that they were still able to compete with young men, while many people of their age would be out of breath after running up a flight of stairs.

The third and fourth matches were more serious than the first two matches. Their techniques and moves were more refined and effective, but neither contestant in each bout won a point. The graduates' experience and the students' better physical condition canceled out each other's advantages. The second-year students had been getting stronger in the past few months, while the two workingmen, who practiced judo twice a week, were experienced enough not to give out any openings. Furthermore, having practiced together many times at the high school dojo, they were quite familiar with each other's strategies and characteristics. After half a dozen *oh-it's-close* shouts, both the third and fourth matches ended up in a draw.

Then, the fifth and sixth matches were the most powerful and spectacular. Ishii and Tomita were in their best condition, but the graduates who had trained on university teams were twice as versatile and powerful. The two sub-captains launched an all-out offensive, respectively, but some time into the games, the *sempai* wrestlers captured a split-second opening and beat their *kohai*s by ippon.

Then, the final match! Coach Arai and I slowly made our way to the marks in the middle of the mat. It was time for a showdown at Okay Corral! Arai was twelve years older than me, but if he felt uncomfortable about the age difference, he showed no evidence at all. Unlike his usual angry face as a coach, his face was rather placid and expressionless, only his eyes glaring like a cobra waiting to jump on its prey. I myself had been, at first, flabbergasted and scared about a bout with the *oni* coach but, by then, was quite excited at the rare chance to compete with our Spartan coach one on one. I could hear my teammates cheering in chorus, expecting me to avenge them all of the tortures and pains that the coach had inflicted.

"*Hajime!*" The referee pronounced at the beginning of the bout, and we grappled with each other. The coach and I assumed the same right-hand posture, with the left hand grasping the opponent's right sleeve and the right hand on the thick lapel of the opponent's judo robe. Actually, we were about the same size and weight and even shared similar techniques and defensive-offensive strategies. I launched my all-out attack against the *oni* coach, not bothering to conceal my vengeful feelings, which soon triggered a rock concert roar in the high school judo studio. Arai himself was still in amazingly good shape for his age, although he no longer actively competed in official tournaments. He tactically blocked my best *uchimata* (inner thigh throw) and other leg techniques, returning equally fast and powerful techniques the next moment. Then, when the match was coming toward the end with neither one of us gaining an effective point, Arai took a firm grip on my *okueri* lapel behind the back of my neck and started to pull me closer to his side with enormous strength.

"Stick it out, Yoshida!" my teammates shouted in chorus. They knew that it was the position that I hated the most, and if the coach, who was familiar with every characteristic of my techniques and strategies, kept on attacking in that posture, I might loosen my grip and get dragged into a vulnerable position. "Stick it out! Stick it out," my friends rooted for me in unison.

Then, Arai pulled me really close to his right flank and tried to apply his powerful *uchimata*. I felt as if I were an animal with its leg caught in a metal trap. All my limbs were paralyzed, and oxygen was cut off from my respiratory system. The next moment, Arai began to turn his body anticlockwise, kicking his right leg all the way up to the shoulder level and reclining his torso forward. *He got me!* I thought. I would be flipped over and tossed into the air the next moment. But when I emitted an almost hysterical battle cry, my body shifted itself slightly to the right. The coach's leg missed the targeted part of my leg. Unconsciously, I was sliding my own body forward to apply an *uchimata*-reversal to counter the coach's technique. Arai's body was lifted off the mat, floated in the air, and then dropped on the mat with a heavy thud.

"*Ippon*," the referee pronounced, raising his right hand above my head. The entire studio roared with deafening applause for the moment.

"You got him!" The students went into raptures about my victory. I could not help shaking my clenched fists above my shoulders to express a triumphant feeling. I knew it was not considered good manners on the judo mat, but just could not help it. My eyes were almost filled with joyful tears.

On the other hand, Arai stood up quietly without any expression on his face, returned to his mark, and bowed to his opponent—one of his trainees—who had just beaten him by *ippon*. Then, he retreated to his position outside the mat.

A frantic jubilation continued for a few seconds, but after all, judo was an event that emphasized the spirit of courtesy and mutual respect more than techniques. The students quieted down soon, especially in the presence of two dozen graduates who had come to the dojo to offer moral support. The referee called the two teams back into the mat, ordered them to line up, and pronounced the graduate team the winner, three to two. We faced and bowed to each other for courtesy, and then faced the *shomen*, or front side, of the dojo and bowed again to conclude the matches.

***

As it was customary, the club had an informal forum after the practice session. The members sat in a circle on the mat, and some snacks and canned beverages were distributed. Another custom was that a huge pot of *shiruko*—or sweet bean soup with pieces of baked rice cakes—was prepared, and the first-year students served it in a bowl to every participant. Gonda announced that an unlimited supply of *shiruko* was available and encouraged everybody to have a second or third helping. Then, some of the alumni members made speeches, making comments on the students' techniques, the current practice system, and the way of club administration itself. As was always the case, some graduates with a sense of humor cracked funny jokes to make everybody laugh. They all commented positively on the training system designed and administered by Arai, and many of them referred to the practice matches that they had just observed, expressing their satisfaction with excellent techniques and offering advice on how to further polish them. My *uchimata*-reversal was referred to several times with nice compliments.

"It was spectacular!" several people mentioned. "And it's an extremely difficult technique to master."

Other people praised the team itself, giving credit to Coach Arai. Arai himself just nodded in response in order to show respect to the speaker but did not volunteer opinions. He had a chance to make his speech as the coach, but he only made a general report on the club's recent activities. He did not talk about his own bout, either. I was suddenly reminded of the saying that Arai often quoted during practice: *The defeated general should not talk about his strategy*. It seemed as if he was following the same lesson himself.

Then, finally, Mr. Gonda, vice president of the school, stood up and offered a few words to conclude the day's scheduled events.

"Well, I'd like to thank all the alumni members for giving up your precious time to come and support the Asahi High judo club. Please continue to drop by and give good advice to the students. If you are fit enough, please join them in *randori* practice. With your support, we'll be building up our accomplishments as one of the oldest sports clubs at Asahi High. I'm so happy that our kids are getting increasingly better and stronger. Though we shouldn't be overly optimistic, we might even be able to accomplish the big goal that Asahi High has been targeting for decades—that is, to go to the national tournament.

"As for the matches today, a lot of people have already made good comments, and I have nothing much to add. But let me take this opportunity to make a few observations as the oldest man in this group!"

Everybody perked up their ears, and so did I.

"The students' general skill levels have improved remarkably in the past four months. Yoshida's last technique was a prime example."

Subconsciously, I evaded his line of sight and cast my head down, as I had already received a series of lavish compliments from other graduates.

"But his sharp reversal technique is the tip of an iceberg, representing the advanced techniques of all members. I must say that no one could perform such a high-level technique without good training partners who are themselves trying hard to master finer, more powerful techniques. Good defensive and offensive moves coalesce to produce that kind of quick, subtle coordination, and the entire group deserves credit for it. The combination of mutual support and rivalry among the club members is indispensable. And again, I'm appreciative of all the people who are here to help them. This club is advancing on the strength of organization.

"Another important point is the coalescence of spirit and physical movement. When it comes to a big tournament—or the crucial moment for either winning or losing in real life—what really determines the winner is one's strong inner desire. This is what a lot of young people today tend to lack. Techniques are important, and physical strength is also indispensable. But what really counts is the exertion of mental energy at the critical moment. You need to learn to control your own mental state in a crisis, and it isn't as easy a task as it might sound. When you are studying a new technique or strategy, you ought to engage calmly in analytical thinking. When you are engaged in intensive *randori* practice, you rely on muscle-visual coordination and automatized movement instead of consciously deploying a strategy. Then, in a bout, you must empty your mind and let your instincts drive you. In order to flip the opponent over on the mat at the crucial moment, you need to exert all your mental, physical, and emotional energy at once. You must have a sort of hysteria to administer coup de grace to your enemy, and it takes a lot of arduous training and determination to exert such power.

"Again, I must acknowledge that Yoshida's reversal technique was a rare accomplishment." Semantically, the sentence was a repetition of what he and several other graduates had already said, but the purposely lowered tone seemed to suggest that he was trying to communicate a different message. After a brief pause, the vice president of Asahi High School added, "I would say it was almost comparable to the unique *sasae-tsurikomiashi* that Arai had beaten all his opponents with in his last high school tournament." *Sasaetsurikomi-ashi* is a leg trip by extending the sole of one's foot in front of the opponent's ankle.

That moment, my downcast head jerked up, and I could not help shifting my line of sight quickly to the speaker's face and then to Coach

Arai. In fact, I could not analytically comprehend the true meaning of Gonda's comment at once but intuitively knew that the head teacher's statement implied that something was wrong with what I had taken for granted until that moment. I strove not to betray my inner feelings. To my relief, none of my teammates seemed to notice the beads of sweat trickling down my temples.

***

We had a two-week break from judo practice to concentrate on our final examinations. During that time, a rumor was going around that Arai might resign his position as the coach after his "humiliating defeat" to the team captain. Ishii and another senior student even bet money on the arrival of a new coach after the exam season.

"He'd been behaving like a dictator and, then, lost a bout to a student," Ishii said while we were walking down the hallway, heading to the classrooms for elective courses. Ishii was taking French, and I was enrolled in the Japanese history course. "You know, he's an arrogant man, and his bruised ego wouldn't allow him to show up again as coach."

"Well," I hesitated to make any comment on that observation. "I don't know. He might or might not."

Mr. Gonda's speech flashed back to my mind. A thought had been nagging at me ever since: there might be a clear difference between what we thought as students and what the teacher and graduates perceived those practice matches as. I could not clearly define the concept yet, but tried not to let it distract myself any further when I had a few more final examinations to finish.

"Hey, is anything the matter, Yoshida? You are sort of quiet."

"Oh, well! I . . . just didn't get to sleep much last night. I was worried about the results of the math exam, you know!"

We reached the classroom where Ishii was going to take the final examination on French. I was going to go farther down to a classroom at the end of the hallway.

"Good luck on your French."

"Thanks, And good luck on your history!"

Then, I proceeded all the way down to the end of the hallway. Across the corridor from my classroom was Mr. Gonda's office. The door happened to be open, and I could see that he was just sitting by himself, not meeting with any other teacher or a visitor. By sheer coincidence, he looked my way, and our eyes met. "Hey, Yoshida, what are you up to?"

"I have a history examination, sir." In fact, I was about ten minutes early for the test, and Mr. Gonda seemed to notice it, too.

"Come on in for a second." He motioned for me to enter his office so that we could exchange a few words.

Gonda suggested that I pull up a chair and sit down. "I know your test is coming up in ten minutes, so I won't keep you long." And of course, Vice President Gonda had important businesses and serious commitments himself. "But we can talk for a few minutes, I guess."

"Yes, sir."

"How's everything at the judo club?"

"Very well, sir." Voicing the other members' concern over Coach Arai's coaching policies flashed across my mind, but instead, I straightforwardly asked one question that I had been anxious to ask.

"Mr. Gonda, I've heard that Mr. Arai and the other *sempais* in his year-group were pretty strong. I was always wondering how they did in their last fall tournament."

"Uh-huh," he allowed a knowing smile. He took out a cigarette, lit it, and inhaled deeply on it before he started recounting the event twelve years before.

"In those days, I was younger myself and used to work out with students all the time. And I must tell you that Arai and his colleagues had been one of the best teams in Asahi High's judo history. They were devoted to their practice, and they were determined to accomplish their goals. And yes, I remember their last tournament very well."

"What was it like?"

"Up to the semifinal, all the five members performed superbly, beating most of the opponents by *ippon*. Then, they confronted the indomitable champion team of Tenryu in the final. When Tenryu and Asai teams lined up, facing each other, everybody was struck by the difference between the two teams' physical sizes. All Tenryu wrestlers were over one hundred kilograms and had the physique of intercollegiate contestants. Three of them were more than 130, and two guys were 190 centimeters tall. On the other hand, Asahi students were all sixty to seventy kilos and around 170 centimeters. It looked like a match between an adults' team and a children's team, and people in the Tenryu camp clearly perceived it that way, too. Though it was the final, the Tenryu guys were laughing and talking to each other with relaxed expressions. Asahi students were, of course, all tense and nervous, like a farmer facing a bear with only a bamboo stick in his hand.

"But when the first bout started, the atmosphere changed a little. The first Tenryu wrestler tried to use his powerful *haraigoshi* hip throw to finish the match at once, but the Asahi student, named Yamada, somehow blocked it and struggled to defend himself, desperately moving right and left. In fact, he had amazing agility. The Tenryu wrestler applied his technique time and again, but he could not capture small Yamada easily. His face flushed in anger and frustration, and his attack became increasingly fierce and relentless. Three minutes into the match, the Tenryu boy's *osotogari* (the major outer leg reap) finally got Yamada and knocked him down on the mat, but Yamada's strong resistance impressed many of the spectators. Some Tenryu graduates were yelling angrily at their *kohai*'s failure to beat the public high school student in a short time.

"The second match went in very much the same, which further irritated the Tenryu camp. Toda was our second wrestler, and he clung to the big opponent like a leech, not allowing him to apply his favorite technique in a perfect form. Again, the Tenryu member's overall physical power and techniques overwhelmed Toda, and the bout resulted in an *ippon* for Tenryu. The third match was more or less the same. Asahi's Yamazaki put up a good fight, but after all, the Tenryu wrestler had twenty times more experience, and he overpowered and defeated Yamazaki by *ippon*. At this point, Tenryu had won three out of the five bouts and was already the winning team, but the remaining two pairs of wrestlers were given chances to compete.

"Then, there was a big surprise. About a minute into the bout, Asahi's fourth member, Okamoto, earned a *waza-ari* with his sharp minor inner reap, capturing a split-second opening. The audience roared with a mixture of shock and applause. The Tenryu wrestler, who'd lost a point, turned into a raging bull and started an all-out attack. He tried frantically to pull Okamoto to his side so that he could apply his *uchimata* or *hanegoshi* and, in the process, accidentally hit Okamoto's head strongly. Okamoto started bleeding out of his nose. He also clutched at his right middle finger with a painful expression. A volunteer tournament doctor stopped his nose bleeding but said Okamoto might have a broken finger. But Okamoto insisted that he was able to continue. The bout resumed, and he somehow kept defending himself, but toward the end of the match, the Tenryu wrestler earned his *waza-ari* point, using his leg sweep to make the scores even. Three seconds after the match resumed, the buzzer sounded to end the fourth bout in a draw, setting off an uproar among the spectators.

"Then, the final bout was between Arai and the Tenryu captain, a 130-kilo regional champion. Arai stood up, exchanged glances with his injured teammate who'd just drawn against a Tenryu wrestler, and advanced toward the 130-kilogram *taisho* wrestler. I recognized a strange mixture of determination and desperation in his expression—it almost looked like a sort of hysteria."

I remembered that Mr. Gonda had used the word *hysteria* in his speech at the forum.

"Then, a fierce battle began. Arai kept moving right and left and used a dozen different leg techniques to break the gigantic opponent's balance. The big Tenryu guy didn't stagger, but Arai's tactic was effective in confusing and distracting his opponent's concentration. Then, half way through the bout, he captured a split-second chance and made the opponent lean widely to his left-front—like a big heavy man tripping over an invisible object in the dark. Arai started to apply his *uchimata* but, then, feeling a strong resistance, turned his body 180 degrees clockwise to apply his favorite *sasae-tsurikomiashi*. The big opponent staggered and sank to the mat with a heavy thud. The referee pronounced *ippon*. It was a big surprise to all the spectators, which was followed by another shocking fact. The Tenryu wrestler could not rise to his feet again. He had a strong concussion and, as the tournament doctor reported, had broken his left knee."

"Is that right?" I was almost terrified by my *sempai*'s big accomplishment.

"Yes. By the way, right after the referee pronounced *ippon*, one of the two corner judges raised his flags over his head and requested a conference. The referee motioned him and the other judge to meet in the middle of the mat. The first judge voiced his concern that Arai might have extended his foot at an unusual angle and kicked the opponent's knee with his heel." A competitor would be penalized if he injured the opponent on purpose. "I could understand the judge's suspicion because it was a really big upset and he probably wanted to make sure about everything. But they decided after all that Arai's technique was effective and perfectly legal and appropriate. The judges returned to their positions, and the referee affirmed his earlier judgment. Arai scored the first win against a Tenryu wrestler. Asahi High could not sink the indomitable battleship, but one Zero Fighter that crashed into it made a big hole right in the middle of its hull."

After a pause, Gonda added his short personal comment. "I was moved and felt I had learned a lesson from the young man. Arai wasn't big. He didn't have unusually good athletic gifts, either. He just kept practicing day after day after day and, when placed in a crisis, emptied his mind and took on the indomitable opponent without a shred of hesitation. He was a role model for all the younger judo club members. At that point, I decided to ask him to succeed me as head coach as soon as he graduated from university and settled into his professional career."

***

Two weeks later, when we stood in the dojo's doorway, we found ourselves looking at the stern face of the same *oni* coach. And of course, a bamboo stick was in his hand.

"What are you guys doing, staring into space like a bunch of stupid monkeys? Can't you see that practice is going to begin in five minutes?" He barked when we were hesitating. "Hurry up and get your *dogi* on, or I'll kick your asses out of my dojo." So it was still *his* dojo after all.

"Yes, sir. We'll get changed in a minute," I responded at once, more positive than apologetic. Ishii and Tomita were a little taken aback, but they followed me as if on a telepathic cue.

I had not yet told my teammates about my conversation with Gonda. I intended to do so afterward, but wanted to reflect more deeply on it myself. Strangely, however, the two sub-captains seemed to have somehow realized that the Spartan coach deserved more respect than they had earlier assumed.

As Mr. Gonda had said at the club forum in July, Arai had a very sharp *uchimata* and had a special tactic of alternately using it and his powerful *sasae-tsurikomo-ashi*—the leg trip in the reverse direction. He had slammed many big wrestlers down on the mat when he was a high school or university student. During the practice match with me, he could have easily gotten me down on the mat by switching the direction of his movement by 180 degrees at the crucial moment. Why didn't he do that? Had he lost his feel in ten years' time so that he could not actually perform it? I doubted it because he sparred with us all the time and always demonstrated his physical strength and agility. One thing I had learned then was that we were always protected, even though Arai wielded his kendo stick and verbally abused us. Bamboo sticks would not break our legs or crack our ribs.

After the practice that afternoon, I shared Mr. Gonda's story with my teammates. The club members then stopped complaining about Arai's administrative policies. For the first time, we learned a lesson without a lecture or the use of a kendo stick: Arai was not a student like us. He was a coach, who worked hard as a professional working man on weekdays at a large corporation. And he was also an educator—a totally dedicated educator. Most of the graduates who had been present at the last practice session for the spring must have appreciated the practice matches from Mr. Gonda's perspective, instead of simply paying attention to wins and losses. Suddenly, the Spartan coach was no longer just a weekend instructor who had volunteered to teach techniques. He was a man with an enormous willpower who volunteered to share his insight to the way of life with his *kohai*s.

Quite a Few Cats

A propeller passenger plane landed on a bumpy runway at Kuh-kuh-kuh International Airport. The city of Kuh-kuh-kuh was across the border from the southern part of China. People spoke a tone language with a complex syntax and wore unique clothes that represented a mixture of several different Asian cultures. However, the life in his hometown was nothing but quiet and eventless. The airport was categorized as an international airport only because there were three weekly flights back and forth to a Chinese airport, where Gnahito Txibdhuzz had just transferred from a Boeing 747 to a propeller plane. The airplane taxied to a disembarkation mark and stopped, and Gnahito descended a universal step onto the tarmac, rubbing his sleepy eyes. Exhausted from his eight-hour flight from Tokyo, he could not help a mixed feeling of relief and depression when he arrived in his homeland. It was his first return trip to his home in almost four years.

Since he started living in Japan, Gnahito's life in Tokyo had been mostly comfortable and satisfactory. He attended Toto Gakuen University on an athletic scholarship and was accommodated in a small but nice and comfortable single room at the university's dormitory located near the campus. The city life was full of excitement, and as a gifted long-distance runner, he had been treated almost like a celebrity. He had participated in several televised marathon relays and made a major contribution to the team's victory and to the advertisement of the school that was known more for its athletic and cultural achievements than academic standards. He had made many good friends, including both classmates and track-and-field-events teammates, and had learned to speak Japanese fluently enough to cope with all real-life communicative situations. He was seriously considering the option of living in Japan permanently if he could find a decent job to support himself after graduation.

However, foreigners always had their own disadvantages and difficulties to deal with, whatever privileged positions they might be in, and life was not all rosy for the star long distance runner. Written Japanese was extremely complex and difficult, and he had to rely on his teachers' and tutors' personal favors to complete all the required courses in four years. From time to time, he received subtle insinuations for being a foreigner, although not outright racial discrimination. He was a tough man and could ignore such unfriendly gestures. However, leaving aside such general problems, what really hurt him was that his position as a star athlete itself did not seem secure anymore. He had injured his knee before the year-end marathon relay of the previous year and had run in poor condition. As he failed to achieve his best time, the team missed the championship. Despite all his major contributions in the past intercollegiate races, his failure in this particular race disappointed the university administration and the supporters tremendously. Then, gone with the lost race was an employment offer from one of the sponsors of the team, a major food products company. His coach explained that the prospective employer had every legal right to take back an unofficial appointment at the last moment when the candidate did not satisfy any of the conditions agreed upon. The twenty-two-year-old athlete deeply resented the unfairness and absurdity of the Japanese company's personnel administration policy, but there was nothing he, or anybody, could do about it.

To add insult to injury, his engagement with his Japanese girlfriend was suddenly at stake because of her family's objection, which was never fully explained to him in plain language. He had been in Japan for almost four years but had never fully understood the inscrutable psychology of the Japanese. It was beginning to destroy his strong pro-Japanese feeling. He had decided to return home, believing it would give him a chance to stand back and reflect on his own position from a different perspective. Although the fresh air and the sight of huge open space back in his homeland soothed his hurt feeling to a considerable extent, he was still bound in a painful dilemma pending his personal and professional future.

His elder brother, Gnachubi, was waiting at the foot of the universal step. At the countryside airport, which looked like a rural high school's baseball ground, people could freely enter and exit the compound without going through a metal detector or the security gates. There had never been a single case of terrorism recorded in the history of this international airport or the city of Kuh-kuh-kuh itself. Therefore, the airport or the government found no reason to invest a large amount of money to install a high-security system or post guards in or around the airport. Gnachubi picked up Gnahito's suitcases and started guiding him toward the family vehicle.

"Did you sleep well last night?" asked Gnachubi. He was not necessarily concerned about whether or not his younger brother had slept comfortably during the flight. It was just a customary phrase that all in their tribe used when they met their blood kin after a long absence—a minor but rigid sociolinguistic rule.

"I certainly did, Elder Brother." In fact, Gnahito had not slept a wink, but again, it was a customary, formulaic phrase to use in reply.

"Good. Now, let's go home. Everybody's waiting for your return." Gnachubi was the second eldest son in the Txibdhuzz family. The social customs dictated that the father and the eldest son in a family wait at home; the role of picking up Gnahito was automatically delegated to the second son.

An ox-driven cart had been parked right outside the main entrance of the airport. Gnachubi deftly loosened the tethered animal and turned the ox and cart around so that his younger brother could climb into the backseat. Then, he started rolling the cart gently; he neither offered more words nor tried to inquire about his brother's experiences abroad during their ride home. When a young man returned from a foreign land, the other members of his family were supposed to offer him a period of tranquility so that he could adjust to the old scenery and customs, that is, unless there was an urgent message to convey. The fact that the elder brother remained silent assured Gnahito that everything was fine back home and all the family members were in good health and spirits.

The official excuse for Gnahito's return home was to attend the memorial service for a distant relative who had drowned in a river while trying to catch a Prussian carp. When fishing by himself, he slipped on the bank of the river and hit the back of his head on a hard rock. When his neighbors found him, he had been submerged in the water unconscious for over an hour. They did not even bother to take him to a hospital beyond the mountain range because the village chief confirmed his death on the spot. In Gnahito's country, the chief of each village had the legal right to pronounce a diseased or wounded person dead, not a medical doctor or a coroner. The tragic news had already been reported in a letter mailed to Gnahito a week before, and there was no need to dwell on the issue during the ride.

Their house was about ten kilometers from the airport. The two brothers drove along the straight dirt road in the desert, and when they came to a fork, what looked like a huge, fat lion was lying on its side with its massive body blocking the passage to the left-hand fork that led to their home.

"Jesus!" Gnahito gasped in shocked disbelief.

It was a total mystery that the region was inhabited by any lions, even if there was a remote chance that tigers might sneak in from a neighboring Asian country. Nonetheless, it looked like a full-sized African lion with a thick mane. At the moment, the animal was facing the other way with its back turned to the two brothers, but Gnahito froze in absolute terror, taking in the huge size of the lion prostrate in the middle of the road.

Gnachubi slowly craned his head to his brother in the back passenger seat and ran his index finger across his lips. "Shh! The animal is sleeping, and it seems like its stomach is full. We'll just ride past it quietly, and there'll be no problem."

There was no scientific evidence that lions could live there, but about ten years before, when Gnahito was still a ten-year-old boy, he had once sighted a lion-like animal at the foot of the nearest mountain. He was with several other children of his age, and they were about a kilometer away from the animal. Everybody in that area had amazingly good vision, and young Gnahito and his friends could instantly identify it as a large wild cat from the distance. They stole away and escaped into a nearby house without attracting its attention. But he vividly remembered the traumatic experience of sighting a predatory animal. Then, nobody else had encountered a *lion* ever since, and he and his playmates soon began to suspect that their sighting might have been an isolated incident, if not an optical illusion. However, now that he had seen it for the second time as an adult, there was no doubt that lions lived in their land. He was now looking at the animal at much closer range. The lion lying in front of him appeared to be twice as large as the first one that he had sighted as a small child.

"We must make a detour, though."

Gnachubi tugged at the ropes and drove the ox to slowly change the direction. Gnahito, a gifted athlete who had demonstrated his valor and strong willpower in big field-and-track events, could not help cringing at the possibility of a fatal mishap. His body stiffened like an iron rod, and he stopped breathing for a long second.

The ox cart swung to the right, its rear left wheel almost brushing the lion's tail, and rattled on. The two brothers took the right-hand fork and headed home along a long way around. Naturally, neither man tried to speak while they were pulling away from the lion. To their relief, the ox did not bellow, obviously registering the presence of a predator in its own way. When the cart was about five hundred meters down the road, Gnahito finally opened his mouth. "Old Brother, has it often happened here recently?"

"Yes! The cats seemed to have suddenly multiplied in the last three years. They suddenly came from nowhere and started breeding. It happened soon after you left for Japan. Now, its population is finally leveling out, but there are more than enough lions to intimidate us all. And as a matter of fact, I saw three of them during my ride to the airport earlier today. Scientists say the general environment in this area is fit for their habitation."

"Jesus Christ! I'm glad you weren't hurt." Gnahito did not use the word *killed*, but had his brother lost his life when he was on his way to pick him up, he would have felt guilty for the rest of his life.

"I was all right, so don't worry."

"And I was just wondering . . ." Gnahito hesitated to voice his immediate concern.

"We may run into a few more lions," his elder brother read his mind, "but at this time of day, they are usually taking a nap after dining on rabbits or boars. At least, we know that much. We just got to be careful not to run over their limbs or tails stretched out on the road." The brother's words did not sound as reassuring in Gnahito's ears as they were clearly meant to be. The Txibdhuzz family was not the richest in their tribe but, at least, had enough land for all the five children. If Gnahito decided to settle in his hometown, which he had been seriously considering during his flight home, his father would probably give him a plot of land to build a house and start a small ranch. But the huge lion that appeared in front of him had shattered his idea of a peaceful, comfortable life back home—an alternative plan that he was considering in case his life in Tokyo did not work out.

"But how on earth do people handle this? Women need to go to the markets every day, don't they?"

"Yes."

"And children must walk a long way back and forth to school."

"Well, it takes some precaution, but you'll get used to it. You'll get used to this kind of environment after living here for a while."

Gnahito pondered his brother's words for a moment. "It seems pretty dangerous to me!"

"But you know something, Gnahito? You have so many automobiles in Tokyo or elsewhere in Japan. We've been really worried about you. I hear that several serious traffic accidents occur every minute and quite a few people are killed or seriously wounded—crushed, flipped up into the air, or run over by those monstrous chunks of metal on wheels." Gnahito did not come up with an apt comment in reply.

"Furthermore, I hear you use a thing called an elevator in tall buildings where you live, work, or study, that can crash any minute! And in the winter, one type of flu sets in after another and goes around in the city. It can make hundreds of thousands of people sick in a matter of a few days while a lion can maul only one or two men at a time. Then, those airplanes! When a plane crashes, though they say it happens very rarely, there's absolutely no chance of survival. I was watching a TV documentary the other day, and the reporter said that in the past twenty years, there have been 150 airplane crashes involving more than a hundred victims each. As the number of flights is rapidly increasing, soon there'll be a dead passenger every nine minutes. Brother, it looks like a real jungle out there where you've been living for the past four years. We've all been really worried about your wellbeing. Compared to the place where you've been, our village is a hundred times safer."

Then, Gnachubi stopped talking, as if embarrassed at his verbosity. After all, it was his younger brother's first return home in four years. He was supposed to give him peace of mind and time for adjustment.

"How many wild lions do you have here?"

"We estimate it to be forty, give or take four or five." In the small city of only one thousand six hundred people, it was one lion for forty people.

Then, Gnahito hesitantly asked the question that he had been anxious—and afraid—to ask: "Has anybody been mauled or bitten to death by a wild lion?"

"Just one!"

So there was a casualty. Even if they might become accustomed to it, there was no foolproof preventive measure against ferocious lions after all.

"We have statistical data to show that there are enough wild animals that lions might feed on for the next twenty years, that is, unless the lions suddenly start multiplying at an unexpectedly higher rate. Animals like boars, deer, and stray dogs aren't intelligent enough to detect and avoid the predators strategically like we humans do. Besides, we now have an advanced course in lifeguard and self-protection, teaching our kids how to predict the appearance of a lion or determine if a lion is hungry."

Gnahito's home county had only one college-level institution, which enrolled about eighty students at a time. All the teachers at the primary and high schools were graduates of that college, and he could tell that their *advanced* lifeguard course was not as advanced as rocket science or quantum physics. But he did not make any comment on his brother's observation.

"And there are several shelters every two kilometers down the road in case you encounter lions when you are outside." People in Kuh-kuh-kuh were generally fast runners, as evidenced by the fact that the city had generated several world-class runners like Gnahito. But running for two kilometers, chased by a lion, was frightening enough a picture.

"There's one over there," Gnachubi pointed his finger at a yellow dome-like metal entrance to an underground shelter. It was about two meters in diameter and had a small transparent shield set in the upper half so that people inside could peer through it at a predator.

"But you know, talking about statistics, I read somewhere that the number of people who are killed in airplane crashes is actually smaller than the number of people who get kicked to death by donkeys in the world. And these wild cats are much more dangerous than donkeys."

"Yeah, but we aren't stupid enough to try to ride on a lion's back while some people in mountainous regions might use donkeys for transportation. Oh, here we go again!"

About a kilometer ahead, Gnahito recognized a speck of object, which, a few seconds later, turned out to be another lion sprawled on the road. His brother made it out more quickly than he did, suggesting that Gnahito's vision might have deteriorated during his life in the city. The shocking realization struck him: "a blind man is more vulnerable to a snake's bite." People with weaker vision were more likely to fall victim to a lion's assault.

Gnachubi did not even try to stop the cart this time; he slowed down but continued to drive past the lion.

"Are we going to be okay?" Gnahito asked in a feeble whisper.

"I hope so. And as a matter of fact, we don't have much of a choice anyway because this isn't a fork. It's a one-way road, and there is no alternative route."

As they approached the lion, beads of cold sweat rolled down Gnahito's temples, and he started trembling out of uncontrollable fear. The lion was not lying right in the middle of the road; it was near the left-side curb. But this time, the animal's head was facing them, and its half-open eyes groggily stared at them. Gnachubi himself sensed a great degree of danger and was white as a sheet. It was then that an old woman, most likely in her eighties, came from the other direction, walking slowly with a cane as support. She did not stop!

She kept on walking in very short strides and tried to hop over the lion's paw tossed out in front of her. She almost lost her balance on landing and staggered! The two brothers held their breath, but she somehow regained her balance and continued to walk past the lion. When the ox cart came close to her, she looked up, smiled with a benevolent expression, and offered what Gnachubi later referred to as a new formulaic greeting: "Boys, there've been quite a few cats these days."

She walked slowly away from the site without turning back again.

Breakup

It was two in the afternoon, and Prelude, a French restaurant where workers at companies nearby had lunch, was now deserted and very quiet. Soft classical music, played for an aesthetic ambiance, accentuated the absence of a crowd. Takeshi and Mayumi sat face-to-face across a small table by the window where none of the other remaining customers was within earshot of their conversation.

"So you know, that's how it happened," said Takeshi in a level tone, showing no perturbed expression on his face. For a brief second, Mayumi even thought that she saw a smile on his lips. "Please don't take it personal, okay, because, after all, it's just human nature, and there was no helping it."

His brief concluding remark, after an explanation about his new girlfriend, insulted her for the second time. *What is more personal than breaking off our engagement to marry another woman?* Mayumi wanted to scream. Then, she did not appreciate his reference to human nature, either, because the expression he used was not only audacious but trite and bland. He could have, at least, prepared a better excuse to break the engagement in order not to hurt her; the reference to *human nature* was hilarious. To her own surprise, however, she was not as angry as she or any other woman in the same situation might be. Although she was indignant at his selfish decision to abandon her and marry a daughter of the director of the department where they both worked, she strangely was not really upset about the unexpected ending. None of the hysterical emotions that movie actresses demonstrated after a melodramatic breakup seized her. *Just like that?* She accepted her ex-boyfriend's words matter-of-factly, perceiving her position as more comical than miserable or tragic.

The two had dated for two years after they started working together in the sales department of Kakubeni Trading Incorporation. Takeshi was three years older than Mayumi, and no sooner had she joined the same department as a new recruit than he started approaching her. With her white complexion, intricately chiseled facial features, and perfect proportions, she attracted all men in the same department, but he made the move before any of his male colleagues had a chance to exchange words with her. First, he initiated a friendly conversation with her on work-related issues and, then, picked up personal topics. Soon, he started inviting her to lunches, dinners, movies, and midnight drives when she was still in the process of adapting to the new work environment. A few months later, he was already expressing his serious desire to marry her, saying that he would not consider any other woman in the world. Her family and close friends advised her to wait and observe his habits and personality characteristics over time, but after his repeated proposal, she agreed to spend the rest of her life with him.

Mayumi was a friendly, flexible type of person, but the older and more experienced people around her had detected a sign of precariousness in her boyfriend's behavior. Her father claimed that he lacked a sense of responsibility after he took her out for a drive and did not bring her home before the time agreed upon. Her mother advised her to take a longer time and carefully consider all possible consequences before making her final decision. Mayumi acknowledged herself that Takeshi had a childish and unpredictable side as many people pointed out. But she accepted his proposal after all because he kept asking her passionately to marry him day after day after day. Mayumi, who was the eldest of three sisters and had been taking care of her younger sisters, could not reject the man who expressed his strong affection for, and a feeling of dependence on, her.

Then, this afternoon, the same man who had literally begged her to marry him suddenly terminated their relationship unilaterally in order to marry his supervisor's daughter: just like changing his order at the restaurant from coffee to iced tea.

"You know, we just fell in love, which was totally unexpected. But before that, I really cared for you and didn't think about anybody else. So please believe me."

His referring to his new fiancée and himself as *we* annoyed her. But she did not bother to respond because there was no sense expecting a person who lived in his own heavens to be sensible.

"It's just that I met this person, and I'm now really convinced we've been tied to each other by a magical *red thread* of destiny."

How romantic, she thought. His selfishness to dump her after two years of dating was unforgivable in the first place, and he was even bragging about the thread of destiny that suddenly tied him to a daughter of Director Mizuno, who had considerable influence in the company. Takeshi and Mayumi still worked full-time for the same company. But at the same time, his brazen speech strangely helped relieve her of the remaining attachment that she might have cherished otherwise.

"Okay, if that's the way it is." Mayumi rose to her feet and fished a five-hundred-yen coin out of her wallet to pay for her coffee. Normally, Takeshi paid for her food or beverages, but she no longer wanted to owe him a penny. He was, at least, clever enough to take the hint and did not protest against her leaving money on the table. While she was exiting from the restaurant, however, her peripheral vision caught sight of his smiling face.

He's so relieved and contented because I didn't make a scene in public. He knew I wasn't the type to raise hell.

What was most convenient for Takeshi was that the company had just made an official announcement that he would be stationed at the New York office for the next one year. Rumor had it that the transfer to an overseas office was a step toward his promotion to an administrative position. Then, on his return to Tokyo, he would be happily united with his new fiancée in holy matrimony. He would not have to face Mayumi for the time being, during which time he hoped the sour feelings would wane to the extent that they could pretend that no personal relationship had existed between them. He certainly knew that Mayumi was not the type to become hysterical or broadcast her past relationship with him to disgrace herself. He took full advantage of her good nature and conscientiousness, and she no longer cared about it. Yet she could not help feeling that he deserved a little lesson before he settled down as a happily married man. In fact, she already had an idea as to how to execute her plan. A key to his apartment clinked in her wallet when she tried to take out the money for her coffee. She did not return the key to its legal owner because the latter never asked for it.

A Month Later

A large group of company employees gathered near one of Japan Airlines' counters at Narita International Airport. They were at the airport to send off Takeshi to New York because he was on an important mission. In reality, however, many of them showed up more out of respect for Director Mizuno, who happened to be his fiancée's father, than for the man who was known for his clever tactics to impress his supervisors and receive personal favors. They all knew he was obsequious to administration.

To his great surprise, Takeshi found Mayumi at the send-off party at the airport! She was standing alone on the periphery of the crowd of company employees who were present. There were so many people that Takeshi could avoid facing her in person or exchanging words with her. Then, as the time for his departure drew near, one of the female employees presented a bouquet to him on behalf of the sales department, and all his colleagues clapped their hands to wish him bon voyage. He was so elated at the celebrating atmosphere that a nagging feeling about his former girlfriend's presence had snapped out of his mind. The call for boarding for his flight came, and Takeshi said a few words to his fiancée, waved at his colleagues, and went down the walkway toward the boarding gate.

When Takeshi was gone, the send-off party broke up, and people headed back to the city in threes and fours. Director Mizuno and his daughter—or Takeshi's fiancée—climbed into a company limousine pulled over to the curb in a pickup area. Some people went down to the parking lot to find their private automobiles, and others bought tickets to board a Narita Express or hopped into an orange airport shuttle bus. Mayumi chose the bus. She went straight to the bus terminal, boarded a departing bus before any one of her colleagues did, and sat alone in the backmost seat. Soon, a few girls from the sales department came on board and seated themselves a few seats in front of her, unaware of Mayumi's presence.

"I was kind of surprised that Mayumi showed up," one girl started in a loud voice.

"Me, too."

"Poor girl! We all know what happened to her, but she herself doesn't seem to be aware of all the nasty rumors going around."

"Oh, sure she does."

"Does she?"

"Yes. I have reason to believe she's heard about all the gossiping."

"And she still showed up?"

"Yes, she still showed up."

"Wow! If I were in her shoes, I'd be too embarrassed to stay in the company. I would've quit right away."

"Right."

"You know something?" the third girl interrupted. "I think what really degrades her position is that she doesn't have the guts to blow up, scream, and yell at the man who treated her like dirt. I'd make a scene in front of everybody and tell them all the terrible things he did to me. I might even threaten to sue him because he really deserves it."

"I'd do, too."

"Well, a selfish man and a naive woman! They are just a perfect combination, though."

Mayumi was listening in on their conversation quietly. *You don't need to worry about it*, she smiled grimly in the backseat. *I have my own plan to straighten it out.*

***

When the airport shuttle pulled into the city terminal at Hakozaki, Mayumi stood up first and walked past her female colleagues. She even turned around, looked into each person's face, and smiled. Naturally, the girls were all stunned and blushed in embarrassment.

"H-h-hi, Mayumi," one of the girls said to cover up the awkward atmosphere. They were not sure how close Mayumi had been sitting and how much of their conversation she might have overheard.

"Oh, we . . . we didn't know you were in the same bus. Otherwise, you know . . . we would have invited you to join us."

"Well, that's sweet of you to say so." Mayumi gave a broad smile.

"You know, we are going to have tea near the city terminal. Do you want to come with us?"

"Thank you, but not today. I just need to make an important phone call, so I'll see you all in the office tomorrow morning."

***

When all passengers disembarked, the girls from Kakubeni Trading stood outside the bus for a while, staring at Mayumi's back until she completely disappeared. Mayumi, however, did not actually stop in front of the bank of pay telephones; neither did she take out her cell phone. She went straight down to the taxi stand and climbed into a cab.

"Ishiyama-cho, please," she declared her destination when the driver shut the door by remote control.

Ishiyama-cho was where Takeshi's apartment was located. He rented a small two-bedroom apartment, conveniently located in the heart of the inner city. And that was where he and Mayumi had spent a great deal of time together before he walked out on her and became engaged to the director's daughter. In fact, he had already signed a contract to purchase a new, larger condominium in the suburbs so that he could move into his new home with his wife after their wedding. No trace of his former girlfriend would be carried over to his new home. But he decided to continue renting the old apartment until his return from New York in order to store all his belongings during his absence. It served more as a storage room, which was probably the reason why he did not trouble to retrieve a spare key from Mayumi. He was more than happy to give it to her as a little souvenir if he could avoid another face-to-face meeting with her. After he moved out of the apartment, the new tenant would replace the lock and keys for security.

Mayumi unlocked the door and entered the dark apartment. When she switched on the lights, she could see some modifications of the interior after her last visit. On his desk was, not surprisingly, a photo of Takeshi and his fiancée smiling and posing together. But the general atmosphere remained the same. Takeshi had never been a person to clean up. Work-related files had been carelessly tossed on his desk and his sofa, and his slippers were flipped out a few meters apart from each other. She even found unclean laundry piled up near the wash machine, that is, despite the fact that he had just left for New York for one year. It seemed that his new fiancée was not the type of person to come to the old apartment and clean up after him, either. But after all, the condition in the room reflected his personality and behavioral patterns, and it was a perfect situation for the little trick she was going to play.

Mayumi silently lifted the telephone receiver and smiled to herself. As she expected, the phone had *not* been disconnected. Takeshi had always laughed when Mayumi tried to economize on living expenses by winding up loose ends, and as she expected, he had not bothered to disconnect the telephone that he would never use in the next one year. She extracted her personal telephone directory from her handbag and started dialing a long serial number.

After a short lapse of time, the distant dial tone started buzzing, and then a recorded message came on in English. Mayumi was an English major back in college and, at least, knew enough English to understand the recorded message.

"The cold pressure system is pushing into the northeast, and the temperatures between the Boston and New York areas will remain in the fifties and low sixties until the end of the week. The weather conditions in the Great Lakes and Canada are volatile . . ."

Mayumi had heard enough to confirm that her former boyfriend's phone was connected to the weather bureau in the United States about five thousand miles away. Then, she slowly put the receiver down beside the telephone, not replacing it in the cradle. She knew the messages being transmitted from the other side of the globe would be played continuously in the next twelve months and the man who had abandoned her for his selfish cause would be in for a big surprise when he returned from New York.

Then, she pulled and closed the dark, thick curtains, switched on all the lamps in his apartment, turned the faucets to run water at full blast both in the bathroom and in the kitchen sink, cracked a refrigerator door open, and turned on the air conditioner in every room. She released the tap and switch for every energy source except for heat and fire, which might set off the fire alarm. She did not feel guilty or worried in the least about the consequences of her little prank. After all, he had always left everything loose, expecting her to tie up loose ends and make up for all his mistakes. She was now just canceling some of the unappreciated favors and undoing the services she had done for him, returning everything to its original position. She associated herself not with a witch that cast spells on people but with the one that broke the spells to change things back to the original forms. It was also time that he learned that "little and often make a heap in time."

Then, she exited her former boyfriend's apartment for the last time, locking away all her bad memories in the loathed man's space. She was now ready to proceed to a new phase of her life.

Ordeal

The government center of Asahi City had a large, dignified main gate made of red bricks. People who walked past it tended to associate it with the remaining relics of the Meiji Restoration. A visitor would check with a security guard and, then, walk between rows of seven- or eight-story buildings lining both sides of the main pathway, which extended all the way to the far end of the compound. Turning right at the far wall and proceeding about fifty meters, he or she would find an inconspicuous two-story wooden house, which was in stark contrast with the authoritative concrete office buildings. This annex was enclosed by a line of cedar trees so that one could get in and out of the building without worrying about other people's eyes.

The plaque above the door identified it as the City Counseling Center. It was staffed by a group of psychiatrists and professors from nearby universities and hospitals. These counselors worked on rotation and attended to people with all types of problems. The service was free of charge because it was a department of the municipal government. Any person who resided or worked in the city was eligible to utilize the service, and outsiders with a referral by a registered doctor, a local counselor, or a schoolteacher were also welcomed. In addition to individual counseling sessions arranged by appointment, the center held a group session every Saturday afternoon. Participants gathered and shared their problems, hardships, and ordeals and offered moral support to each other. The counselor in charge served more as a coordinator than as a mentor or doctor.

One Saturday afternoon toward the end of May, a regular group session was held. It was a rather small session with only five participants, who had not been previously acquainted with each other. Ms. Kamata, a secretary, provided each participant with a name tag that identified him or her with a pseudonym and guided them to sit in a circle. That day, they were seated in the order that they would be asked to speak, although group-session participants were often encouraged to sit where they pleased and talk spontaneously. When they were all seated, a fleshy man of about fifty stood outside the circle and pronounced the meeting open.

"Folks, welcome to this meeting," the fat middle-aged man said when the wall clock indicated the opening time. "My name's Satake. I am here to guide you through today's session."

Although some of the participants had utilized the center several times in the past, none of them was familiar with this middle-aged man. They could see, however, that he was the counselor in charge for that weekend. He had a tinted pair of thick glasses and was dressed in a loosely fit blazer coat and pants. His voice was guttural, and his movement slow.

"Please sit in a comfortable position and try to relax. You're going to share your problems with other people just like talking to your friends or family. Telling others your problems is a good way to alleviate your suffering, and I'm sure someone can offer words of advice or, at least, give you a hint to solve your problems."

Without any further preamble, Satake introduced the first speaker. "Mr. Igarashi, would you like to talk about your experiences first?"

"Y-y-yes," Igarashi responded hesitantly.

Satake retreated a few steps and slumped in a large chair set in a corner of the room.

Igarashi was a thin twenty-eight-year-old man with a pale complexion and looked clearly stressed and depressed. His problem was that he had lost his girlfriend whom he had been dating for seven years since they were freshmen in university.

"After graduating from university, I joined a printing company, and I've been working very hard ever since. It's a rather small company with only thirty employees on the payroll, not a fancy corporation. I worked in a small office from nine in the morning till nine at night, buried in miscellaneous work. My routine involved proofreading the typed pages and keeping track of orders or products to deliver. The tasks were extremely tedious, but I worked hard in order to save money for marriage. My fiancée and I had agreed that we'd marry as soon as I got enough money for a nice apartment and a honeymoon in Hawaii. But one day, she suddenly stopped replying to my phone calls and text messages. At first, I just thought she was busy, but when I finally got through, she canceled our next date, saying she didn't feel very well. She didn't agree to schedule another date, saying it was hard to tell when she'd be free again. Soon, she stopped answering my phone calls, e-mails, and text messages completely. I could later see that it was her way of indicating that she was losing interest in me.

"Then, about a month later, I got this I-met-this-guy-by-chance confession from her. Her new boyfriend was a Keio graduate and a son of a golf course owner. He drove a brand-new Mercedes and already had a large house of his own in the suburbs. I could see why she no longer cared about a small condominium that I was trying to buy in twenty-year installments. But anyway, I knew that my train was going and that I had no chance of getting her back. I despaired and tried to hang myself in my apartment room."

"But it didn't work, did it?" Another participant interjected. Otherwise, Igarashi would not be there.

"As a matter of fact, I wasn't smart enough to pull it off."

"It was fortunate you failed."

"I tried to hang myself at midnight, hooking my neck on the rope I tied to the raft. But I didn't tie a loop properly, and the rope caught my windpipe, not the arteries. I choked and had a lot of pain, but I didn't lose consciousness. I flapped my limbs and hit the wall repeatedly. The next-door neighbor was woken by the violent bangs and jumped out of his bed. He fetched the landlord, and they opened my door with the master key. The two cut the rope and got me down on the floor. I was already unconscious, but they resuscitated me by performing CPR. The landlord's wife called an ambulance at once, and I was taken to an emergency hospital. Fortunately, because of the neighbor's and the landlord's quick action, I recovered without suffering any aftereffects."

Igarashi also reported that he had been traumatic ever since, started drinking heavily, and developed sleeping problems. When he finished recounting his story, his eyes were filled with tears. A grown man crying like a small child was not a pretty sight, but the other participants gently offered their words of sympathy.

"I'm so sorry to hear that."

"It must've been really traumatic, but I'm glad you survived."

"I'm glad you suffered no permanent physical damage afterward."

Satake rose from his chair again, stood behind Igarashi, and gave him a friendly tap on the shoulders. "Well, we'll come back to Mr. Igarashi's problem later and discuss how we can best help deal with his problems. But now, let's hear from Ms. Kato as the second speaker."

He turned everybody's attention to the woman sitting next to Igarashi. Kato looked a few years older than Igarashi—perhaps in her early thirties. She had a large bandage above her left eye and wore a large surgical mask, which, in combination, covered two thirds of her face. So it was difficult to determine her real age. She wore no makeup and looked totally defeated. "Folks, I referred to her as Ms. Kato, but I'm using a pseudonym to protect her privacy."

Anonymity was agreed on before the participants signed up for the session, but Satake affirmed this rule for the only female participant for the day.

Kato had kept her head down most of the time when Igarashi was speaking, but she finally looked up when her name was called, dabbed her eyes with her handkerchief, and started speaking in a low voice.

"I feel sorry for Mr. Igarashi who missed a chance for his marriage. But I must tell you that married men or women aren't always happier than those who haven't married. Look at me if you need any evidence." She sobbed for a while until she finally looked up and started talking again.

"I married my boyfriend soon after I graduated from junior college. For the first three months, it was full of sweet feelings and excitement. Then, we began to see a huge gap between our personalities or between what he expected of married life and what I'd naively hoped for. He'd expected me to be a devoted wife who would do housework perfectly, make love to him whenever he wanted, and wait for his return until late at night. But I worked myself and was often too tired to do all those things. When I neglected something, though, he became sulky and complained that I was insensitive to his feelings. His sullen glare at the breakfast table began to hurt me. He himself often barhopped until past midnight, saying it was part of his job to keep his customers company. He also needed chances to impress people who might help him with his future promotions. But his drinking really took away a large portion of his salary every month as he did it so often. Our original plan was to save a major portion of my salary for buying a house in the future, but we ended up spending it all to pay the rent and the utility bills. We both became increasingly frustrated over time, and when I protested against his spending, he started beating me. We live in a concrete apartment building, and the neighbors don't know what is happening inside a locked door. I'm really scared because he might kill me one of these days soon." She started sobbing again.

"Why don't you just leave him?" one participant said.

"Yes, you should do it at once or seek shelter somewhere. If there's no one to turn to for help, you can even stay with us for a while," another offered.

"Well, Mr. Igarashi and Ms. Kato," Matsumoto, a man who was sitting next to Kato, started speaking without waiting for a cue from Satake, the organizer. "I'm really sorry for both of you. But you have no reason to despair because things can be much worse."

"Well, everyone," Satake stepped in and belatedly introduced the third speaker who was anxious to take the floor. "Mr. Matsumoto was supposed to speak next. Mr. Matsumoto, would you like to start now?"

"Yes. I'm thirty-five years old and just recently lost my job as a salesman. The securities company I was working for started restructuring, and they needed to kick out several employees to make up for a serious financial loss. Unfortunately, I'd made a couple of minor mistakes in my business transactions, and my supervisor, Tsuruta, compiled a list of my problems and mistakes and submitted it to the administration. But actually, I was framed. I knew that he personally didn't like me, and I'm sure he embellished my mistakes and problems to make me look like a really stupid and worthless worker. And based on his report, the company fired me—or permanently laid me off as they put it—along with several other not-so-useful employees."

Igarashi, Kato, and the other participants perked up their ears and listened.

"To me, it was totally out of the blue. I knew that the company was in financial trouble and needed to cut costs in every area, but I just never thought they'd really fire me. I'd been working hard since I joined the company at twenty-two, often spending weekends in the office and sacrificing a lot of my private life. I'm married, and we have two small children, but as I was often forced to work on weekends, I rarely went to see my son's baseball games or my daughter's ballet performance. Then, this guy, Tsuruta, used a neat trick to kick me out of the company. By firing me, he himself probably got credit for contributing to financial streamlining. He is a typical kiss-up-kick-down guy who gets himself promoted by flattering his supervisors and treating those in lower ranks like dirt."

"Yes, I acknowledge there are people like that," someone concurred.

"As a matter of fact, our relationship had gotten worse two years ago. A year before April, he was appointed as an assistant director of our department. We all despised him for his sneaky personality, and a few other guys and I always talked about his selfish behavior when drinking beer at a nearby bar. But, one evening, one of Tsuruta's underlings happened to be in the same bar, and Tsuruta learned through him how we bad-mouthed him. He soon reported to the director that we were a discontented party that might soon lead a revolt, and based on that report, people at the top started assigning us extremely difficult tasks as punishment. I was the hardest hit because I was described as the main instigator."

According to Matsumoto's story, the administration placed him in charge of several companies on the verge of bankruptcy, whose stocks had become completely worthless. There was no way to profit from transactions with them; their executives were being sued by their clients and business associates. Matsumoto's narration went on and on, but the main point of his predicament was that he had two children in elementary school and could not find a new job to support them and his wife.

"If this thing had happened a little earlier, like when we hadn't had kids, I could have found a different company more easily. I might have even gone back to a university and retrained myself to go into a completely different trade."

"Right," someone nodded in agreement.

"But now, I can't afford to pay the tuition."

"Have you considered legal action?"

"I consulted a friend's friend who is a lawyer. But he said it'd be difficult to ask for a big compensation because the administration didn't leave any evidence that it was a case of personal punishment against me. The company would insist it was across the board."

"You said a couple of other people were dismissed, too, didn't you?" said another participant.

"Yes."

"Then, why don't you join forces to tackle the problems? You can either sue the company together or help each other restructure your own lives."

"The problem is, all the other guys have already been saved by somebody. Some guys received small inheritance from their parents, and some got help from their wives who agreed to work till they'd find new jobs. Or their elder brothers and sisters helped them find different jobs. They've found individual solutions to ride out this crisis. But I'm an only child, and my father is a retired company worker. He and Mother live on social security. My wife has no work experience, and her parents are more or less the same as mine. We're supposed to take care of them, instead of getting help from them. My savings have completely run out, and I have no special expertise or experience to put my life together."

"Sorry to hear that."

"We're going to be evicted from our apartment at the end of this month, and I can't even provide proper meals to my family."

Matsumoto dropped his shoulders and cast his eyes down like an old defeated boxer.

He turned to Igarashi with a pathetic expression. "Your problem is nothing compared to mine. At least, you still have a job, and if you ask me, it's a good thing you don't have to worry about a family to support now that your girlfriend has left you."

Then, he turned to Ms. Kato. "I'm sorry that the savage man brutally beat you. But your problem can be solved quickly: just divorce him. Hire a lawyer and ask him to finish all the procedures on your behalf. You don't even have to meet him face-to-face. And you make your former husband pay for the way he treated you. It would provide you with a nice allowance to prepare yourself for your new life."

Matsumoto had recounted his own experiences, hoping to console the younger people, but both Igarashi and Kato could not help feeling that their *sempai* was mocking their misery and predicament.

The fourth man, whose name tag identified him as Yamazaki, nodded deeply at Matsumoto's comments but offered his personal view that differed slightly. "But your situation doesn't seem totally hopeless to me, Mr. Matsumoto. I have pancreas cancer. My doctor recently diagnosed it as terminal."

All participants froze at a mention of terminal cancer.

"I'm fifty, and I can't complain much about my illness. A couple of decades ago, men were supposed to retire at fifty or fifty-five because that was pretty much close to what was then believed to be man's longevity. But what I'm seriously worried about is my family. We have two children, one in high school and one in university. Mr. Matsumoto, I know you must take care of your small children, too, but the cost for raising and educating children reaches its peak when they start attending high schools and universities. Tuition at private schools is highway robbery. And of course, you can't just make them go to school, sit for classes, and come straight back home. You need to give them some allowances and let them participate in extracurricular activities, field trips, and various events and activities. Even their commuters' passes and cell phone bills alone would add up to twenty or thirty thousand yen per month. You'll understand it when your children grow a little older. Life in general is far more expensive today than a few decades ago, and it's most expensive when your kids are in school. And the coup de grace is my medical bills, which took away all my savings. The company kept me on the payroll for one year, but I was finally suspended. I haven't paid off the housing loans, and my wife is also prone to sickness, complaining of high blood pressures and stomach ulcers. Now, I'm really a dead duck."

There was a long silence in the room.

"By the way, my father passed away ten years before," Yamazaki added, "and my mother is bedridden in a nursing school. I wonder what will happen to her if I die."

There was another awkward silence.

"Mr. Matsumoto," he turned to the previous speaker again. "Your problem is still quite manageable. At least, you are healthy and strong. All you have to do is just find a new job. Scour the entire city for work, comb through the wanted ads in newspapers, and talk to all your acquaintances who might be able to help you. It's hard to bow down and beg people for help, but you can do it if you put your mind to it. Drop your vanity, and take any job that is available. I'm sure you'll find some job or meet someone who can help you. I acknowledge it's rather difficult in the present economic climate, but you can start as a deliveryman at a parcel delivery service or an attendant at a convenient store."

Participants were expected to help, console, or encourage one another by sharing their experiences, but ironically, the episodes recounted by those who suffered more tended to insult those who suffered less.

The fifth man named Wada, forty years of age, followed up on Yamazaki's story. "I'm truly sorry about your disease, Mr. Yamazaki. But at least, your children will soon be big enough to take care of themselves. University students, if not high school kids, can even work part-time and go to school. In addition, with the lump sum of money you receive at retirement, you can stick it out for a few more years. And hypothetically speaking, if worse comes to worst, your family can collect life insurance money after your departure. I'm truly sorry for your illness and your financial predicament, but I still don't really think you're at a dead end."

Wada started to tell his own life story. He had made a fortune as an entrepreneur in his late thirties but then failed and had gone into a huge financial debt. He knew that he could not pay back the borrowed money in several lifetimes and would soon be on trial for multiple fraud, tax evasion, and theft charges. The police and the prosecutors were not the only parties that were chasing him for punishment. Some of the money loaners had hired crime syndicate members to hunt him down, threatening to physically hurt his wife and children.

"At least, your relatives and friends are sympathetic and willing to support you. But I am confronted by enemies on all four sides, hated by my associates that I cannot pay the money back to, and distanced by relatives and friends. They're angry that I've brought disgrace on all of them and caused them all the trouble. My wife and children no longer live with me. I can't blame them because they are traumatic after a series of intimidating phone calls and visits by sinister-looking men. They don't want to be involved with me anymore. It's totally my fault. But, Mr. Yamazaki, in terms of the degree of suffering, I'd say I've suffered at least three times more than you just described. No offense, but it's much worse than having a terminal disease."

All the earlier speakers were astounded at Wada's speech and had no comment to make on his comparison between his and other speakers' problems. They remained silent for a long second.

"I've thought of killing myself many times. When I stand on a station platform, waiting for an express train . . ." He suddenly choked on his words and started sobbing. Nobody knew what words to offer to this person who found himself in an ultimate predicament.

Then, Satake, the mediator, rose from his seat slowly and made his way to the center of the circle. He removed his tinted glasses and slowly turned around to look every participant in the eye. When he completed his 360-degree turn, everyone's face was white as a sheet as if they had just seen a ghost. His right eye was a glass ball. Then, he clumsily bent forward and tucked up his long pants to reveal his prostheses. This time, the participants let out a feeble exclamation of "Uh" in unison. Particularly, Wada, the last speaker, stared at his artificial legs with his mouth agape.

Satake started speaking in a gentle tone. "Folks, I heartily appreciate your hardships—and your effort and courage to talk about them. I extend my deepest sympathy to all of you. But believe it or not, I've got practically all the problems you've described.

"I have lost my job three times, went into a huge debt, and was divorced by my wife who's now taken full custody of the children and would never let me meet them again. I'd been chased by members of crime syndicates for a long time until I finally had a terrible accident and lost my legs and my right eye. It was reported as an accident, but I'm convinced that it was a clear act of terrorism. It was their idea of punishing me and teaching me a lesson."

All held their breath.

"I was riding my motorcycle on a rainy day. I'd sold off my car, and the motorcycle was my only transportation. And I wasn't aware three dark sedans were stealthily following me. When I came to a deserted section of a highway, one car suddenly overtook me and cut in front of me, another one closed in on my tail, and the third one flanked me and suddenly rammed me against a guardrail. The hit men, hired by a money loaner, punished me in the meanest and cruelest way. I don't know whether they intended to kill me or cripple and let me live and suffer for the rest of my life. But, either way, I must say they've been most successful, achieving their purpose."

Everybody in the room stared at the one-eyed man with no legs, reliving the terrifying scene in their minds.

"But I know one thing for sure. Each ordeal is hard for the person who is experiencing it for the first time. When you get one problem after another, you'll get used to it and eventually become numb. Looking back, I feel that my first broken heart back in high school had hurt me more than the divorce by my twenty-year wife, and my failure in a university entrance examination had tortured me ten times more severely than my bankruptcy. As a teenager, I thought it was the end of the world. The amputation of my legs drew everybody's attention and much sympathy, but strangely, it was far more tolerable than the first broken bone that I'd sustained when I was practicing judo in junior high school.

"Folks, the severity of problems is a matter of comparison—either between or within individual persons. It's a matter of personal perception and subjective judgment. If you lower the threshold and look at your predicament from a slightly different perspective, anything can be tolerated. After I lost my money, my family, and my legs and one eye, I was accommodated in a sanatorium—an institution for deranged people. I despaired and wallowed in self-pity for months. More than once, I attempted to take my own life. But about a year later, when I was still accommodated at the institute, I started reading books with my good eye and taking correspondence courses. That was one therapy that a counselor suggested to divert my attention from my sufferings. After all, I had nothing else to do, so I read for hours every day. My vision out of the remaining eye deteriorated to some extent, but it was better than lying in bed like a vegetable. Time passed, and six years later, I qualified myself as a psychiatrist."

Wada and Yamazaki both looked Satake in the face and nodded deeply.

"Are you here as a participant?" Wada then asked.

"I don't see any reason why I can't be both a counselor and a participant. After all, the only practical purpose I can serve in society may be exposing myself as a prime example of loss and failure and sharing it with you guys so that you might have an idea where you can go from here."

Igarashi and Kato had a smile at the ends of their lips.

See All Evil, Say No Evil

The intersection where the fatal accident occurred was only twenty meters from the apartment building where I lived, and as a matter of fact, there had been two similar accidents before as if warning me of the serious physical threat closing in on me. Every morning, I turned right at this intersection onto Park Street and walked about fifty meters down to catch a commuter bus. In the late afternoon or early evening, I returned from work, got off a bus on the other side of the same street, walked back fifty meters in the reverse direction, and turned left to cross the same intersection to reach my home. Being able to return home in the early evening was an advantage for a civil servant working at a municipal government. This intersection did not seem to have any unusual characteristic feature. The road was fairly large with two wide lanes on either side, and there was no prominent obstacle that might intercept drivers' line of sight. The volume of traffic was normally not very large, either. Looking back, however, there must have been some invisible factor that confused or distracted drivers even if it had evaded the pedestrians' notice.

The first crash that I had witnessed involved a sedan and a young man riding his bicycle, and the second one was a collision between an SUV and a motor scooter. The two collisions occurred on exactly the same spot in the almost identical fashion within the space of a week. And both accidents took place at about the same time of day—

approximately 6:30 p.m.—when I had just returned from work. As it was in early summer, there was plenty of daylight left.

In the first accident, the bicycle rider pulled away from the curb and tried to cross the center divider to make a U-turn when an automobile, which had just negotiated the corner, came up from behind and struck the wheels of his bicycle, flipping him violently up into the air. The man on the bike made an acrobatic tumble, seemed to levitate a few meters above the ground upside down, and came crashing down on the asphalt surface with a heavy, unpleasant thud. There was no doubt that the bicycle rider received a strong impact and probably had a concussion, but from the spectators' viewpoint, it was as spectacular as a movie stunt. People immediately gathered around the fallen man to check his condition.

Not surprisingly, he was bruised all over the body and bleeding out of his nose and mouth. But fortunately, he had landed feet first after a complete tumble; the tires of the bicycle hit the concrete surface first and provided a cushion to the falling rider. People tried to help him up to his feet, but he could stand up by himself and, although a little disoriented, declared that he was not seriously wounded. When an ambulance arrived, he climbed into it unaided.

Then, a week later, exactly the same fate fell on a *soba* delivery man riding a motor scooter. He was riding his soba-delivery scooter with a metal bowl-container fixed behind his saddle. The container, which had multiple beds inside to stack several noodle bowls, was suspended from a short metal arm with built-in springs so that the impact and vibration from driving was absorbed and the soup of *soba*, or buckwheat noodle, would not spill. I happened to be familiar with the structure of the equipment because a curious business associate from abroad had once asked me what that strange-looking box attached to a motor scooter was, and I had done quick research to be able to explain it in English. The soba delivery man had just pulled away from the curb after finishing his delivery and tried to make a U-turn, just like the earlier victim had. Then, he was struck on the right flank by an SUV, which was traveling at a cruising speed of about forty kilometers per hour. It was the normal speed for city roads but fast enough to exert a strong physical impact on a two-wheel driver.

I was rooted to the spot in shocked disbelief until a woman who ran a fruit and vegetable shop two doors down came and regarded me with a strange mixture of concern, apprehension, and suspicion.

"Oh, my goodness! You are always passing by when this thing happens."

"Well, you know, I live right over there in Mejiro Heights. But yes, it's a strange coincidence that I've seen it twice."

"I'm telling you, young man, you better watch out for yourself."

I had thought that the woman might fetch a handful of salt and toss it around my feet for purification. She did not actually perform a salt-tossing ritual, but I could see what the woman was implying. A number of people, especially those in older generations, believed in evil spirits that haunted certain places or certain people. This vegetable shop owner was clearly suspicious that either the land around the corner was haunted or I might be accompanied by an evil spirit.

Was this place a passageway for dead souls? I questioned myself in my mind, imagining a mysterious world of the dead spirits. As a small child, I used to read a lot about the netherworld. *I really hope I'm not possessed by any weird thing.*

I preferred not to get into a debate with the woman over the existence of dead spirits. I had bought apples and pears from her several times in the past, and we had talked a couple of times. But exhausted from a heavy day's work, I did not want to be involved in a long, heavy conversation with her at the moment. All I wished was to return to my apartment, take a shower, and indulge in a tall can of cold beer. So I lightly nodded at her advice and walked away. Then, a week later, *my accident took place!*

***

That afternoon, I was heading back to my apartment just as on any other working day. Suddenly, I felt a gigantic chunk of metal slammed at my back and felt as if I had been pushed off a bluff from behind and made to plunge into the valley, tumbling and spiraling. I found myself floating upside down in the air for a long moment until I landed headfirst onto the hard surface. *Headfirst*—that was one notable difference between my case and the two previous accidents that I had witnessed as a passerby. I blacked out and was soon sucked into the dark, silent vacuum. When I came around, the surrounding scenery looked completely different. The entire place was dark, chilly, and soundless. There was no ambulance or rescuers around, and I did not see the woman from the local fruit-and vegetable shop, either.

In place of any of the familiar faces, a skinny man in his forties or fifties, wearing a white robe and a white triangular headband, was standing before me. He had a calligraphy brush in one hand and a ledger in the other hand. At first, I thought that I was prostrate on the ground but soon realized I was standing erect, face-to-face with the man. He was a scrawny middle-aged man who was approximately as tall as I was.

"Welcome," the man pronounced his words in a flat tone.

I did not know what to say, not having the slightest idea who the man was and where I was.

"I am Number 4, and I'm supposed to sign you in."

"Sign me in for what? And where the hell am I?"

"You are entering the infernal regions." The sky came crashing down.

After all, the vegetable shop owner was right! Did an automobile suddenly emerge out of nowhere and strike me from behind, just as in the cases of the bicycle and motor scooter riders? Am I, Nobuo Toyama, really dead at age twenty-five? If so, it had been such a short life with an abrupt ending.

Then, the white-robed man, whose name tag affirmed his identity as Number 4, proceeded to read out my name in the ledger. "I understand you are Nobuo Oyama, twenty-five, a resident of 2–402, Mejiro Residence, Sancho-me—"

"Toyama," I corrected it at once, noticing he had mispronounced my name. My address and the name of the apartment building were also different. The man looked into his book and emitted a weak exclamation, "Uh!"

"To-ya-ma is my name," I repeated.

"Are you . . . are you sure about that?" Suddenly, his tone was a half octave lower, and his expression was clearly troubled.

"Yes." How can anybody be mistaken about his own name even after suffering a concussion? "As a matter of fact, many of my teachers back in school made the same mistake, calling me Oyama. It's very easy to drop the first voiceless plosive."

Now, the man's face turned ashen. "Oh, my God! How could I have done it?"

"Done what?"

"I . . . I'm terribly sorry, sir. But I seem to have picked the wrong person."

I felt the blood draining from my head. The seriousness of the situation sank in, although it was difficult to define it in clear language. "Hey, what the hell is going on?"

"Someone by the name of Oyama was doomed to enter this netherworld today, but you, carrying a very similar name, happened to pass by, and I . . . I just thought it was him."

"Does this often happen?"

"No, absolutely not! I've never made this kind of mistake, but, oh my God, I'm in deep trouble. I might be stripped of my position and credentials."

"Wait a minute. How does that precisely affect *my* well-being?" I was not concerned about the man's job or position because my own life was clearly at stake or might have already been taken away.

Number 4 looked at me in the face, sobering up from his confusion and emotional turmoil. "Sir, I acknowledge my terrible mistake, and I sincerely apologize to you because you've been brought to this place by mistake. You actually don't belong here—at least, not as of this date."

I contemplated the matter for a second. The physical impact of the crash had been so strong that I was still a little disoriented, but I was gradually regaining my ability for some logical analysis and reasoning. "Wait! I just hope you aren't implying you can't send me back to the living world?"

The man inclined his head. "I'm afraid I can't."

"Jesus Christ!" I was suddenly furious. "Why? Why can't I go back?"

"Because, in this world, you can't move backward just like no one can travel back in time in the human world. One can only travel in a linear order, and there's no such thing as *going backward*."

"You mean, you mistook me for someone else and brought me down to hell. And you say you're not going to let me go back, even though you admit it was your fault."

"I'm afraid that's exactly the case."

"Oh, dammit! Dammit!" I choked on my words, shocked and angry.

Then, after an awkward moment of silence, I protested again, "Listen. I'm only twenty-five. I have a job and a lot of professional responsibilities. Besides, I haven't even cleaned up my apartment, either."

I was concerned about the personal letters and a few dirty magazines hidden in my desk drawers. My family and relatives would see them when clearing out my apartment.

"It just isn't fair. Oh, oh, no. Oh, no! I can't take this, you idiot!"

Number 4 was frozen at my outburst, clearly acknowledging that I had every right to blaspheme against him. Then, when I paused to catch a breath after raving, he ventured a suggestion. "Would you allow me to talk to my supervisor? He might have an idea."

"Do whatever you ought to. I just don't want to stay here for good—not even for another hour. Just get me out of here."

Number 4 retreated into the darkness and, a few minutes later, came back, accompanied by an elderly man. His supervisor wore the same white robe, but his headband had three purple stripes stitched on it, apparently signifying a higher administrative ranking.

"Sir, I truly regret that my subordinate brought you down here by mistake. I looked into your profile and confirmed that it was a totally different person that was doomed today. It was 100 percent our fault."

"So can I go home?"

"You might, but there is a certain condition you need to comply with."

"Listen," I was enraged again. "You admit it's 100 percent your fault, and how dare you impose a condition on my departure?"

"I can understand your resentment, but as Number 4 here mentioned, there's no *way back* in this region of space-time. People will normally come in and stay for good or proceed to the deeper parts of this world."

"What happens to me now?"

"If you really wish to return . . ."

"Let's just put it behind us," Nobuo spat out. "I *am* going."

"If you really wish to return to your original place," the supervisor continued, ignoring my emotional outburst, "we'll just have to escort you all the way to the end of this world and sort of push you out through a wormhole. You may suffer a mild concussion when you are thrown out of this place and hit the ground back in the living world, but I assure you that you won't have any serious aftereffect. You'll be physically fine."

"Physically fine? Then in what way can I possibly be *not* fine?"

"During the trip, you'll be passing through the scenes you'd find rather disturbing. Of course, since yours is a special case, we'll manage to guide you through a shortcut, but you'll have to witness the ugly endings of some people whom you crossed paths with in one way or another. You'll have to see them, but once you are back in your own world, you won't be allowed to tell anybody what you've seen here."

"I've heard the proverb: 'See no evil, hear no evil, say no evil'."

"It's a misquote. The correct one is, 'See all evil, say no evil'."

Leaving aside the different versions of the proverb, I could see the point. I knew how painful it would be to know a big secret and not to be able to repeat it to anybody. However, I did not seem to have any choice but to follow the man's suggestion.

"All right. But just one question!"

"What is it?"

"You said I'll see people that I've crossed paths with in the past. But you mean in the area where I live—or lived—presently? The particular section of Tokyo where I've been living in the past several years?"

"No. All the places where you've ever been, including your hometown. This world isn't divided up in accord with the arbitrary geographical boundaries in the human world. Saving the complex explanations, I'd just say you have your own universe."

The supervisor's words gave me a weird feeling and considerable anxiety. Nonetheless, I would rather be an Urashima Taro who had returned from the undersea palace of Dragon King with a sacred souvenir box containing the compressed passage of time and all secrets. Even if I were not permitted to open the sacred box, or recount my experiences to my friends and family, I still preferred to see them in person and in real time, instead of being left behind after they passed over.

"Oh, what the hell! Let's get moving."

***

I was guided along a narrow dirt road, which soon came to an old bridge that spanned a river. The length of the bridge appeared to be about the same as the Ohashi Bridge in my neighborhood. I estimated it to be approximately two hundred meters long. The major difference was that the bridge that I was obviously supposed to cross was very narrow and made of wood. There was barely room enough for one person to walk at a time, and I was frightened by the fact that there was no safety guardrail on either side. The long bridge arched over the river like a rainbow, and there were no pillars supporting it, let alone a cluster of modern suspension wires stretching from both shores. The sight of this unusual bridge sent shivers down my spine and made my knees buckle.

However, I could see that the river itself was not very deep because several groups of people were fording it. They were moving slowly toward the other shore in three orderly lines, which gradually diverged in different directions. The three groups of people were clad in similar flimsy *yukata*-like robes, but the colors of their robes differed from group to group. One group of people wore white robes, another group had red robes on, and the other group was in black. I noticed that the people wearing black robes were moving more clumsily and staggeringly than the other two groups, and I soon realized that their hands were tied behind their backs. The way they tottered and walked in zigzags suggested that their feet might be shackled.

"Who are those people walking across the river?" I could not help asking, although it was not very difficult to guess who they were.

"They were sinners and criminals in the living world and are now forced to cross the river on their own feet."

"The River of Three Crossings?"

"Yes."

"Why do they have different-color robes on?"

"They are classified into three categories according to the gravity of the sin they committed before death. Those in white committed minor crimes, such as petty theft, shoplifting, and luggage theft. They were mostly very poor and were forced to steal food and daily necessities for survival."

The white-robed criminals waded into the river in single file and walked across the water slowly but steadily. I recognized a pathetic expression on their faces, but they looked comparatively composed. It might have been evidence of resignation, but at least, they did not seem to be in severe pain.

"How about the women in red?" I had noticed by then that those in red were all female. They were heading to the other shore through a slightly different course.

"Those women are what you call prostitutes in your world,"

Number 4 stated in a flat tone. The women showed a mixture of resignation and relief on their faces, and some even had a faint smile.

"They violated a major ethical code that women shouldn't violate, but they didn't steal or hurt other people."

"What's going to happen to them?"

"Well, they must struggle to cross the river, fighting against the current. It won't be easy, but not an ordeal. But after all, that's the extent of the punishment they deserve. Once they reach the other shore, they will go through some rituals for redemption and will eventually be put to rest."

"Sounds like a rather light punishment."

"You know, they were sinners by your social standards, but they aren't even mean and wicked. Instead, some of them are quite caring and compassionate."

"This seems like a rather nice world for prostitutes."

"The fact that they had relationships with many men for money cannot be condoned. But, in a sense, those women played an indispensable role in society, giving comfort and affection to men who were spiritually deprived. Their existence was appreciated by a sizable population of people."

"How about those in black?"

"The condition is different for those guys. They were really obnoxious men and women. They betrayed their friends and associates or stole money from innocent or helpless people, using dirty tricks. Worst of all, many of them pretended to be decent human beings, law-abiding citizens, or even role models who contributed to human society. They were loathsome creatures and need severe enough punishment.

They first labor in the river, sinking and floating for a couple of years."

"That long?" The river looked only about two hundred meters wide in my eyes, but obviously, the distance between the two shores must be far greater than it appeared from the bridge.

"Yes. As you can see, they are first forced to walk against a very strong current. Along their way, there are many pit holes on the riverbed, studded with rugged rocks and long, thick needles to pierce their feet."

Looking closely, I could see that the black-robed men and women who had progressed half way through the width of the river were submerged in water up to their noses or eyes. They were struggling not to drown. It was now clear that they were tied to one another by rope, and when one person stumbled and sank, those around him or her were dragged underneath the surface. They popped their heads, gasping for air, but were soon pulled underwater by the weight of the others.

"Then, some of them will be taken to a coal mine deep in the mountains and forced to dig tunnels for a very long time. It will take them a couple of centuries to pay back their dues."

"Wow!" I was speechless for the moment, imagining the way the black-robed guys would be tortured after their present ordeal across the river.

"But for more serious offenders, there are different rituals in store."

I suspected that I was doomed to see the *rituals* for the worst sinners but did not make any comment for the moment.

"Well, shall we go, Mr. Toyama? I thought you were anxious to move on." Number 4's words shook me out of the reverie.

"Yes."

I was acrophobic and terrified of the high bridge that was neither supported by wires or pillars nor equipped with safety guardrails, but I had no alternative but to move on. I took one careful step on the narrow bridge at a time, trudging like an old sick man who was not confident about his leg strength or balance. Then, after a few steps, I abandoned my vanity and started crawling on all fours, instead of walking erect and taking a risk of plunging into the river crowded by hundreds of criminals. Number 4, who was escorting me, had no trouble with the bridge at all and walked erect on his feet. His relaxed posture reminded me of construction workers who were trained to walk on scaffolds built around a tall building.

Then, after we crossed the bridge, the path gradually sloped up and turned into a mountain trail. It was pitch-dark, and the visibility was extremely poor. I could hardly see ten meters ahead, let alone glimpsing the top of the mountain. It might be just a large hill or a three-thousand-meter-high mountain range. I had no idea how high it was. Number 4 took out a small lantern out of nowhere and shone the dirt road to guide me in the general direction upward.

"It's going to be a long walk, so please brace yourself."

His words made me nervous and wary, but I tried not to betray my anxiety. I was determined to leave that dark, eerie world, no matter how long the trip might turn out to be, and would not want to show any sign of fragility after declaring my firm determination to Number 4 and his supervisor.

"All right, but I was just wondering what's going on at home," I asked in an intentionally flat tone.

"Are you afraid your family and friends might be worried about you?"

"Sort of."

"Don't worry about that. By the time you get out of this place and return to the living world, only a few seconds will have passed. It'll have been just a few seconds after the traffic accident!"

"Is it like the duration of time that I was flipped up into the air and then slammed down on the ground?"

"Something like that!"

Obviously, time had been stalled ever since I was accidentally sucked into the deceased people's world.

I was tempted to ask the reason but stopped short of doing it, assuming that I would not fully understand his explanation full of jargon and unfamiliar theories anyway. It would be wiser not to waste my energy over incomprehensible technicalities when I had a mountain to climb. We trekked the narrow road for hours and then came to a steeper mountain trail where there were a number of logs neatly laid in parallel, forming a flight of stairs. I had seen similar log steps in parks and shrines where the crossties provided foot traction. Then, Number 4 gave me a warning while shining his lantern around my foothold.

"Be aware that walking up these steps might be a little trickier than it seems."

"Okay."

"This is what we'd call Stage One. And I advise you not to turn back until I tell you to do so. Just look up ahead and move on. I'm telling you this for your own good, and you better trust me."

"Fine with me!" It was clear that something uncanny would be going on around, or behind, me as I walked up the stairs, but I chose to save my breath.

"And of course, when you finish climbing, you *must* see the entire stuff, whether you like it or not. But till then, just believe my words and don't bother to look back."

The flame in his lantern suddenly dimmed. I groped my way with my feet, first lifting the right foot and trying to establish a foothold on the dark stairway covered in dirt. When I shifted my weight forward onto the first crosstie and tried to lift the left leg, I could not help gasping because of a strange feeling of discomfort. "Oops!"

What I had thought to be a log sagged under my weight like a sand bag or a bunch of damp, tightly bound straws.

"Yes, I know it feels funny. But don't let it worry you for the moment till you finish climbing the steps. Again, you'll have to see them when you get to the top, but not now!"

"How long will it be?" I could not help asking.

"It's a flight of a hundred and eight steps."

Number 4's words weighed on my mind. Ascending more than a hundred steps would be a serious physical workout even in the daylight. In total darkness, it might turn out to be an endlessly long, arduous trip. But again I steeled my mind, trying not to be overwhelmed by the discouraging thoughts. I advanced my left foot, keeping my balance low, and took another heavy step forward. After a few more steps, I had a distinct feeling that I was walking on some soft, soggy material that I had never stepped on in my life. And every now and then, I thought that I heard a squeaky sound—or groaning—responding to the pressure of my weight. I felt that I had been made to step on something forbidden. But I remembered Number 4's warning and tried, for the moment, not to pay any more attention to the objects underneath my feet. I was not a private detective or a news reporter covering the mystery world. All I desired was to leave the place and return home.

"That's it. That's it. Keep on going." Number 4 was very supportive at each and every step, giving me moral support. "You are doing very well, Mr. Toyama."

Then, when we reached the top of the steps, Number 4 instructed me to slowly turn around. "Now, you must turn around and see it because it was our agreement."

I shifted my line of sight downward in the direction that Number 4's finger pointed. I had been in pitch darkness, but now the log steps shone like light-emitting diodes.

"Jesus!" I almost had a heart attack. What suddenly came into my field of view—stretching all the way down the slope of about thirty meters—were a hundred human bodies, laid in parallel with each other to constitute a flight of stairs. It was not a flight of log steps; it was a flight of *human* steps! I had been forced to walk on human bodies, each of which was bound hand and foot and partially buried in the ground. They had been turned into human crossties, incapable of any voluntary movement.

"I know it looks unusual in your eyes. And weird it is! But don't be sorry for those guys you've walked on. They were incorrigible sinners who trampled innocent people's rights and feelings or manipulated others for their egoistic purposes. Some of them stole innocent people's savings and indulged in luxuries. Others betrayed their best friends or played nasty tricks on his colleagues in order to win promotions over them. Because of their egocentric conduct, many conscientious people were driven to bankruptcy or suicide. Now, these guys deserve to be trampled on, punished, and shamed."

I was transfixed, completely lost for words.

When I partially regained my composure, I hesitantly asked, "Are some of the black robe guys I saw crossing the river going to—?"

"Yes, some of them will end up here, though some might be taken to other places for a more severe punishment. It all depends on the type and gravity of their sin back in the living world."

I kept staring at the bodies that lined the downward slope.

"Now, let's go. You still have a long way to go."

***

We continued to trek the narrow dirt road for another hour—or what seemed to me like an hour, to be more exact. It was a long tedious hike, but I could, at least, use the time to make my heartbeat subside. An experience of walking on dead human bodies had really unnerved me.

"Are you ready?" Number 4 asked, as if reading my mind.

"You mean for the next stage?"

"Yes, for the second stage."

I held my breath when a tall camphor tree came into view. A thick branch extended horizontally, and I could see something hanging from it—and some movement underneath. The object was tied to the branch by a piece of rope and dangling helplessly about a meter above the ground. When I got closer, it turned out to be the body of a man hanged in an old-fashioned execution style.

"Look at him closely."

The man looked already dead—or completely unconscious—having suffocated from the pressure around his neck. To make the scene truly gruesome and grotesque, a pack of snarling dogs were jumping up and down to snap at his feet, genitals, and abdomen. The flesh on every part of his lower body had been shredded to ribbons, and his bones below the knees were exposed while the frenzied animals continued to desecrate the corpse.

"You know that man, don't you?"

When I looked closely, my eyes threatened to pop out again. He was a delinquent young man named Okada. He had lived in the small town where I had been born and raised, approximately three hours away from Tokyo. When I was a high school student, that is, a little before I moved to Tokyo, this man, two years older than me, had often been seen hanging around in the downtown area or aimlessly driving his SUV around. My hometown was a small peaceful town in a mountainous area where there had not been a single case of murder before. Okada's father was a carpenter, and Okada himself had started his career as an apprentice. But after his coming of age, he had stopped working with his father and started wandering as a delinquent. Then, seven or eight years ago, after I moved to Tokyo, there was a report of an incident involving a local junior-high-school girl. The girl suddenly disappeared on her way home from school, and very recently, word was out that the police had finally determined the murderer. The identity of the murderer was still being withheld because the police investigators had yet to produce crucial material evidence for his arrest, but the local people had all suspected that Okada was somehow involved.

"Was he actually the one who abducted her?"

"Yes, he took her to a deserted place in his car, raped and killed her, and abandoned her body deep in the mountains."

"Holy shit!"

"The police finally found enough evidence that he had murdered her, though her body wasn't found. He was arrested and tried, but he never seemed remorseful. So, they executed him."

"So soon?"

Normally, it would take at least two or three years before an execution was carried out even if the suspect did not show a sign of contrition or did not bother to appeal.

"In fact, the execution would take place a few years *later* in your time." Number 4 explained that there was a significant time difference between the living world and the underworld.

"I see. And do the dogs keep snapping at his body to strip him of all flesh and skin?"

"Perhaps. But we'll turn the animals away as soon as the girl's body is discovered. Then, this guy might be allowed to rest in quietude."

"You mean, he'd be entombed or something."

"No, there's no such thing in this world. Besides, he doesn't deserve it. He'd be just left undisturbed, hanging from the tree, so that he would eventually be mummified. But, as you know, he hid the girl's body deep in the mountains after committing a hideous rape and murder, so it'll be a while before the body might be finally found. Until then, he'd be exposed to the canine teeth for punishment. The dogs would render him completely skeletal, though the head and upper torso might remain because the animals can't reach them."

"That is, he'll continue to be exposed and humiliated."

"Yes, and again, he deserves it."

I could understand, and agreed to, Number 4's statement, but I was just too horrified when I pictured his skeletal body hanging and being abused by the animals for months, or years, to come.

***

After another hour of trekking with Number 4, I found myself in front of a cave. Number 4 explained that it was a tunnel that led to the summit of a mountain and to the exit from the netherworld.

The moment I stepped into the tunnel, however, I was overwhelmed by a sickly, damp air. A strong sulfuric odor stung my nose, and the tunnel made me feel as if I were buried alive deep under the ground. When I proceeded for about three or four hundred meters, fighting against the pungent smell, the ascending tunnel leveled out. We came into a fairly wide-open space, which seemed like a midway rest area. After proceeding a few more steps, I was suddenly dazzled by the bright red light, which, as I got closer, turned out to be a bonfire. A gigantic cooking pot was placed above the fire, and the boiling water was sending up thick plumes of steam—the scene that I could not help associating with the story of Ishikawa Goemon.

Goemon was a notorious thief in the Edo era; he stole from the rich and gave the stolen items or money away to the poor and underprivileged. Legend had it that, when arrested, he had been boiled to death in a public execution. Exactly as in the story of Goemon, a middle-aged man was writhing in pain in the simmering, hot water.

Seeing it first-hand, though, was a truly horrifying experience, and I felt that the heat radiating from the boiling pot would scorch my face and hair.

"You know that man, don't you?"

"Well . . ." Thick columns of steam rising from the pot made it difficult for me to recognize his face.

"I hope you've been careful enough with your money not to be involved with the likes of this guy." Number 4 dropped a hint.

"Oh, yeah, I know him!"

He was the former president of Yamashi Credit, a notorious consumer-credit company. As far as I remembered, he was currently on trial for the use of heavy-handed tactics for retrieving the loaned money. The media reported that he had lent money at outrageously high interest rates, taking advantage of business administrators or individual citizens swamped in financial quagmires, and made his subordinates use *yakuza*-like tactics to terrorize those who were slow in paying back the loans. A group of his former employees filed a suit against him after one of their colleagues committed suicide, which triggered a nationwide class action to press charges against his company.

The main office of Yamashi Credit was near a railway station ten minutes from my apartment. Although I commuted to my office by bus, I occasionally caught a train at the railway station when heading out for a personal appointment. And I had once literally crossed paths with him in front of the office building that housed his company. In fact, I had physically run into him. Yamashi had pulled his Rolls-Royce to the curb, climbed out, and crossed the pedestrians' pavement to enter the office building. As he darted out in front of me, we almost collided with each other. I tried to dodge him, but his elbow hit my stomach. He clearly noticed it, but instead of apologizing, he gave me a dirty look as if I were the one to be blamed for blocking his passage. I still remembered his hateful, disdainful expression and his condescending manners.

"I thought he was going to be taken to court."

"He was *as of a week ago*. But he somehow threw the investigators off the scent when they came to his office with a search warrant and attempted to flee the country. While the police were still moving heaven and earth to find him, he sneaked around and made it to a small port under the cover of darkness, obviously trying to escape in his own sailboat. But that's where we arrested him. We caught him on the seaside highway and drove his Rolls-Royce off the road. He plunged one hundred meters down the cliff to a death valley."

I was speechless for a long moment, scared and, at the same time, impressed by the efficacy of the dead world's law enforcement system. On the other hand, when I reflected on the man's wicked and loathsome personality, the idea of his shiny Rolls-Royce turning into an ugly junk was a rather amusing diversion.

"Hmm!" I was a little puzzled by one anomaly. "So you can actually manipulate events in the human world."

"If necessary."

"But you didn't help the police find the body of the girl that Okada had hidden?"

"Why should we do such a thing? He's just suffering from the sin he'd committed."

"Right, right!"

He pointed his finger straight to the man in the Goemon pot. "This guy deserves this, doesn't he?"

Before my own death, I had repeatedly seen the forty-two-year-old moneylender's face on the news. When TV reporters with microphones were chasing him, this man literally thumbed his nose and climbed into his chauffeured limousine.

He surely deserves the severest punishment, I acknowledged to myself. But the sight of a man being boiled in a large pot was just too gory and gruesome. A crew of executioners—black, dwarf-like creatures—took their positions around the pot. Their right hand was crooked like a scythe, and the index and middle fingers on the left hand formed a pair of large scissors. There were also executioners with hands shaped like hammers or spears. A pair of horns was sticking out of each creature's head. Their eyes were extremely small and almost invisible, but they were obviously sharp enough not to miss any move by the man being punished. Yamashi tried to pop his head above the simmering water time and again, gasping for air, but one of the black creatures with an iron hammer was sure to strike his head and shove it under the hot water. When the tortured man lost his consciousness, another executioner dragged him up above the surface, and yet another executioner plunged a spear into his ear. They did not allow him to expire so easily. Instead, they kept drowning and waking him alternately in endless repetition.

"Did Yamashi cross the river in a black robe?"

"Yes. But don't bother to reason why the man who was supposed to toil in the river for years is already here. It's just that your concept of time doesn't apply here."

"All right." Overwhelmed by the barbaric sight of a boiling execution, I did not have room for further debate or speculation.

The punishment was indescribably brutal. However, now that I had seen the sinners being tortured at the second and third stages, I was more concerned about what the last scene might be like.

***

I turned away from the Goemon pot and, following Number 4's navigation, started walking again through the tunnel.

"For your information, Goemon, the notorious thief in the Edo era, didn't actually end up here," Number 4 offered a tip of information.

"Is that so?"

"Yeah. When he arrived in this world, he was placed in the white-robed group." Number 4 talked as if it had been a very recent event. As Number 4 indicated, I had realized by then that the concept of time in the living world did not apply to the world of the dead. "He was then put to rest after a certain ritual."

After about a hundred meters of walk, the cave narrowed again, and another hundred meters ahead, it came to a dead end where a ladder was propped against a towering rock wall.

"The ladder is for you," Number 4 announced. I could see dark splotches on the cliff face. When my eyes adjusted to the dim lighting, I recognized those dark shadows as humans clinging to the wall and trying to scale it. Their hands and feet were blistered and bleeding, and they repeatedly slid down after ascending a few centimeters.

The ladder prepared for me was tilted at an approximately 60-degree angle but, strangely, stretched endlessly up into the sky without being bent under its own weight. The legs of the ladder were placed only a meter away from the rocky wall, and it did not make any physical or mathematical sense in terms of the length of the ladder and the angle at which it was propped against the wall.

"Go ahead and climb it, and you'll get to the final stage."

"Will there be other weird stuff up there?" I could not help asking like a nervous young boy who was waiting to enter a dentist's examination and treatment room.

"Weird it is, from the living people's perspective," Number 4 answered in the affirmative.

Breathing in deeply, I put my right foot on the lowest rung and grasped the one at chest level with my left hand. The ladder reminded me of a gymnastics class in high school where we were required to scale a wall studded with rungs and rings to hang onto. I had always cringed from that event, but here, I had no choice. When I mustered my strength and tried to pull myself up by the right hand, however, I actually felt as light as air. Number 4 himself simply levitated and came up after me without even holding onto the ladder. I gained altitude very fast, although the humans—or half-mummified bodies—on the wall frightened me when my peripheral vision captured them. A hundred, two hundred, and three hundred rungs slid downward beneath my hands and feet, and I soon went up to the top of the cliff and crawled onto the plateau. This easy, swift climb suddenly gave me a reassuring feeling that I was approaching the end of the dark passage through the infernal regions—except, of course, for the upcoming final display! On the elevated area that I climbed onto, the entire land was barren and frozen, and the ground was covered with a layer of ice, which was in sharp contrast with the swelteringly hot place where Yamashi was boiled in a large Goemon pot. It was still pitch-dark, and although Number 4 guided me forward with his lantern, I could not see a meter ahead of me and had to rely on his verbal command for each step to take.

"Now, take ten steps forward and turn right." Number 4 gave me instructions, which I followed. "Take another ten steps, turn to the left, and take five steps. Yes, that's it."

I found myself standing in a chamber equipped with an alcove. The chamber was obviously meant to accommodate a small group of visitors. "Now, you get down and sit on your knees."

Following his command, I clumsily sat on what seemed like a *tatami* mat and peered into an alcove, or framed den, which looked like a display stage for a freak show at a carnival. My eyes adjusted to the darkness with time, and the object on the stage itself started to emit faint light. When I made out what was inside, I froze and was transfixed by the unusualness of the image presented in front of me.

Is this the man who committed the greatest sin in our society?

I was looking at the most hideous ending of a human. He was crucified on the concrete wall, a thick pile driven into his throat. Each of his limbs was pinned to the wall with a thirty-centimeter nail. His eyes, nose, and bowels were gouged out, and lizards, rats, and insects were creeping in and out of all the cavities and crevices, extracting and feeding on the remaining organs inside. It was the ugliest and most gruesome ending of a human being. With his eyes and nose hollowed out, I could not easily identify the man. But with the lapse of a minute, the shredded pieces of what seemed like a surplice revealed his identity.

He was the highest-ranking Buddhist monk named Kosho—the most celebrated person of my home prefecture. In fact, he was not just a monk but a hero of our home city; he had put the small unknown city on the map. With more than three hundred thousand full-time followers, he was requested to lecture at universities and hold seminars at nationwide conventions throughout the year. His lectures, speeches, or seminars were often broadcast on TV and were available on DVDs. He was not just a Buddhist monk; he was a famous scholar, a published author, and a practicing doctor who had developed his own discipline of holistic medicine. His novel philosophies about life and death brought about a great sensation after hundreds of aged or ailing people reported that their chronic diseases had been completely cured when his hand touched the affected parts. Although his followers had built a palace in Shibuya Ward of Tokyo and transported him from place to place in a limousine so that he could cope with his murderously heavy schedules, he was known to lead a very frugal life himself and was thus respected as a truly charismatic leader. A huge population of people admired him like a deity, and there was a rumor that he was preparing to run in the next parliamentary election in order to reform the corrupt political system of the country.

"But why . . . why is he here? I thought he was the most respected and trusted person in our society."

"On the contrary, he is the biggest liar on earth, having deceived thousands of thousands of people, using his dirty tricks. He'd swindled innocent people out of their life savings. He collected tons of donations, saying that the money would be sent to starving people in Africa and India. In fact, with the collected money, he built a palace in Shibuya to entertain rich, influential people."

"Did he *order* his followers to build a palace?"

"Of course."

"I heard he lived very frugally."

"That's full of crap! He treated himself to expensive wines and dishes every day and housed a dozen concubines in his palace. He also indulged in the collection of expensive garments, masterpiece drawings, and hilariously high-priced Japanese swords, purchasing them all with the money he'd stolen from innocent people. Starving children in Africa didn't receive a penny. Not only that, but he murdered dozens of people who tried to leave his organization or file a suit against him or his syndicate. As a matter of fact, he had such extensive influence that his disciples and followers included prominent scientists, highranking police officers, and powerful lawyers, and they covered up all his criminal conduct. The victims could never take revenge against him or prove themselves to be victims. But we knew it all and decided to handle him ourselves."

"You mean, a little later?"

"Right! You've ended up in this place at an inopportune timing, but yes, from your perspective, historical events have been chronically scrambled."

I was staring at the man's figure for a long moment while he was moaning in his death throes; on his face was the most pathetic expression that I had ever seen. And I realized that a really weird phenomenon was taking place. A deep scar suddenly emerged on the man's face, running vertically from forehead to chin, and the skin and a layer of muscle beneath it were ripped open sideways. It looked as if a thick leather jacket was being turned inside out. Then, the man's face turned into a plump, middle-aged woman's. The head and body were still penetrated by the pile and long nails and were being abused by small animals and insects. But the entire body was blurred for a moment and then turned into a clearly different image.

"Who is that?" I exclaimed to myself, groping in my memory for a person that matched the image. The distinct feeling that I must have seen her somewhere in the past made me extremely uncomfortable.

"I guess you spent a lot of time watching TV when you were a teenager."

"I supposed I did." In those days, I had far more free time to spend in front of my TV set.

"Who was your favorite TV personality?"

I gasped at the shocking realization. "Damn it! I don't believe it!"

It was Kaoru Tachibana! She had started as a TV newscaster. But with her charming expressions and perfect proportions, she debuted a few years later as an actress and singer. She had been my idol when I was a high school student. Half a dozen life-size posters of her were posted on my walls. She was several years older than me, and what I really admired her for was her versatility: reading news on TV as a newscaster, starring in popular dramas and movies, composing and singing songs, and writing bestseller essay books. She was also known as a world traveler, fluent in English, French, Spanish, and Chinese. Then, she ran in the parliamentary election and was elected. That was when a rumor circulated that she had an incorrigible, manipulative side.

"What happened—or what is going to happen—to her?" I was becoming accustomed to the time discrepancies. It was obvious that she would eventually be appointed to a highranking administrative post in the government.

"A good question! Her final position was popular culture minister, a new position that the last prime minister created for her. In fact, the prime minister who pulled strings for her had gotten his own position as head of the nation with the help of his uncle who was a former prime minister. But the opposition parties protested against the nomination of Tachibana in chorus and kicked her out, criticizing her lack of political expertise and integrity. 'You can't fool all the people all the time,' as a former US president said. Her reputation turned from a role model for working women to a weather vane and to a political whore. It was one of the reasons why the prime minister himself was forced to resign a few months later. But anyway, the point is, she never made efforts to make society better or help people. Instead, in the process of her relentless ascent, she kept backstabbing her colleagues and deceiving her supporters. She never contributed to the betterment of society. Instead, she damaged the country's politics irrevocably, interfering with the conscientious people's efforts to resolve various social problems."

"How would you classify her as a sinner?"

"I think political whore is a perfect term for her," he said in a flat tone. "She didn't have to work as a prostitute for money, of course, because she was born to a very wealthy family. But she was a typical kiss-up-kick-down type. She flattered people with influence and treated those of lower rank like dirt. She never hesitated to slander those who might be an obstacle to her promotions. We have dealt with a number of humans like her in the past, but she was the most despicable."

Then, the woman's image blurred and took the shape of yet another person—a military commander in his fifties. I studied his descriptive features closely but could not identify him.

"I don't think I've ever seen him!"

"Not in person or on the TV screen, of course, because he died before you were born. And I know today's young people aren't seriously concerned about the historical personages during the wars."

I groped for a hint in my memory, and a few seconds later, the missing pieces of a puzzle fell into place. "Admiral Musashi!"

"Correct! And you can see what crime and sin he'd committed. He sent hundreds of thousands of promising young men to battlefields, knowing they'd be mercilessly blown to death. He ordered his subordinates to put teenagers on old, half-broken Zero Fighters or in Kaiten suicide submarines with the mission of crashing into enemy battleships. He put forward a fancy philosophy to make young soldiers believe they could cause a divine wind to blow off all evil enemies and would go to the heavens after martyrdom. His conduct has set the worst example of moral and ethical violation in the world so that people in other parts of the world started doing copycat jobs."

"Like nine-eleven and suicide bombers in Iraq or Israel?"

"Yes, and probably more to come in the future."

"But how can I be related to him? I don't believe I crossed paths with him. We didn't even live in the same period."

"Your direct supervisor's name is Teruyoshi Musashi, isn't it?"

"Right."

"He's a great-grandson of the admiral."

"Holy shit!"

I was in a trance for a long moment until Number 4 addressed me again in a low tone, "Now, you can see why those guys don't even have their own figure or identity anymore. They have turned into an unrecognizably rotten cadaver of the most egoistic souls in human history."

"What bothers me, though, is that the seriousness of the crime doesn't seem to match between the three people. In my opinion, the woman you call a political whore can't really be compared to the general who caused hundreds of thousands of young people to die."

"I can see your logic. But in this world, we consider the gravity of sin, not crime, and how much they were hated by other human beings. Sin is by far the more reliable criterion than crime when we have to judge who the worst person in this world is."

I could see Number 4's point.

"But anyway, we thank you for your patience, and I would extend my sincere apology once again to you concerning your accidental involvement. We now let you go. Please look straight down at the mat underneath your legs."

Suddenly, the *tatami* mat on which I was sitting was pulled down with tremendous momentum, and I dropped straight down by what seemed like fifty, one hundred, or two hundred meters as if in a crashing elevator in a tall building. I was sucked into the vacuum without being able to emit a word of exclamation, and when I opened my eyes, the woman owner of the fruit-and-vegetable shop was bending over me and looking down into my face. "I told you, young man! Thank God you are still in one piece!"

A Tent by the River

"There they are, again!"

Satoshi jogged through that scenic spot by the river every day, and it was not rare for him to find a camera crew shooting a film there. He knew it was a popular location for movies and TV dramas but stopped to make sure what they were doing, remembering his agreement with his friend Keiko. Keiko, his university classmate who lived in the vicinity, had never seen a filming location and had entreated him to let her know on his next sighting.

"I've got to call Keiko!"

Jogging ten kilometers was part of Satoshi's daily physical fitness routine. As a graduate student, he spent hours every day reading books or working on his research projects. His eyes tended to be strained and his back stiff, so he committed himself to an hour of physical exercise every day: running outside in the late afternoon or early evening. As usual, he had been running along his favorite waterfront route and was just about to cross the bridge to return to his home. The filming in progress was on the western side of the river, whereas his home was on the eastern side. He would not normally bother to stop and watch it himself, but Keiko, who was an avid viewer of TV dramas, had expressed her strong desire to see a film being shot on location.

Satoshi knew exactly where the nearest pay phone was. He made his way to the booth, picked up the receiver, deposited the prepared coins, and dialed her cell phone number. He heard a few dial tones, and a female voice—not Keiko's voice but what sounded like a recorded message by a professional announcer—clicked in: "This is Keiko's answering service. Please leave a message after a beep."

"Gosh, she's never there when I call her with good news!" he grumbled to himself. But at least, she seemed to have finally put her phone on the answering service so that he could leave a message as evidence that he kept his promise to call her. On the past few occasions, he had heard an endless series of dial tones or had gotten a mechanical message that her cell phone was either out of transmission range or the power had been turned off. He left a voicemail message, reporting the time and place of the filming, hung up, and resumed his jogging. Chances were slim that she would pick up the message soon enough and come over to the movie production site at once, so he did not bother to wait long for her arrival. He had fulfilled his obligation as a good friend and neighbor. His mission was accomplished. Before leaving, he took a quick look at the young woman who seemed to be a starring actress. She was very beautiful in her own way and might even be a famous actress, but because he was not in the habit of watching TV dramas regularly, he could not identify her.

"It's ironic," Satoshi smiled wryly. "People like me, who don't care about those dramas or TV personalities, keep running into filming locations, but Keiko, who's crazy about them, keeps missing a chance."

Satoshi and Keiko were both students at Seito University and happened to be enrolled in the same French course. Satoshi was a graduate student who majored in economics and took French as an elective foreign language. He needed to read articles and books written by French scholars. Keiko was a Japanese literature major, taking French as part of the requirement for her bachelor's degree. They often sat together at a desk up front. Satoshi always arrived early to sit near the teacher's podium, and Keiko tended to come to the classroom just in time and ended up sitting up front because there was no other empty seat left. During their conversation at recess, they found out that they lived in the same neighborhood near the Sumida River and picked up a couple of local topics. Then, he mentioned his routine jogging and the fact that he had sighted many filming locations.

"From what you've said, it must be *A Love in Tokyo II*." When he described one of the locations that he had seen, she could immediately tell the name of the TV drama, which he had only heard of and had never watched.

"Well, as I said, I don't watch a lot of TV dramas, and . . ."

"Yes, yes, that must be it."

"I saw a young, skinny actress with shoulder-length hair."

"That's Miku Yamazaki. And did you see a tall man—about 185 centimeters tall—with long, yellow hair?"

"You mean the weird guy with a piercing earring on his right earlobe?"

"Oh, yes, yes, yes! That's Hayate Kondo! Oh, yes, He's my favorite actor."

"Is he?"

"Yes. Will you please, please let me know next time you see it?" She begged him to contact her on her cell phone in case he saw another location. He had no reason not to accommodate her request.

"Sure!"

"Oh, I might get his autograph, or shake hands, or even take a snapshot with him!" She was ecstatic and engaged in her optimistic imagination.

"I didn't know seeing actors at a movie location would mean so much to you."

"I'd kill for it, Satoshi. When you see a location again, would you call me on my cell phone whatever the hour?"

"I will, if that's what you want."

"Oh, thank you! I'd hop on my bicycle and shoot over to the site."

The only problem was that he, as a conscientious person, felt so strongly committed to the agreement that he had to repeatedly interrupt his jogging and call her. He would have to keep doing it until her dream of seeing a movie production in person was fulfilled.

***

Their neighborhood was a beautiful residential area located on the waterfront. A long, wide strip of pavement—along either shore of the Sumida River—stretched over several kilometers. People who worked or lived in the area enjoyed a leisurely walk on fine days, and amateur photographers spent time taking pictures of the scenery tinged with different colors of sunlight at different times of the day. On the eastern side of the river where Satoshi and Keiko lived, there was a bank of high-rises—including thirty- to forty-story ultramodern residential towers—which constituted part of a picturesque urban landscape of Tokyo. The developers had taken over a huge land area where a major steel maker's factories used to be located and turned it into a new residential area. There was also a new suspension bridge designed by a famous French architect.

Although a large number of people visited this metropolitan scenic spot, either from neighboring areas or from faraway places, the entire waterfront area was so large that it was never crowded to the extent that a filming activity might interfere with walkers' or joggers' passage. It was one of the reasons why TV or movie companies tended to choose this site as a perfect place for filming. They could obtain permission to shoot a film there more easily than to do so in the middle of downtown Ginza.

Another nice feature of this neighborhood was that there were very few pavement dwellers. When the first group of high-rises was built, the local residents saw a few homeless men on the waterfront. Some were lying on benches, and others slept in cardboard boxes under the bridge on either side of the river, but the city government seemed to have taken countermeasures at once. Police officers started patrolling the area frequently, and the maintenance staff in charge of the public areas fixed metal armrests on each bench, sectioning it off into two or three separate spaces, so that nobody could sprawl on it in the lying position. *A nasty trick*, the homeless might have thought, but people were relieved that one security threat had been removed or, at least, put under control. Again, a few pavement dwellers had been seen loitering, but interestingly, they never stayed there very long. They drifted in from somewhere, stayed there for a couple of days, and soon disappeared. There was no sign of a formal complaint filed by either residents on the eastern shore or business administrators on the western shore.

***

However, when Satoshi started jogging again along the riverside, he was reminded of one notable exception: a blotch on the perfect urban landscape. While he started climbing a slope toward the bridge, he noticed a small, new tent pitched near the bottom of the slope. The tent looked almost brand-new, and a middle-aged man in his rather clean jeans and T-shirt was sitting nearby, smoking. He was in his late forties or early fifties and about 175centimeters tall. His hair, streaked with gray, was trimmed short, and he was obviously in good shape and health. Satoshi had seen him several times in the past, but with the appearance of the new tent, this homeless person's existence was suddenly projected. The man had always possessed a stack of plastic containers, in which all his clothes, provisions, and other belongings seemed to be stored, and a bicycle was propped on its kickstand near the plastic containers. It was quite a lot of property for a pavement dweller, Satoshi thought. But the new tent attracted his attention the most.

When Satoshi ran past the man, stealing a glimpse of his tent, the latter obviously noticed, turned toward him, and even showed a faint smile on his face. The man was clearly familiar with the young runner who had been jogging through the area all the time. Satoshi nodded in recognition but just continued to jog along his course. He was not interested in any intimate relationship with the homeless, whether he was friendly or not friendly.

During their brief encounter, however, he recognized a character—and a sign of intelligence—in his expression.

He might have held a decent job and position before he ended up here. Perhaps, he failed in stocks or real estate transactions when the bubble economy collapsed.

Satoshi soon tried to dismiss it out of his mind, though, because he needed to finish his jogging and get back to his studies.

I just hope he wouldn't set a bad precedent, inviting more homeless guys into this area.

***

After seeing the new tent for the first time, Satoshi started paying more attention to the man than before. Sometimes, his tent was not seen, probably folded up and stowed away in one of his plastic containers. One afternoon, Satoshi saw the man listening to a CD player, but he was using a pair of earphones in order not to bother people who walked or ran through the area. The player was placed on top of his stacked containers, and he was standing as if trying not to give an impression that he was taking up extra space. There was never any litter around his place, not even a cigarette butt. Satoshi was impressed by his tidiness. But he still could not help worrying about the possibility that this single individual might draw other tramps and establish a homeless colony in this nice neighborhood. A man with great personal charisma, whatever his present position, would often make other people gather around him and act in concert.

As days went by, Satoshi, as a regular jogger, began to perceive the homeless man or his tent again as just part of the background scenery along his jogging course. And to his relief, the man did not seem to be drawing homeless companions from other areas. Occasionally, he was seen with one or two other men in rags, sitting on the steps or leaning against the river guardrail. They were chatting and smoking together in a rather relaxed and friendly way, but for one reason or another, new tramps never settled in the area. They were seen with him one day but were gone the next day. As far as Satoshi remembered, several different individuals came, and each drifted away in a day or two.

Satoshi secretly nicknamed him a homeless gentleman and continued to run past him with a mixed feeling of puzzlement, amusement, and slight respect. But, of course, watching the homeless was not his major concern; he was there to run for his good health.

If he ever paid attention to anything during his run, it was, instead, to people on the more glamorous side of society. While jogging, he could not help glancing at men and women in dark business suits, getting in and out of the big corporate buildings. He was hoping to join one of the large corporations after obtaining a master's degree in economics. Movie locations, although he was not as keenly interested in the entertainment business as his friend Keiko, was another glamorous part of city life.

Because he jogged along the waterfront pavement every day, he saw a filming crew almost every week, a rather good sighting rate outside of movie or TV companies' studios. And one late afternoon, he finally got hold of Keiko on her cell phone while the filming was in progress. She was delighted at his call and came to the site in five and a half minutes.

"Oh, thank you so much, Satoshi. I really, really appreciate it," she expressed her gratitude, beaming with delight. No sooner had she caught her breath than she spotted and identified the starring actor. "Oh, my goodness, it's Kento Hayakawa! I'm a big fan of his."

They watched the location together, Keiko explaining who the actors and actresses were and what drama they were shooting. She was as fluent and informative as a movie commentator. Although she did not have a chance to talk to, or shake hands with, her favorite actor, she was enchanted to see him at close range.

However, the movie production was a slow-going activity as the director ordered the actors and staff to redo the same scene over and over again. So, after watching it for a while, the two students left the site and started strolling down the waterfront together, picking up casual topics. Then, there *he* was again! The homeless gentleman was smoking, sitting at his place, but that moment, a totally unexpected incident took place right in front of their eyes! A large black automobile pulled over on the traffic road up on the embankment. The road ran in parallel with the riverside walkway but was elevated by about five meters. The car screeched to a halt, and a group of four big men, all in dark suits, climbed out of the car, walked down the slope, and headed straight to where the homeless gentleman was sitting. One man was about the homeless man's age, although a little shorter and much stockier. The others were all younger and heavyset. All the four men had their heads close cropped and wore sunglasses. Satoshi and Keiko were both stunned at the intimidating image of the men. *Is it another TV drama on location?* he almost thought for a moment and, then, instantly dismissed the idea.

The homeless gentleman rose to his feet when surrounded by the big men, and they talked for a few minutes in low voices. None of them raised their voices, but they kept talking with serious expressions on their faces.

"They look like crime syndicate members," Keiko whispered to Satoshi, frightened at the sight.

"No, I think it's an arrest," Satoshi said. "The heavyset guys must be plainclothes police officers."

"Or isn't it by any chance a different movie production?" In fact, it was what Satoshi himself had thought when the men in dark suits first arrived. But there was no camera crew following their movement.

"I seriously doubt it because there's no camera crew around him. Besides, I've been seeing that guy for some time, and I've always been suspicious about his background."

Satoshi felt that pieces of the puzzle suddenly fell into place. The man must have been a financier who had turned into a fugitive after a heavy tax evasion or his failure to pay off the debts. He looked like neither a brutal murderer nor a sneak robber. Instead, the image of an aggressive businessman who had driven himself into bankruptcy after trying to execute an overly ambitious business venture perfectly fit the lanky man now surrounded by dark-suit officers. But, of course, Satoshi was a graduate student, neither a financier nor a veteran detective. What had exactly happened to the man was completely beyond him.

Soon, the men with close-cropped heads escorted him up the embankment toward the car, forming a human enclosure around him. They did not handcuff him, but they kept a tight formation around him while they walked so that he would have no chance to escape.

***

The man climbed into the limousine and slumped in the backseats. He undid the top two buttons of his shirt and loosened the laces of his sneakers. "Gee, it's cool and nice in here!" he appreciated the air-conditioning in the car.

"Captain Hayashi, would you like something to drink?" asked the oldest of the dark suit men who sat with him in the backseats.

"What have you got, Igarashi-san?"

"We have iced tea, coffee, orange juice, and wine." Igarashi opened the lid of an icebox.

"Wine will be great."

"Certainly!"

Igarashi poured wine into a plastic cup and courteously handed it to Hayashi with both hands. It was served in a plastic cup, instead of a nice wine glass, but Hayashi appreciatively accepted and gulped it down. His face turned red at once.

"Gee, it's pretty good! I haven't had good wine for six months."

"Hope you'll make up for your lost time, sir."

"As far as good wine and *sake* are concerned, I definitely will!" Igarashi refilled his plastic cup.

"Where would you like to go, first, Captain Hayashi? Do you want to go back to your apartment in Akasaka and get changed before your meeting with the Governor? Or shall we take you to the police department which is nearer? I can get an extra uniform prepared for you by the time you get there."

"Well, if I can borrow a uniform at the headquarters, that'll be fine." He sipped his wine and stared into space for a second. "After all, what have I got back in my apartment? My wife and daughter are gone, and there's nobody waiting for my return."

"Well, as a personal friend, I'm truly sorry for what happened to your family."

"Well, a traffic accident is a traffic accident. There was nothing anybody could do about that. But thanks for your kind words."

"In my official capacity, though, I must say we were most fortunate that a man of your rank and experience volunteered to take on this mission on behalf of the department."

Captain Hayashi did not make any comment on his colleague's words.

"We never thought the situation would get so complicated. At first, there were just a few tramps, and the patrolling officers drove them away. But then, a group of homeless men started to live in a hidden area under the bridge, and the group soon began to grow large enough to colonize the neighborhood. Complaint calls flooded in from east side residents. Then, two large firms on the west side threatened to take legal action against the city that allowed drifters to settle in the area. The governor delegated the dirty work to the police, but we couldn't, of course, brandish our sticks or thrust our pistols at their temples to force them out because they hadn't done anything bad enough to be apprehended. Besides, if we kicked them out, they would just go to a neighboring park, and people there would start filing the same complaints. It's really a cat-and-mouse game. We had to deal with the situation using a secret tactic. But the problem was, no officer with experience and abilities would volunteer to live there as a homeless man himself and scare them away in a subtly intimidating language."

"Or persuade them to move into the homeless shelter," Hayashi added.

"Yes. And you handled the guys perfectly. I don't know how you did it, but you sent dozens of them to the protection center. Those bums are normally pretty stubborn and refuse to go there."

"Partly because they don't fully understand the benefits of the center. They feel they are just being thrown into an animal cage."

"Or a jail-like rehabilitation center where they have no freedom or privacy," Igarashi paraphrased it. Historically, the same neighborhood was home to a notorious training center for unemployed laborers, which was, retrospectively, categorized by historians as a type of prison.

"Well, I acknowledge that ninja tactics are my favorite skill area. I've spent years perfecting techniques to move people from one place to another without using a kendo stick or a karate chop. In fact, that's how I moved ahead in my career and made it to captain at age forty-two," he chuckled with a jocular expression.

"But again, thank you very much for volunteering. You've really saved the police department and society."

"You were right that no one is stupid enough to take on this kind of job, except for someone like me who doesn't have any home to return to! My large apartment isn't my home anymore. So being there or being out here on the waterfront didn't make much difference."

Igarashi remained silent for a second out of respect for the man who had not fully recovered from his family tragedy. "If it's any consolation, though," he said in a soft tone, "your promotion has been officially affirmed, as I just reported out there. You'll be the new head of our police department. Governor Ishiyama will officially appoint you to the position when you get to his office."

"All right! And thank you!"

"Naturally, there'll be a big bonus, too. You said you were going to buy a new apartment near your parents."

"Yes. That's my plan. Oh, by the way, will you pick up that small tent I was using and send it to my present apartment? I really liked it, and I want to keep it as a souvenir."

"Sure. I'll have someone deliver it to your place. Maybe, you can use it on another mission."

"Oh, come on! Knock it off!"

"I'm just kidding, sir." Both laughed.

"And about the bicycle and the set of glasses and plates, please return them to the Sumiyama Securities with words of thanks. They've been most courteous and hospitable throughout the time."

"I'll take care of the matter myself after we drop you off at the governor's office."

Top of the World

I had expected it to be a rather uneventful Saturday at our office, contrasted with the hustle and bustle of the last several months. A few employees were in the office to tie up loose ends, but most people took the day off. We had been working on the construction of a thirteen-story residential building, which was finally coming to its completion. The next stage was to have subcontractors move in and furnish the interior, but all in all, we could see the lights at the end of a tunnel. Right from the very beginning, this particular construction project had entailed a number of problems. Before the foundation was to be laid, there had been a strong protest from the neighbors, claiming that the new building would shadow their houses and shut them out of sunshine. There was also a fatal accident involving a worker early in the construction process, and my good colleague who supervised the pertinent section had been prosecuted for negligence and forced to resign in disgrace. But we struggled through to finish the building, and I took a morning off myself for the first time in ten months. When I arrived at the company and walked into the office at 12:10 p.m., the few people working that day were out for lunch except Uchida, a chief architect. He was my same-year colleague at the company and had been a good friend of mine. At the time, he was sipping a hot cup of coffee alone in the sitting area. A folded newspaper was laid on the coffee table.

"Were you waiting to go to lunch with me?" In fact, I had already eaten soba noodles near the subway station.

"Well, actually, I wasn't. My wife fixed a *bento* lunch for me, and I've already eaten it. But come over here for a second! I wanted to show you something."

I noticed an uncharacteristically grave expression on his face. By nature, he was a relaxed type of person with a great sense of humor, who cracked silly jokes even at a serious business conference. "What is it?"

"Isn't this the guy who came into this office last week?" He opened his newspaper and pointed at a small article on the third page.

I read the headline and the first few sentences and froze at the name Shingo Saotome. The words *crash* and *killed* glared.

"I remember you told me he was a kind of TV personality."

"Y-yeah." I snatched the paper and tried to read the entire article. While I was reading it, Uchida explained it like a simultaneous interpreter.

"It seems like your friend killed himself, driving his new Nissan at 120 kilometers past midnight, after consuming a lot of alcohol at a bar. He crashed head on into a utility pole."

I remembered the shiny, latest model Fairlady that he had driven to my office last week. It was typical of him to drive around a plush sports car even when he was heavily in debt. But as far as I remembered, one thing he could justly boast of was his semiprofessional driving skills. One hundred and twenty kilometers per hour should be his normal cruising speed, leaving aside the issue of inebriation.

So you did it, bastard! I stared into space and cursed at my dead friend in my mind. *Goddammit, you really did it!*

***

Shingo Saotome, whose real name was Koichi Tanaka, was my old classmate back in high school. He was 180 centimeters tall, boasted a sporty long hair in those days, and often played the guitar in front of his classmates. He was also a very good basketball player, although he never joined the high school basketball team, saying that he hated the regimentation of sport teams. Because his birthday was in April, he obtained his driver's license earlier than anybody else in the class and started driving his father's car around at the beginning of the third year in high school. Of course, he kept it a secret to the teachers, but many of his classmates knew it and admired him for it.

Koichi, another boy named Akio, and I used to hang out after school. In retrospect, the three of us had distinctly different personality characteristics and completely different values and worldviews. Looking back, I could not even believe that we had spent so much private time together. But at any rate, we hung out at local karaoke studios, fast-food restaurants, and the only discotheque near JR Toyama Station. In a small town one hundred kilometers north of Tokyo, there were few entertainment establishments for high school students, but we went to all the available places together. One late afternoon in the summer, we were chatting in a little corner of the school playground. Koichi passed around a cigarette package and suddenly said, "You guys want to go to Harajuku?"

"Sure. I know it's a fancy place," Akio said.

"Then, let's go."

"When?"

"Right now."

"Jesus." It was already five in the afternoon. "It takes two hours just to get to Tokyo."

"Two hours to get to Tokyo, and we still can spend a couple of hours there and catch the last train back home."

So that we can brag about our adventure and about our hairbreadth jump into the last train to the classmates tomorrow morning: I could see what he was plotting to do.

I had committed a number of minor offenses as a high school student and often behaved in the way that my parents disapproved of: smoking a cigarette, cutting classes, drinking beer at a karaoke studio, or riding a motorcycle before obtaining my driver's license. They were all part of my adolescent rebellion against my disciplinarian parents. But missing the last train and roaming downtown Tokyo past midnight was not my idea of being cool and independent. We might even be expelled from the school when our delinquent behavior was found and reported to the school principal.

"Do you want to go?"

"Oh, I don't know."

"Come on, Satoru. You are like a chick that never learns to fly off the nest!" Koichi teased me in a way that always irritated me.

I turned to Akio in search of an excuse to stay away from trouble. "What do you think, Akio?"

"Well, it sounds like fun, but I don't have money."

"I've got enough money. I can loan you the train fares."

"Oh, all right," Akio answered without thinking carefully. Whereas my father was a physical education teacher at a prefectural high school, Akio's father had inherited a farmland from his parents, and his hobbies were playing mah-jongg and flirting with bar hostesses. Because of his father's influence, Akio himself tended to act without considering the consequences of his moves.

"Are you serious?" I protested, frowning at Akio's betrayal and his careless decision.

Koichi was a friendly man and was always good company, but another reason why his classmates gathered around him was that he always had a large amount of cash on him for a high school student. He often treated his friends to hamburgers and coffee or ramen noodles. He said that he had a small job, running errands for an automobile repair shop and sometimes bragged about collecting thirty or forty thousand yen by winning pinball games at a *pachinko* parlor. He said that he cheated on his age and entered the establishments. It was true that he had deft fingers and had a strong intuition for gambling, but I always suspected that he was exaggerating his own earnings. He probably received more allowances from his parents than other boys of his age. I had heard that his father was a long-distance truck driver and his mother worked a night shift at a local hospital. They left Koichi alone a great deal of time and, to compensate for their absence, spoiled him with a larger amount of money to dispense. One of my other classmates once said that his mother was not a registered nurse, but I never learned exactly what her professional position was at the hospital or how hospitable nurses were ranked. Nobody in the neighborhood or at the school knew much about Koichi's family, and Mr. and Mrs. Tanaka never showed up on class observation days. Academically, Koichi was by no means a model student in class but made himself popular with his classmates in his own way.

"Hey, Satoru! You want to borrow some money from me, too?"

In fact, I happened to know exactly how much money I had in my wallet at the time. I could afford to buy the train tickets back and forth to Tokyo, eat a light meal, and still bring back about four thousand yen after the trip. I would not usually carry so much money around, but I was hoping to buy a few music CDs of my favorite singer on my way home, and that was why I had a fairly large amount of cash on me. But at any event, now that the other two had already voted to make a trip to Tokyo, I no longer had a good chance to escape without being called a coward or traitor.

"As a matter of fact, I've got just enough to pay for myself."

"All right, then. Let's go. I'll buy you some food and drinks when we get there."

"Oh, that'll be nice!" Akio responded with a carefree expression.

***

We put our bags in coin-operated lockers at Toyama Station and hopped into the next semi-express train for which we did not have to pay additional express fares. But before we boarded the train, there was a minor incident, which, in retrospect, I should have paid more attention to. When we were buying train tickets, Koichi stole a glimpse into my wallet and said, "You actually have a lot of money, Satoru!"

"Oh! It's just that I was going to buy some CDs later in the day. I usually don't carry this much money."

Koichi allowed an uncanny smile on his lips, which strangely bothered me. Then, he stepped forward to the ticket counter to buy one-way tickets for Akio and himself.

When we arrived in Tokyo, Koichi bought us hot dogs and Coca-Cola just as he had promised, and we walked down the streets, eating and drinking.

It was in early summer, and although we arrived at Harajuku past seven o'clock, there was much sunlight left. The shopping area was crowded with young people. But to my own surprise, I took an instant liking to Harajuku! Everything was novel and fascinating. A variety of fancy shops lined the streets, and people were dressed in colorful, fashionable dresses, symbolic of the city life I had dreamed of as a country boy. I even forgot about our argument for or against an adventure to the city two hours before. Then, when we came close to the Jingu Bridge near the gate to Yoyogi Park, we saw groups of teenage boys and girls dancing to tape-recorded music in unique costumes. For the first time in my life, I saw what was known as Takenoko-zoku (bamboo-shoot clan) dancers firsthand. They looked just about our age and, therefore, could be high school students themselves, that is, unless they had already dropped out, seeking too much freedom and entertainment and neglecting their studies.

Koichi turned to me and grinned. I could see what he was trying to say: *I told you, Satoru. If you don't venture, you'd never see all these fascinating things in the real world.*

Some of the young dancers' faces were painted red, yellow, and white, and their hairs dyed in weird colors. Some of the clothes and accessories that they wore were more bizarre than unique or fashionable, but I still appreciated the originality that they expressed in their own way.

"Pretty neat, huh!" Koichi said.

"Yeah," I nodded noncommittally. Again, the area seemed to represent the culture of city teenagers that I had only read or heard about until then, but their dancing did not impress me as an artistic performance at all. I had always been interested in various genres of music and dances, and I had had a few years of dancing and gymnastics training from professional instructors at the suggestion of my father. So I knew a little more than those *kids on the street*. "Do they always dance this late?"

"I think they usually do it during the day, like Saturday or Sunday. But obviously, some do it in the evening, too."

"I like this kind of dancing," Akio said, again not thinking deeply. "It's cool, and it seems like a good way to blow off steam."

The first group that we saw was performing an amateurish version of Cossack dance, the next group was doing a mixture of tap dance and aerobics with big feathery hoods on their heads, and yet another team was repeating a series of hand-and-foot movements that resembled imperfect karate techniques. The only common factor was that they created something new out of mixtures of different dances and exercises. Yet one or two groups among them were attracting more attention than others, and quite a few people stood or squatted in front of them as an audience.

"What do you think, Satoru?"

"Huh, I think I can choreograph a much better one."

"You do?"

"Sure!"

"Hey, I have an idea. Why don't we form our own dancing team and come back here to dance? I can recruit a couple of other guys in the class to join us. And a few cute girls, too."

I knew that Koichi, a handsome tall boy with a knack with words, could recruit pretty girls easily. I also had to admit that he was endowed with certain leadership qualities in spite of his self-centered side that often grated on my nerves. But most importantly, I really liked the idea of choreographing or coaching my own dancing team. My father was a PE teacher and gymnast, and my mother used to be a music teacher before my sister and I were born. Unlike my elder sister, who had always done as they told, or expected, her to do and advanced to a prestigious music university, I just wanted to decide my own future based on my autonomous thinking and was, at the time, groping in the dark. That was why I tended to rebel against them whenever they seemed to dictate my life. Yet deep down inside, I was beginning to feel pressured to commit myself to seriously studying for entrance examinations and preparing for a professional career in the future. So the idea was to have one big party to blow off steam and then return to my studies. I knew enough about dancing and music to choreograph a bamboo-shoot-clan dancing team and thought it was a great chance to express my feelings and creativity. We could even demonstrate the same dance performance at the high school festival afterward.

"All right. Let's do it."

But on our way home, Koichi did something that I did not like. In retrospect, it might have been the beginning of our doomed relationship, which deteriorated and, in due course, resulted in a permanent breakup.

We moved back to the area near Harajuku Station, and Koichi guided us through some of the sideways lined by fancy shops advertised in fashion magazines and travel guidebooks. He then stopped in front of a women's accessory shop and said, "Guys, may I just stop by and buy a couple of things? I want to buy something for Mari."

"Yeah, but please be quick. We don't seem to have much time before the last train."

"Don't worry. I'm not stupid enough to forget about the departure time."

A number of fancy accessories and customed jewelries were displayed in the store window, and I could see that Koichi had always intended to buy some presents for his girlfriend and probably a couple of additional things for the other female friends that he associated with. Akio and I squatted at the edge of a pedestrians' street and waited, chatting on trivial matters. At the moment, the two of us were practically shut out of the exciting and glorious culture of Harajuku because we could not afford to do shopping. As I feared, Koichi took a much longer time than he said he would. And when he emerged out of the shop, we were dumbfounded at the two large shopping bags he was carrying.

"You bought all those stuff?"

"Well, Mari would be mad if I went to Tokyo and didn't bring back anything nice for her. And it'd be nice to get some compliments for everybody. Don't you guys want to buy anything?"

"I don't have money," Akio shrugged his shoulders. We already knew that he did not have a single yen in his pocket. I did not even bother myself to reply to Koichi's question. I was carrying some cash, but it was what I had saved hard to buy new CDs.

"Come on. Let's go. We got to hurry to catch our train."

We dashed toward Harajuku Station. We had to take a train on the Yamanote Line first and, then, transfer at Ueno Station to a local train that would take us back to Toyama. Panting for breath, we finally reached Harajuku Station's ticket vendors. There was only thirty minutes before the last train back to our hometown would depart, approximately the time required for the trip from Harajuku to Uneo. Then, when I was taking out my wallet, Koichi said something totally unexpected in a matter-of-fact tone. "You know I spent too much money for shopping, and I've only got enough money left for my own ticket."

"What am I supposed to do now?" Akio was shocked.

"Satoru, you want to buy him a ticket?" he said with a smirk, which disgusted me. He had shrewdly figured out how much money was left in my wallet and had decided to exploit it.

"But you said you'd buy his ticket, and that's why we agreed to come here."

"Oh, come on! You have money. You buy him a ticket. No big deal! Remember I bought him the first one-way ticket."

"You said you'd lend him money for a *round* trip."

"Don't be so petty."

"No, I'm not. It's a matter of principle."

"All right. I acknowledge your principle. But whatever your principle, we've got to jump in the train and head back home. Come on, Satoru. You aren't saying we're going to leave this poor guy out here, are you?"

I was furious at the way he framed me. Time and again in the past, he had manipulated people in similar ways, but I was outraged when he did it to me in person at the remote city a hundred kilometers away from home. But there was really no time for further argument.

Reluctantly, I took out my money and bought two tickets.

"And don't forget I brought you guys food and drinks, too."

I was sickened at the blatant way that he demanded gratitude for his favor. And of course, Akio was famous for his failure to return the borrowed money. So during the train ride back home, I clammed up, sore and pissed off, and did not speak a word with either of my classmates. But Koichi kept talking to Akio about friends and sports and cracked silly jokes to make him laugh, as if laughing at my sulky mood.

***

Three weeks later, we found ourselves back in Harajuku as a new *Takenokozoku* dancing team. The sour feeling between Koichi and me had lingered for a while after our first trip to Tokyo, but with time, it was amended to some extent, particularly when we had a common goal of accomplishing a new dancing project.

During the three weeks between our first trip and our debut as dancers, I had devoted myself to the choreographing. Again, I was mad at what Koichi had done to me, but once I had set a goal, my pride did not allow me to do any slipshod work. I stayed up until two every morning to study literature and videotapes of professional dancers, and I even consulted my father, a PE teacher, for expert opinions. I told him that we were preparing for our dance performance at the school festival. Then, after class every afternoon, we danced in a small corner of the school playground. I had turned into a proud dancer and choreographer of a new dancing team, and I even designed the costume for everybody and made arrangements to have them tailored within the limited time and budgets. Akio ran errands to collect materials, following my commands, while Koichi demonstrated his own gift for recruiting pretty girls as charming additions. We all appreciated his efforts for staffing the team, and he complimented me, time and again, on the way I coached the team.

"You are doing a splendid job, Satoru," he said repeatedly. "And you've got a real flair. I really don't know what we'd do without you."

After all, Koichi was a smooth talker, and I always found his compliments halfhearted. Yet nobody would be offended at words of appreciation for his hard work.

Out of the twenty boys and girls who were somehow involved in the plan, eight—including five boys and three girls—actually decided to make a trip to Harajuku. We all lied to our parents, saying that we were staying over with one of our former classmates who had moved to Tokyo. The official purpose of our visit we fabricated was to attend this Tokyo friend's birthday party. We arrived in Tokyo the previous night in order to take the best spot in front of the Yoyogi Park and camped out. We were united as a strong troop, advancing to the front, fully prepared for the big day. And we even had a stroke of luck on our first day in Harajuku. To be more exact, Koichi did! When I looked back several years later, I wondered what exactly he had really been scheming to do in the first place when he first invited me and Akio to the first trip to Harajuku.

Once we had lined up and assumed our positions, all our mundane worries evaporated. We forgot about school, relationships between the members, and the fact that we lied to our parents; we just danced, frantically rocking and swinging. Despite all personal feelings, our movements were perfectly synchronized, which reflected our common desire to dance beautifully, demonstrate our idea of creativity, and attract passersby's attention as credit for perfect performance. The audience around us grew incrementally larger during one performance and over a series of performances. There was even a big applause after we finished the last round.

"Excuse me. May I ask you a few questions?" A young female TV reporter came up to us after the last performance, accompanied by her camera crew. Junko Yamaguchi was her name; I instantly recognized her because she was my favorite newscaster. But the moment she addressed me, Koichi stepped forward and literally snatched the microphone away before I had a chance to respond. For him, it was perhaps just like a dexterous move in a basketball game to intercept an enemy player carrying the ball, except that I was supposed to be on the same team with him.

"Sure. I'd be happy to speak on behalf of our team."

"Are you the leader of this group?"

"Yes, though we've all been working together." Koichi glimpsed my frowning face and, then, immediately turned back to the reporter.

"We were really impressed by your dancing. It's really novel and dynamic, and we've never seen such a perfectly synchronized performance."

"Thanks. We've done a lot of research, and we . . . you know, everybody contributed in one way or another."

"Are you the one who choreographed?"

"Well, more or less, yes though, as I said, we all did it together."

I inched toward Koichi and glared at him, although I was not sure if he noticed or cared about it.

"How about the costume?"

"Again, we all thought about it together."

You bastard! I thought. But he had already taken the floor as speaker of the group, and after all, he was the most eloquent—and also the most nice-looking of the male members. I was irate at the way he treated me, but there was nothing that I could do anymore unless I wanted to step forward to contradict my colleague who had declared that we were a closely bonded team. It would serve no purpose at all except turning me into a jerk who would not act in harmony. Koichi always manipulated his friends by placing them in a morally self-contradictory position.

"We videotaped your performance. Would you authorize us to edit and use it for a broadcast?"

"By all means."

"And can we film you and your teammates in close-up?"

"Of course. Come on, guys!" he turned to the rest of us. "We are going to hold each other's shoulders and pose. Okay?" He drew other members on either side so that he would be standing right in the middle. I was unconsciously moving to the leftmost side, away from him. "Hey, guys, smile. A big smile!"

The cameraman turned toward us and started rolling his TV camcorder.

The filming continued only for a minute or two. Then Ms. Yamaguchi had a quick conference with the man who seemed to be a director and then turned back to Koichi. "Is there a telephone number or something that we can reach you at? We may want to talk to you again regarding the production of our TV show."

"Oh, sure, sure!" Koichi was quick in response and scribbled his telephone number on a piece of paper that Ms. Yamaguchi produced. "If you want to know more about our team or dancing style, please call me. I'll put the info together and send it to you on the double."

"All right!" Yamaguchi smiled at her interviewee's offer.

"I can even put together everybody's bio if you want."

"We might prevail on you to do that."

No sooner had the camera crew left than I turned into a raging animal. I throttled him, pushed him against a utility pole, and cursed, "You bastard!"

"Oh, what's the matter? What the hell are you so upset about?"

"Don't give me any more crap. You know exactly what I mean."

Koichi still pretended innocence, shrugging his shoulders.

"Listen. She specifically asked who choreographed, and you said, '*We* worked together.' She asked who designed the costume, and you said, '*We* all did it together.'"

"Didn't we?"

I tightened my grips on his throat. "Knock it off. You know who did all the work, and you stole the credit. Listen, Koichi, I don't care about anything else. Just for the sake of argument, I might even forget about your stealing money from me—like you did three weeks ago. But this is a completely different matter. As far as the creative work is concerned, I won't let you cheat on me. I'm the one who worked hard till late at night to put this thing together."

"So you want to tell them now."

"I should have, except that you let them go before anybody had a chance to speak!" Actually, I no longer cared about it. I acknowledged my stupidity to fall for his neat trick. All I wanted was to break up with this despicable man permanently and never to see his smirking face again for the rest of my life.

Then, Koichi, instead of looking contrite, gave a knowing smile and said in a deliberately indifferent tone, "Don't take it so personal, Satoru. Life is a game."

That moment, I pulled him closer with all my might and delivered a head bat against his forehead. All the other members of the team were stunned at our confrontation, and nobody dared to mediate. I thought he would strike back and that we would get into an ugly fistfight in public. I was ready to fight that loathsome, despicable man until either of us would be dead. Although he was ten centimeters taller and ten kilograms heavier, I was a raging beast that could crunch a lion's head off.

He did not hit back! I loosened my grip on him, picked up my bag, and headed back home alone. That had been the last that I saw of him in person, that is, before he audaciously showed up at my office for the first time in fifteen years.

***

A month later, Koichi was recruited by Tommy's Junior Company, a prestigious talent agent that had produced many popular male TV personalities and singers that could skyrocket TV audience ratings and fill up the Tokyo Dome or Japan Martial Arts Center with their fans. Heavyweight promoters with huge political and financial clout staged large-scale concerts for the recruited teenage boys who danced and sang on the stage. With no prominent artistic gifts, the young men primarily used their physical charm to draw large female audiences rather than polishing their musical and theatrical techniques.

When Koichi was first interviewed on a TV variety show under the name of Shingo Saotome, a group photo of our Takenoko-zoku dancing team was shown for a brief second. It was a shot from the video back at Harajuku. But in any event, that was the only time that Koichi, or Shingo, ever referred to his old buddies' existence. Apparently, the Bambooclan dancing was a meaningful but minor phase of his life that he soon decided to put behind. It was just a springboard that helped him jump onto the professional treadmill, and he obviously regarded his childhood friends or former classmates as completely irrelevant to his debut in the glamorous show business. He soon accomplished a quick ascent as a new star, appearing in one popular TV show after another, and although I loathed his crafty and manipulative personality, I could not help admiring his aptitude for show business. He had a flair for attracting the right people's attention at the right time and never missed a chance to win recognition in the world where he lived.

Singo was no longer an ordinary high school student; he was a big star—a celebrity. Being chased by fans and reporters everywhere, he soon stopped attending classes and officially withdrew from school by the end of his last year in high school. Because he started his fancy career as a TV personality, a high school diploma no longer meant much to him. Obviously, he never considered the possibility that his popularity might wane in the future with changes in audiences' tastes. He started his new social life with famous actors and singers and the powerful media people whereas his singing and dancing skills never improved to a noticeable degree after the time of Takenoko-zoku dancing. Now, he was a man on a different planet, totally beyond our reach, except that we heard about him on occasion from Mari. She married Koichi soon after she graduated from high school but was friendly enough to keep communicating with us as old-time friends. In fact, I did not care for the endless episodes of his celebrity life she recounted. However, one episode that I heard from Mari about five years after we lost contact with him caught my attention. It was a truly tragic incident for Mari and was brought to our attention a month before she filed for divorce.

***

A year after his debut, Shingo married Mari, who had just graduated from high school, which caused a big sensation in the media. He was, at the time, rising to stardom as a TV personality; therefore, their wedding was broadcast on TV, and their photos dominated the tabloid papers' front pages. In fact, it might have been the prime of his private and professional life as his glamorous career in show business was set to decline soon. The same was the case of hundreds of young actors or singers with little talent and a stroke of great luck. After all, he was neither an opera singer nor a ballet dancer who had spent years of arduous training to learn high-level artistic techniques. And during his period as a rising star, he developed a millionaire's spending habit. He and his wife moved into a mansion in Dennen-chofu where celebrities, baseball stars, and high-rank politicians resided. They traveled abroad first class whenever he had a few days' vacation, and he bought a new sports car every year. He earned tons of money, but he always spent more and eventually fell into a trap awaiting many young actors who had prematurely risen to a high socioeconomic position.

Then, this unexpected incident took place in his private life, which triggered the overnight celebrity's downfall and eventually put an end to his ephemeral success and happiness. It looked like an isolated occurrence on the surface, but when I later reflected on Mari's report on this happening, I could not help but suspect that there was a cause-and effect relationship between his personality traits and his destiny. From my perspective, Koichi—the gambler, traitor, and idol with fake charisma—deserved the fatal consequences. It was a pity, however, that his innocent preschool son was involved in the disaster.

One windy winter afternoon, Koichi tried to take out his three-year-old son for a motorcycle ride.

"Hey, Ichiro. Want to go for a ride?"

"Oh, no, Koichi! It's just too dangerous," Mari protested in an uncharacteristically strong tone. "And the wind is pretty strong."

Koichi had made many enemies, but he and his wife had miraculously gotten along with each other due to special glue factors. It had been so at least until that afternoon.

"He may fall off the seat and get seriously injured or even . . ."

"Oh, no, no! He's my son, Mari. And it's very important to teach him at an early age that a man must have guts for success. Life is a game—a serious game to kill or to be killed—and only those who are bold and tough will make it to the top."

"But he's only three years old. And if something happens, it's too late."

Those were the first harsh words I'd ever flung at him, Mari later told us old friends. She had always cared for him and respected his decisions, that is, even after she began to hear severe criticism about his haughty attitude from his personal acquaintances. But she just could not yield on that particular point, having an ominous premonition.

"You want to go, Ichiro?"

"Yes. No. I don't know. Daddy, I'm scared . . ." the boy whimpered.

"He says he's scared. So please stop it," Mari pleaded.

But Koichi looked away from his wife and glared down at his son who was trembling on the small saddle behind the driver's seat. The word *scared* had stung him. "*Scared* is the last word that a man should ever utter. You said you wanted to go for a ride." The boy did not respond.

"What the hell is that? You said you wanted to go, didn't you?"

"Yes."

"Then, stick it out till the end."

"Koichi, please, don't," Mari protested again.

"Hang on tight, Ichiro!"

Koichi mounted his motorcycle himself, ignoring his wife's words, and stepped on the gas pedal. The engine roared into life, and as he leaned forward, the motorcycle darted out like a missile with the front wheel lifting off the ground. The reverberating muffler and a sudden air pressure made him forget about everything for the moment except the road ahead. Then, a few seconds later, he heard a faint sound of a crying voice behind him. He ignored it and kept on driving for a few more seconds until he finally looked over his shoulder to see his wife crouching on the ground and covering her face. He shut down the engine and brought his motorcycle to a screeching halt. Thick meandering tire prints were left on the asphalt. It was no longer a faint crying voice that he was hearing from behind; Mari's was screaming like an air-raid siren, which carried over the distance. Then, his peripheral vision caught a bulky black-and-red object on the ground—around the midway point between himself and his wife.

"Jesus Christ!"

His three-year-old boy had been thrown off the backseat and was now lying in a pool of blood like a ragged, abandoned doll. They called an ambulance, but the boy died on his way to the hospital.

Koichi and Mari divorced after an ugly battle in court, during which time young people's preferences in popular music, dance, and dramatics changed quickly. Shingo Saotome could not concentrate on his work and ride out his first major professional crisis. And despite his declining popularity and his responsibility to pay alimony and other compensations to his former wife, he continued to spend money like a feudal lord who owned a gold mill. There was soon a rumor that he was borrowing heavily from consumer-credit companies. As Mari no longer lived with Koichi, we no longer had updates on his exact whereabouts, except that he occasionally appeared on minor TV shows. A few years later, he disappeared from the public eye completely. It was not very difficult, however, to imagine what a heavily indebted man's life was doomed to be in the end. And when I saw him in person last week for the first time in fifteen years, I was convinced that my speculation had not been wide of the mark.

***

"It's been a long while, Koichi!" I said to my high school classmate who showed up at my office with no warning. It was an odd statement because I had never expected or hoped to meet him again, but that was all I could say to the ghastly pale man who had appeared from nowhere. Again, I hated and despised this sly, egoistic man and could not bear the sight of him. Yet I was no longer a teenager. I had a professional position and did not want to turn into a hysterical, revengeful jerk in front of my colleagues and subordinates. Besides, a thirty-year-old woman who had ushered Koichi into the office was already telling the other people that he was Shingo Saotome, a former teenage idol. Shingo—or Koichi—was in his jeans jacket and pants; he was gaunt, and a few days' stubble showed around his mouth. I even saw streaks of gray in his thick hair. "What can I do for you?" I asked, suppressing all my conflicting emotions.

"I . . . I'm sorry to intrude into your work place like this, but I'm in trouble."

I can see you are in trouble, but what does it have to do with me? I wanted to say.

I had decided long ago that it simply was not worthwhile to meet him again for the rest of my life. His being in trouble was the last thing that I would have cared about. But again, I was not a high school student anymore, and my common sense dictated that I deal with all visitors to my office in a civilized manner, regardless of his personal or professional backgrounds. I showed him to a sofa in one corner of the office and even asked a secretary to bring a cup of tea for him.

"What kind of trouble? Money?" I could not help being sarcastic because I knew that he deserved it. Moreover, I was beginning to feel that he would soon be acting like a beggar.

"You know I was hoping to get a major contract toward the end of last year, so I borrowed some money from a place called Alfa Consumer's Credit, but things didn't turn out the way I expected."

Koichi seemed to have concocted what he believed to be a credible story with some embellishments that would draw an old friend's sympathy. He was clever enough to know that I did not want to be bothered by the details of his financial destitution. I had to admit that he was also intelligent enough to grasp the present power relationship between him and his old classmate.

"Listen, Koichi. I'm not a rich man, and I have a family to support. I have to pay all the bills and dues as a member of society."

"Yes, I understand. I knew you'd have every right to refuse my audacious request."

"Then, why did you come?" I spat out my words on the spur of the moment, aware that I was turning meaner than I had intended. Deep down inside, I wanted to grab him by the scruff of his neck, throw him out on the street like a stray kitten, and pitch a pinch of purifying salt to drive off any evil spirits that he might have brought to my work place. But again, my colleagues were present.

He did not answer at once. After a long minute of silence, he sheepishly admitted, "I . . . I just don't have anybody else to turn to for help." That was more or less what I had guessed.

"How much do you need?"

Koichi stated the amount of money that he urgently needed. Sitting across the coffee table from me was a total loser; there was not a trace of a shrewd, manipulative man who had always bluffed, cheated his friends, and bragged about his trophies. Needless to say, there was no evidence of a former TV star with fame and riches. I suspected that the evil spirit might still remain deep inside him, but the sad fact was that he could no longer afford to worry about his appearances, begging for money from his childhood friend whom he had openly insulted in the past and had never tried to communicate, or make amends, with.

"Any collateral or security, in case you couldn't pay me back?" A mean side of myself kicked in again.

"None," he said, downcast.

After throwing another contemptuous glance at him, I wrote a check and handed it to him. Then, when I walked my old friend to the exit of the building, I was shocked to find his white, brand-new sports car pulled to the curb.

"Huh! TV stars need to drive fancy cars even when they're insolvent," I practically yelled in a burst of anger, convinced that the money that I had just loaned him would never come back. He might even spend it at a nightclub a few blocks down.

"I . . . I was trying to get rid of it."

"That sounds like a sound idea!"

"Yes, I'll soon get rid of it." Then, after a short silence, Koichi expressed his appreciation again. "Thanks again, Satoru. I really appreciate your help."

"Drive carefully" was all I could say, holding back my anger and disgust.

He pulled out, slightly inclining his head through the window at me.

The next week, Koichi kept his words on one thing and did not on the other. He did not pay me back the loaned money; he just got rid of his plush car in his own way.

On the Sunny Side

The twenty-five-story twin towers of Sumida Insurance Inc. stood on the riverfront like a majestic castle. They were solid buildings with thick concrete walls so that people who walked past were likely to have an impression that all employees inside were carrying out their tasks quietly and leisurely. In reality, the buildings contained dozens of battle zones. Young workers were running up and down the floors, supervisors were shouting orders to subordinates like army sergeants, and many heated discussions and debates were in progress day in and day out. Some were engaged in extremely important business negotiations with outside parties, on which the company's future hinged on. Kiyoshi Hashimoto and his same-year colleague Takashi Matsumura had just been in an extremely difficult business transaction with a tough client. Fortunately, their business negotiation had been successfully concluded, and the two young men courteously escorted their client out of the company building, flanking him like secret police agents guarding a VIP. The man whom they were seeing off was Mr. Abe, a vice president of Toyo Instruments. Abe slid into the backseat of a black limousine that had been waiting in front of the main entrance.

"Thank you very much, again, Mr. Abe. We wish you a safe drive back to your office."

The two young insurance company employees stood to attention and bowed deeply to their business customers. Toyo's vice president leaned back in the comfortable wide leather seat and lifted his right hand in response to their salute. Abe was a frail old man in a dark tailored suit, but from their first-hand interactions with him, the two Sumida employees learned how difficult it was to deal with this particular person. At the moment, however, he was obviously in great humor, flashing a big smile.

The car pulled out of the turnaround, but Kiyoshi and Takashi maintained their deeply declined postures until the limousine disappeared around the corner. Then, they finally lifted their torsos and exchanged glances with an expression of relief and triumph on their faces.

"A great job, guys," said Tanaka, their immediate supervisor who had been standing by. He tapped the two young workers on the shoulders and congratulated them. Sumida Insurance had just gotten a major contract from Toyo because of the two young workers' hard work. "You did an excellent job."

"Thank you, sir," the two courteously bowed to him in unison.

"Why don't you take a short break, have a cup of coffee in the cafeteria or take a walk outside?" A stack of miscellaneous work was waiting for them back in the office, but Tanaka offered them a few minutes of freedom as a small reward.

"Thank you, Mr. Tanaka. We appreciate it."

"All right. Now, I have an appointment in Yokohama, so I'll see you guys on Monday morning."

"Good day, sir."

As their supervisor retreated, Kiyoshi and Takashi congratulated each other again.

"That was a tough job. Thank God we made it!"

"Yes, a mission accomplished!"

In the past month, the two had made many trips to Abe's office and spent hours and hours to persuade him that the policy that Sumida offered was by far superior to those prescribed by its rival companies including Yasui and Tsunetomo. Toyo Instruments manufactured special cranes and ground-digging instruments and required a special workmen's accident insurance that covered particular types of accidents at its factories or the construction sites where its customers used those machines. Accidents were comparatively rare, but each accident involving a heavy piece of machinery tended to entail heavy casualties. Thus, the premiums would be accordingly high as compared to the general insurance policies for accidents and disasters. Vice President Abe had invited all major insurance companies to bid for the contract. Young as they were, Kiyoshi and Takashi made ceaseless efforts to demonstrate the advantages of Sumida's plans and defeated the competitors to win a big contract. It had been a major accomplishment for young workers only six years into their employment, and their excellent job would be reflected in their monthly performance reports. Instead of having coffee at the cafeteria, the two chose to sit on a bench by the Sumida River and have a long, relaxing chitchat.

They perched on a bench on the riverfront pathway. On the other side of the river was a plush residential quarter studded with ultramodern residential towers. They knew by hearsay that some of those high-rises housed star baseball players, movie stars, and TV newscasters. The buildings themselves displayed special architectural designs and were believed to have very high real estate values. In the late afternoon or early evening, amateur photographers set their tripods on elevated areas and took pictures of the cluster of beautiful high-rises and the artistic suspension bridge designed by a famous French architect. The bridge had been opened to traffic on the same day as the great Tokyo Bay Bridge had. The crews from movie or TV companies were often seen shooting dramas on location in one corner or another. This scenic spot in the megalopolis, not crowded by commuters and passersby, was convenient for movie producers because it was comparatively easy to obtain permission to set their heavy equipment and engage in filming activities. The sales department of Sumida Insurance, to which Kiyoshi and Takashi belonged, was on the twentieth floor of the company building and commanded a magnificent view of the river and the bridge. Sitting in their office was in itself a luxury as they could enjoy the ambience of a high-class metropolitan area. Yet the employees tended to find an excuse to step outside in order to be relieved from the hustle and bustle of the workstations.

"The big job is done. Why don't we celebrate it over a couple of beers after work?" Takashi suggested.

It was Saturday. The young employees were often required to work on Saturday to clear backlogs of work, but it was much easier to escape at an early hour than on busy weekdays. They might leave the office at five and spend a few hours at a bar in Ginza or Yurakucho.

"I'd love to, but not tonight."

"What are you up to?"

"I'm going to get up early tomorrow morning and take my family to the Ancient Capital."

"Oh, is that right? You know, my girlfriend and I went there."

"Did you?"

"Yeah. It was a lot of fun—and educational, too! I'm sure your kids would love it."

"I hope so."

"How old are your children now?"

"Kohei is five, and Yuko just turned three."

"Time flies. It feels like I was sitting at your wedding reception just a few days ago."

"I feel the same way."

"So they are getting bigger and more active, I guess."

"Yeah! They are often out of control."

"Don't complain. It's evident they're growing up as healthy children."

"I guess it is," Kiyoshi gave a wry smile.

"So they keep clamoring for things like going to the new theme park?"

"Exactly."

"But this Ancient Capital is a great choice. It's more authentic and educational than Disneyland or USJ."

Kiyoshi had already taken his wife and children to Disneyland in Urayasu several times and made one weekend trip to Universal Studio Japan in Osaka.

"You said you took your girlfriend there?"

"Yeah. We were there when it first opened. They reconstructed the old, sixth-century capital of Japan, building the replicas of palace buildings, old temples, and residences of the nobility. It was pretty impressive."

"That's what my wife says. She picked up some information on the Internet. But don't tell me more. I'm really looking forward to finding it out myself."

"Right! I won't tell you any more."

"But they charge a pretty good admission, too."

"They always do that at that kind of place. But you are lucky to have two beautiful children. You should willingly pick up the tab."

"Oh, maybe. But I'm warning you you'll soon be buying four or five tickets yourself, instead of two."

"Perhaps."

"When are you going to marry?"

"Oh, a year after the next, I guess!"

"Why do you wait so long?"

"Just to save up enough money. I was trying to buy one of those apartments." Takashi pointed his index finger at one of the residential towers on the other side of the river.

"New Century Tower?"

"Uh-huh."

"I hear Actress Tachibana lives there."

"Yes. And Matsumoto, an MVP baseball player, too."

"I heard all the units were sold out before the construction of the building was completed."

"Yes, they were, in spite of the exorbitant prices. But now, some people are already moving out," the prospective buyer grinned.

"Is that right?"

"Some are beginning to realize they can't handle the bank loans after their hasty purchases. More ambitious investors are trying to buy something else by selling their new apartments."

"Huh!" Kiyoshi was amazed at the inside information that his friend had gathered.

"I believe it'll be a good investment for my future even if I have to borrow a lump sum of money from a bank. And I can't miss this chance when the prices of the apartments are coming down to a reasonable level."

"How much is it? I'm curious."

"Seventy-eight million for a three-bedroom—a big discount from the original ninety."

"That's a real bargain. Have you actually seen the room?"

"Yes. The one I checked out was superb. It's on the thirtieth floor and commands a panoramic view of the inner city and part of Tokyo Bay. In the summer, we'd be able to watch the Tokyo Bay firework display sitting in our living room."

"Wow, that'll be cool."

"Yes, it's really like a castle in the sky."

"I hope you'll really get it. And tell me more about it when you move in there."

"Absolutely! And of course, you are invited to come and visit."

"I will, especially for the firework display. And you know something? I was actually thinking about an upgrade myself because it'd be better to move into a higher-grade residence at an early chance, instead of paying bank loans for the second-class apartment."

"Oh, your present apartment is anything but second class. It's really nice in its own way!"

Soon after marriage, Kiyoshi had purchased a brand-new three-bedroom apartment in an eastern part of Tokyo. He had received a small inheritance from his father and used it as down payment.

"Not a bad place to live in, but I'm trying to plan a wise investment."

"But you got your BMW, too."

"I know what you mean. I got my BMW. It took away a huge portion of my savings."

"Don't you think you got to save money?"

"Yes, I got to save money hard. I admit that. And I've got my family to provide for, too. But another reason why I'm considering a better apartment is that Tomoko wants to enroll Kohei in a private elementary school. She says that the families of most kids attending that school live in the above-seventy-million houses and apartments in Seijo, Dennen-chofu, Azabu, or whatever fancy area of that rank."

"Does it affect the kid's admission to a private elementary school?"

"Not officially, but it does in one way or another—just like my BMW that might impress my business associates when I go to a golf course." As a close friend, Takashi knew that Kiyoshi had originally wanted a Mercedes.

"Hmm! Interesting!"

"But anyway, I really hope you'll get that real estate for you and your fiancée. This area is really one of the most beautiful parts of metropolitan Tokyo."

"It definitely is," Takashi agreed.

"The only thing that bothers me is the presence of those tramps." With a scowl on his face, Kiyoshi jabbed his index finger through the air in the direction of a man who lay lethargically on the riverfront walkway, bundled up in rags. Right next to him was a cardboard box, a common convention that served as a homeless man's bedroom. It was placed against the wall underneath the suspension bridge, but at the moment, he was lying outside the box. Kiyoshi and Takashi were sitting about fifty meters away. The tramp seemed to be sleeping—or hibernating—obviously in his effort not to waste any of his remaining energy. A small parcel of his belongings was tossed by his side. Kiyoshi could see that, in that particular position under the bridge, the tramp would be sheltered from the wind and rain. On a hot sunny day, he could keep off the strong heat and sunshine and enjoy a nice breeze from the river. There was also a rather clean public bathroom nearby, and it seemed to be a perfect place for the homeless.

The loser's wisdom, Kiyoshi thought. The sight of the homeless man strangely disgusted him for a reason he could not clearly define himself.

"Those guys really ruin the sight. Otherwise, this place is an impeccable environment."

"But at least, there aren't many of them in this area, and the few who are here are pretty quiet. They don't bother us by wandering around or spreading their stuff to block pedestrians' passage."

"I know. But a handful of them are more than enough. The police should take measures to drive them away or throw them into a homeless shelter somewhere."

"I hear that welfare people from the municipal government come from time to time and advise them to go to a protection center, but they tend to refuse to go to the center."

"Why?"

"They want their privacy."

"What privacy? It's just ridiculous for those dirty creatures to ask for privacy! Give me a break."

"Oh, come on, Kiyoshi! You don't have to be so harsh on them. I know they are incongruent with the beautiful scenery, but they didn't ask for it, either. They probably just had a series of misfortunes in the course of their lives and ended up losing their homes."

"It's their problem, not ours!"

"I know. But they might have even worked hard and held decent jobs before. In this day and age, it's easy for anyone to miss one step and lose his position and property overnight—like a company that goes bankrupt or undergoes personnel reshuffling. The same misfortune might fall on anybody."

"All right. You are the humane and conscientious person, and I'm the jerk. But whatever it is, they are losers. They lack self-discipline and willpower. They didn't push themselves to work hard. That's why they ended up as tramps." Kiyoshi pointed his index finger, again, straight at the homeless who was lying like a dirty bag of garbage. Then, he flipped his finger from right to left in a quick, sweeping gesture as if trying to openly insult the loser. His finger movement also looked like an umpire's gesture on the playground, trying to expel a foul player.

"Gee, you are really tough on them!"

"I guess I am. But you know, they have healthy, strong bodies, yet they don't try to stand up, find work, and pull their lives together. That's why I don't like it. Why don't they bus tables at a restaurant or work at a construction site?"

"I don't know. Perhaps, they can't even find such mediocre jobs because the economy is really bad. And there's a possibility that they were working hard in a large company's office like us but suddenly got fired because of some problems on the administration side. Then, they were involved in unexpected incidents and didn't know how to find a different kind of work because they were really dedicated to highly specialized types of work. Just like us, you know, they might have been handling highly technical stuff, faithfully following the supervisor's orders. We were lucky to join a large company fresh out of college, but we tend to take it for granted and fail to consider contingency plans in case something goes wrong. If something happens, we might end up in their position ourselves."

"Oh, don't say that. I acknowledge you've made your logical point, Takashi. And again, I admire your humane and compassionate personality. But personally, I would fight and crawl out of the quagmire—unlike those bums! Those guys don't have the guts. And that's why I can't stand the sight of them. This isn't the place for the losers. They should just go away."

"All right. You made your point, and let's not talk any more about it."

"Right! But let me, at least, tell you this. When we have families, we must fight to death to protect them."

"Yes, I agree on that."

"You'll really understand it better when you have kids."

"I'm sure I will."

However, Kiyoshi himself had a big surprise in store a few days ahead, which would give him a thunderbolt of insight concerning his own biases and prejudice. Fortunately, his company did not go bankrupt or suffer a serious enough financial problem. Neither was he kicked out of his company. Nonetheless, Kiyoshi was destined to learn more about unexpected incidents in human society, and he was forced—or was given an opportunity—to reconsider his own life philosophy.

***

The theme park was a grand-scale replication of the sixth-century capital of Japan in Asuka in what is now the prefecture of Nara. A major developer, whose headquarters was located in the Kansai district, had purchased a large land area about one hundred kilometers north of Tokyo. People were puzzled why this particular theme park had been constructed near Tokyo, not near the ruins of Asuka in Nara; no clear-cut explanations were offered by the developer, sponsors, or the host prefecture. In fact, before the park was opened, no one had ever heard of Goroyama. The park literally put the small town on the map. But at any rate, this new park named the Ancient Capital was larger than the combined dimension of Tokyo Disneyland and its later addition known as Disney Sea. The Ancient Capital was widely advertised, and visitors flooded in from all over the country immediately after its opening and crowded all roads and transportation facilities that led to Goroyama.

Naturally, the park was a hot topic among small children, and Kohei, enrolled in a kindergarten, had been clamoring for a trip there.

The total price of the tickets for the Hashimoto family, including two adults and two children, amounted to more than thirty thousand yen, and since it was a ninety-minute train ride from Tokyo, they also needed to pay the train fares back and forth to Goroyama. Moreover, staying in the park all day, they must eat at overpriced restaurants or cafeterias in the park.

"If we buy a couple of small souvenirs for the kids, it'd be sixty to seventy thousand yen in a single day," said Kiyoshi, doing his fast math.

"I know, but this is a really special occasion for them," Tomoko argued. "Many of their friends have already been there and are planning to go again."

"Yeah, I know it."

"We can order cheap meals in cafeterias." The visitors were not allowed to bring in the food purchased outside, but she pointed out that the prices of the meals varied from restaurant to restaurant and from dish to dish.

"Right."

"I'll also try to make up by saving money for the rest of this month."

"Well, all right. We'll worry about the expenditure later. As a matter of fact, I don't mind making at least one visit myself."

Kiyoshi himself was curious to see a few pavilions that his colleagues had mentioned, and Tomoko was excited about the new theme park herself, hoping to share her experience with her friends at the children's schools or in the neighborhood. All in all, the trip was going to be a special event for the family.

Tomoko originally suggested that they drive to the place, but Kiyoshi insisted that they take trains because the weekend traffic jam would be appalling. He also knew by hearsay that it would take at least another half hour to find a parking space in the crowded theme park. Furthermore, as he had been working hard all week in the office, he preferred the public transportation system that would allow him to take a nap on the way home.

Despite the expensive admission fees, however, the Hashimotos were fascinated at the new theme park when they arrived there. The park, a reproduction of an ancient Japanese capital, imparted a far more exotic atmosphere than Disneyland or Universal Studio Japan, reflecting many foreign cultures brought in by the immigrants during the pertinent era. All the scenic setups, buildings, and people's costumes were authentic replications of those in the Asuka era—evident that the designers and architects had done thorough research, consulting experts in history and cultures. Every pavilion was made of high-quality wooden materials, not a prefabricated structure comprising plastered walls and steel pipes.

The entrance passage itself constituted the first attraction of the park. The moving walkway that carried visitors from the gate to the pavilions was camouflaged as a dirt road in the dark. The passage was built in a long tunnel—or gigantic tube—enveloped in white chilly fogs spewing out of numerous holes in the walls. A number of pale white-and-blue light bulbs embedded in the ceiling flickered and twinkled like distant stars. Soft background music—performed with Japanese *koto* harps and *shakuhachi* flutes—produced an aesthetic ambience, and it changed gradually from a modern tune to those which represented various ages in descending order of time. Then, when it came closer to the attractions area, the roof of the tunnel displayed increasingly brighter stars, which subsequently merged with a yellowish orange orb that turned out to be the sunrise—or the dawn of a civilization—in the distant past. Awaiting the visitors at the end of the time tunnel was the ancient Asuka Palace itself. A wave of soft vibrating sound tinkled people's ears for a few seconds, and then it was suddenly dead silent.

When visitors stepped off the moving walkway, a soft female voice from the speakerphone courteously directed them to walk ten meters up a gentle slope and stand on top of an elevated area—a hill that overlooked the replicated ancient capital spreading over a large expanse of land. Clusters of beautiful wooden buildings emerged before the visitors' eyes. According to the park map, it was the entrance to Zone A. Zone B was not in sight; the visitors could reach it by riding a tram shaped like an ancient type of ox-drawn carriage for five minutes.

Unlike the commercial centers of present-day Tokyo or Osaka, there were, of course, no high-rises in the ancient capital, but all the flat architectural structures were surprisingly large-framed and wide in horizontal dimension, resembling the thick-pillared temples or mansions owned by wealthy families in rural areas. The roofs were covered with expensive-looking *kawara* tiles decorated with beautiful motifs, and whereas the roofs were dark brown and black, the walls and pillars were painted in pure white or bright red. They were residences of the nobility during the Asuka era.

"The buildings are huge!" Kiyoshi exclaimed, and his wife and children nodded in agreement. "I read somewhere that recent studies have revealed that the ancient capital was much larger than it had previously been believed. I think that these replicas reflect those new research findings."

"I think you are right," said Tomoko, "and it's gorgeous. And it'll be a lot of learning both for the children and for us."

"I expect it is."

"I wonder how many of those pavilions we can visit within a day."

"Let's go and find out. We don't have a minute to waste."

The two small children were already tugging at their hands, forcing them to race against the other people who had arrived at the park with them.

"Let's go, Dad and Mom. We'll be late."

"All right. Let's go."

A pair of gate towers welcomed the visitors into the simulated ancient capital. The streets and avenues were quite wide for an era in which there were no automobiles, and they formed a grid of high geometric precision. It seemed that the core section of the ancient capital had been meticulously designed before construction unlike haphazard additions in downtown Shibuya or Ikebukuro. The sizes and colors of the houses were intricately coordinated with one another. Large public buildings, which included temples, government offices, and other public facilities, were surrounded by comparatively small ones that were obviously residences or minor public service buildings. The major buildings serving important governmental functions were purposely enclosed by auxiliary buildings and properties as part of the defense mechanism.

The Hashimotos joined a line to enter the nearest pavilion, which depicted an agricultural revolution in the Japanese archipelagos. While they were waiting in line, a procession of people dressed in colorful traditional costumes came around. The parade was quiet, not accompanied by loud music bands and lit-up floats. Several large ox-driven carts proceeded along the thoroughfare, escorted by an entourage of men and women in silky high-quality kimonos. The second passenger cart was remarkably larger than the others.

"Who is he?" Yuko immediately spotted a distinct-looking man on board and asked her father.

"Wow, it looks like Crown Prince Shotoku himself!"

"Who is Prince Shotoku?"

"He is a famous personage in the sixth century. As a member of the royal family, he brought Buddhism from Korea and taught moral lessons to people in this country."

"Oh, I know him," said Kohei, who had recently read a children's book on Japanese history. "And his image is on a ten-thousand-yen note."

"You are right, Kohei. His face is on an older version of a ten-thousand-yen note."

"Was he famous?" the three-year-old girl asked an innocent question.

"Yes, and he was an extremely bright person. They say he could respond to seven different people who addressed him at the same time. He understood several foreign languages, too, including Korean and an ancient language in India known as Sanskrit."

"Wow."

"Look at the people who are following him. Have you noticed something?"

When the five-year-old boy was wondering, his mother gave a hint. "Some people are dressed in Korean dresses."

"Are they?"

"Yes, Asuka was a cosmopolitan city in that era. People from many different countries visited or came to live in this land. They spoke different languages and brought different cultures and traditions of their native lands."

"Did they speak English, too?" Kohei knew that his mother was an English major in college.

"Probably not," Tomoko laughed.

"English-speaking people were from Europe, and Europeans didn't come to Japan in those days," Kiyoshi explained. History had always been his favorite subject in school.

"But instead, it's believed that Chinese, Mongolians, Koreans, and people in Southeast Asia and the Pacific came to Japan. They are our ancestors."

"Like great, great, great-grandfathers of Akebono and Asashoryu?" The five-year-old boy referred to two sumo grand champions who were from Hawaii and Mongolia, respectively.

"Yes. And we'll definitely have to go around to the Journey from the Korean Peninsula later," Kiyoshi reminded them of one of the most widely advertised attractions. Another *time tunnel* would take visitors to the Korean Peninsula, letting them travel backward in time and tracing the immigration routes.

"I want to see the World of Legendary Gods," Kohei named his favorite. He was a manic of deities and supernatural heroes. "Can we go there?"

"Of course. I know you won't leave this park without seeing it."

"You can write about what you see today in your composition homework," Tomoko suggested.

"I will. I definitely will."

In the first pavilion named The Agricultural Revolution, visitors rode in a gondola that levitated a few meters above the ground and moved slowly along a prescribed route, which enabled the spectators to observe how people learned to grow rice in paddy fields. The process by which a new agricultural method was introduced was chronologically displayed. First, a group of missionaries and immigrants from the continent provided the local farmers with sample grains or rice seedlings and showed them how to plant and grow rice in paddy fields. The technology for irrigation was introduced, and the farmers engaged in collaborative farming projects, which eventually changed Japanese people's lifestyles and the societal structure. It was the beginning of the agriculture-based life on the ancient Japanese archipelago. The robotic machinery, objects, and paintings by gifted artists and advanced computer graphics made the scenes look amazingly vivid and realistic. The panoramic view was truly spectacular, and the visitors had an illusion of being on an old Japanese farmland in an ancient time.

Whereas The Agricultural Revolution was basically a museum where visitors quietly observed the objects on display, other pavilions presented more dynamic attractions, such as a bloody battle zone in which ancient clans fought each other for the full sovereignty of the country. In the pavilion of Taika Revolution, the visitors found themselves standing among the soldiers who smashed their swords against each other's. Arrows were shot in barrages, which appeared to come flying right at the spectators because of three-dimensional projections.

As expected, the theme park was fully packed, and the Hashimotos had to wait in a long line at each popular attraction. Nonetheless, they tried to see as many attractions as possible within the day because they knew that it would be difficult to come back again in the near future, considering the expensive admissions and Kiyoshi's tight work schedules. They tended to lose track of their time as they rushed from one attraction to another. At around two-thirty, they finally decided to take a lunch break and rest for a few minutes.

"We still have to go around to Zone B," Tomoko reminded Kiyoshi. Whereas Zone A was composed of pavilions of different shapes and sizes as in any other theme park, Zone B looked just like the ruins of Asuka Village in Nara. In the present-time Asuka Village, the remains of old temples, mausoleums, and uniquely shaped stones called Oni Ogre's Chopping Board, Oni's Lavatory, Monkey Stone, and Tortoise Stone are scattered over a large area; between them were rice paddies and private residences. The replicas of all those objects were concentrated within the park. By walking around, visitors enjoyed the pastoral scenery of present-day Asuka, somewhat downscaled, but each stone or object constituted the entrance to an underground chamber that featured a particular historical event or legend. There were also multimedia presentations of academic issues that interested not only children but also the adults who liked Japanese history. About twenty such underground museums and attractions were in Zone B. One of them was a huge underground attraction that displayed robotic representations of mythological deities. At another major attraction, visitors rode on a roller coaster and traveled to different regions and eras of the Korean Peninsula.

Time flew! The Hashimoto family enjoyed all the novel and mysterious attractions to the fullest until they realized that it was the closing time. They reluctantly exited and started heading back to the train station, which was about a fifteen-minute walk. Kiyoshi and Tomoko made a point of leaving the park in enough time to catch a train back to the city. Naturally, the two children—a five-year-old boy and a three-year-old girl—were exhausted by then. When the exciting excursion came to its end, they suddenly felt overwhelmed by the physical fatigue and stress from hours of walking and standing in line.

First, Kohei threw a tantrum. The exit gate was congested, and while waiting in line, the boy lost his patience and insisted that he could not walk anymore, so Kiyoshi ended up carrying him on his back. Tomoko trailed after her husband, carrying three bags of souvenirs in one hand and holding her daughter's hand in the other. Thus far, Yuko had been handling the daylong trip better than her elder brother partly because she skipped one attraction and took a short nap on her mother's lap in a rest area. But she had her own problem. A few minutes after they exited the park, the little girl suddenly came to a halt and said, "Mom, I need to go to the bathroom!"

"Can't you just wait till we get to the station?"

"No, I won't last."

"Why didn't you tell me before we got out of the park?"

"At that time, I was okay."

"Tomoko, there's no use arguing over the call of nature. Why don't you just go back one block? There was a public bathroom right outside the exit of the park."

"All right. Will you hold these bags until we come back?"

"Just put the staff down by my feet. I'll keep an eye on them," he said, pointing with his chin toward his feet. He was still bearing a big boy on his back.

"We'll be right back." Tomoko pulled Yuko's hand and headed back to the bathroom.

However, their trip to the bathroom took much longer than Kiyoshi had anticipated, and he was a little irritated at the long wait. At the time they left the park, a large crowd of people was heading toward the railway station, but most of them were gone. The remaining people walked past them at a quick pace and disappeared into the darkness. About ten minutes later, there was practically no one in the area except Kiyoshi with his son on his back. He felt strangely uncomfortable being left behind in the dark in a faraway rural area.

There might have been a long line in front of the women's room, or the little girl might be dawdling. It was fifteen minutes later that Tomoko and Yuko finally caught up.

"Were the bathrooms crowded?"

"There were some waiting in front of us, but Yuko took a long time herself."

"Come on. We'd better hurry. The last train was around eleven-thirty, I believe." The family started trekking toward the station again.

They had to ride trains for one and a half hours back to the city, and it would be nearly one o'clock in the morning when they arrived home. Kiyoshi was generally quite punctual, disciplined through his tight work schedules at his company. But it was, after all, a private weekend excursion, and he was not so keenly conscious of the train departures from the theme park.

Then, when the family reached Goroyama Station, they found the area eerily quiet and dark.

"Excuse me," Kiyoshi found a station clerk, who was about to retreat to the office, and asked him. "Hasn't the last Tokyo-bound train come in yet?"

"The last train arrived and left a few minutes ago," he said in a polite, businesslike tone.

"Pardon me?"

"The last train just departed."

"But . . . but I thought there's an eleven-thirty train."

"We have an eleven-thirty train only on weekdays."

Kiyoshi and Tomoko were speechless for the moment in shocked disbelief. They looked at each other, and then, Kiyoshi addressed the station clerk again. "What are we supposed to do now? Is there an alternative means of transportation back to Tokyo?"

"I'm afraid not, sir." The station attendant's response was immediate—evident that the same incident had happened many times in the past.

"But I don't understand. So many people were here visiting the park—just until a few minutes ago—and you say there's no other transit system at all. It's just . . . not practical."

"I know. We might increase the train runs in the future, and a developing company is considering long-distance midnight buses, too.

It may be implemented in a few years, but at present, this is the way it is."

"Is that right?"

"The last train was fully packed," the attendant added as if to emphasize the importance of the train company's service. Clearly, he was not so seriously concerned about the wellbeing of a stranded family.

"But what are we going to do now?"

"Well, you may want to stay at the Grand Hotel." The station attendant pointed at a tall building across the street. In fact, there were actually three hotels near the station, including the Grand Hotel, which had been newly built to accommodate visitors to the theme park. Not surprisingly, the Grand Hotel that the station clerk recommended was by far larger than the other two. It was a twenty-story building, and Kiyoshi had read about it when he looked up the theme park on the Internet before the trip.

"Well, we might as well. Thanks."

For a brief second, the idea of catching a taxi flashed across Kiyoshi's mind, but Tokyo was nearly a hundred kilometers away, and he could easily estimate the approximate taxi fare to cover the entire distance. The price would be exorbitant, and it was commonly believed that late-night taxi drivers would often overcharge their customers. On the other hand, he could not think of any convenient place where he and his family might seek shelter near the park, such as a coffee shop or an all-night movie theater. After all, it was a new theme park constructed on what used to be an abandoned land mass one hundred kilometers north of the metropolitan district. Furthermore, looking around, he found no taxis at all, either waiting for customers in front of the station or circulating in the area. The taxicabs might have been there earlier, but there were none at the time. They might have disappeared shortly after the departure of the last train, picking up the passengers who had narrowly missed it.

"What are we going to do now?" Tomoko turned to her husband again with a concerned expression. "If it's not so awfully expensive, we should check into the hotel. But . . ."

"How much money do we have now?" The married couple opened their wallets, looked at the remaining bank notes, and did the fast math. The total amount of cash that they had on them was about fifty thousand yen.

"And you've brought your credit cards?" Tomoko asked.

"Well, as a matter of fact, I haven't. We had enough cash for the admission and trains, and I didn't even seriously consider using the plastics."

His failure to bring credit cards was another unfortunate incident, but Tomoko suspected that her husband might have left them at home on purpose, determined not to spend too much money in a single day. That was one trick he sometimes used in order to restrain himself from overspending, and she approved it herself as a sound strategy to save money.

"Why don't I go to the front desk and ask?" the husband suggested.

"Yes, please do that."

"Let's see . . . which one should I try first?"

"Just a minute!" Tomoko flipped out her cell phone. "I think I can access their Web pages and find out their pricing and vacancy."

"Good idea!" Kiyoshi appreciated the technological device and his quick-witted wife's decision to utilize it. "Find out how much they charge at each hotel."

"That's exactly what I'm doing." She got the Web page of one hotel after another on the tiny display of her cell phone and checked the vacancies and the prices. A minute later, however, she made a rather disappointing report. "Well, the two of them are fully booked up."

"Which ones?"

"Plaza Hotel and Goroyama Inn. There doesn't seem to be a single vacancy. Perhaps, tourist groups from remote districts like Osaka or Fukuoka might have taken them."

"I'll bet they did. It's only natural for tour groups to choose the most inexpensive accommodations."

"So, the Grand Hotel is the only possibility, isn't it?"

"It seems like it. It's a huge hotel made for this theme park, and they probably have plenty of rooms." A minute later, her face beamed triumphantly. "Yes, they have vacancies."

"Check the pricing."

Tomoko scrolled the price list on the small display, which showed the prices for single, double, and triple rooms.

"Here! For a triple room, it's thirty thousand yen per room." She let her husband look at the price list with his own eyes.

"Hmm! That's pretty expensive."

"But not unexpected for a resort hotel of this type," his wife commented. "Besides, the big consolation is that it says *per room*, not per person."

"So, it's like in America."

"Right. And it says guests can check in any time of day. What do you say?"

"Let's see," he pondered the issue for a moment. "It's now almost twelve, and the first train is around five."

"Yes, I see what you mean. Killing time somewhere and hopping on the first train would be another alternative."

If it had been nine o'clock, instead of twelve midnight, Kiyoshi and Tomoko would have just accepted the price and proceeded to the check-in procedure at once. They would have enjoyed the luxury of spending time in a nice and comfortable hotel room. The next day was a regular work or school day, and they would have to check out early in the morning to head back to Tokyo, but they could, at least, have a sound sleep. They exchanged glances, silently weighing the discomfort of staying outside overnight against the large cost for staying in a hotel for five or six hours.

"Why don't we wait for a while and see if we can survive a few hours of exposure?" Kiyoshi proposed the economical option.

"It sounds like a good idea." Tomoko was fully aware how much money they had already spent that day. They must save money if they hope to enroll Kohei in a private school next spring and to move into a larger and better apartment.

"If we can somehow put up with five hours' waiting, we can save a lot of money." In fact, they had already waited for hours in line for attractions and might as well wrap it up as a big waiting day. The children might drop off to sleep in their parents' laps soon, Kiyoshi thought optimistically. His wife nodded her agreement to his suggestion. "And if it doesn't seem to work, we can always go to the hotel."

"Right. We can always go to the hotel if it doesn't work."

They huddled together on a bench in front of the station. Kiyoshi made a quick trip to the bank of vending machines to get a couple of beverages and ice creams to pacify the children. "It's just a couple of hours. You guys eat your ice cream while I'm telling you stories, okay? And before you know it, it'll be time to hop in the first morning train and head back home. Kohei, you haven't ridden in the first morning train, have you?"

"No."

"It's really nice and refreshing, you know. The train is almost empty, and you've got an entire car to yourself. You'll see the dawn outside the window, which is spectacular. It's like another big ride in the theme park."

"It may be more fun than rides in the park because it is a real-life thing," Tomoko seconded her husband's suggestion, smiling.

"Okay. I think I'd like it," the five-year-old boy accepted it as an interesting option.

"How about you, Yuko?"

"I like it, too," the three-year-girl agreed innocently.

However, in a matter of ten minutes, the young children started to recognize the reality of staying outside all night.

"Daddy! Mommy! Aren't we going home?" Yuko asked in a whimpering voice, obviously intimidated by potential problems, which she could not define as a child. "Why aren't we going home now?"

"We missed the last train."

"I want to go home. I want to sleep in my house, not outside."

"Listen, okay? We missed the train, and there won't be any way to get home until morning. But as I said, it'll be no big problem because time will pass very quickly. Besides, Mom and Dad are with you."

"You can sleep on my lap, Yuko." Tomoko took off her cardigan sweater and covered the little girl's shoulder like a blanket.

"But I want to go home. I want to go home now." The girl was persistent, and her voice turned into a shriek.

"I said we *can't*," Kiyoshi raised his voice. He could understand that children were not as patient as adults. Their concept of time was quite different, and five hours probably seemed like days. However, fatigued from walking and waiting for a whole day, he could not control his own irritation. "The train is gone, and there is nothing we can do. Can't you understand it?"

"Then, why don't we go to a hotel?" Kohei offered his smart idea in support of his younger sister.

Although his wife had accepted his logical alternative to save money, the young children did not share their parents' internal struggles and voiced their honest feelings out loud. And it hurt Kiyoshi because he himself desperately wished to accommodate his small children in a comfortable place but could not easily afford it.

"Just shut up," Kiyoshi snapped in anger, his face flushed crimson. He then glared at his little daughter without intending to do so. Yuko looked down and started weeping. Kohei, her elder brother, remained silent with his head cast down, clearly afraid of triggering another outburst of his father's anger. "Your mother and father are just discussing what can, or must, be done. Besides, we missed the train because you needed to go to the bathroom."

The next moment, Kiyoshi regretted losing his temper and was more miserable than the children. He had not intended to mention Yuko's trip to the bathroom, either. His long, hard week at the insurance company was taking its toll, and he was way past the point of exhaustion. Nonetheless, he was seriously ashamed of losing his temper. At the same time, he realized for the first time that he had never been burdened until then with the obligation to take care of his children all day long. He had often spent time with them on weekends, but he normally only engaged in a few hours of entertaining activities so that the children regarded him as a nice and understanding father. He had never been forced to raise his voice to his children because Tomoko played the role of a strict parent, struggling to keep them in line. He had to admit that it was why he did not understand the children's psychology as well as his wife did.

The night air turned chilly, and the wind started blowing. It was late summer—or early autumn—but because the weatherman predicted a fine weather for the whole day, they had not brought any thick clothes. They were all wearing thin, half-sleeved shirts. Only Tomoko, who hated the air-conditioning in the trains or buildings, chanced to have brought her cardigan.

"Why don't we move over to the bench near the hotel?" Kiyoshi suggested. "There we can, at least, keep ourselves from being directly exposed to the chilly night air."

"Sounds like a good idea," Tomoko seconded his suggestion without making any comment on her husband's explosion.

The family moved to a bench that was placed right behind the back of the hotel and huddled. Branches of the trees that surrounded the hotel served as a roof or large umbrella above their heads, and a lukewarm air that was blowing out of the ventilation hole in the hotel's outer wall served as a heater. It was a somewhat more comfortable place than the bench in front of the station where they were exposed to occasional gusts of wind.

Kohei dozed off for a moment out of exhaustion but soon woke up and said, "Mommy, I'm cold."

"Just try to be a little patient, Kohei. Okay? We'll soon be able to ride a train and go home." She didn't have another cardigan to offer to him.

The five-year-old boy did not whine or sob like his sister, but his weak voice showed how much he needed protection in the overnight refugee-camp situation.

"Maybe, this is too much for the kids." A few minutes later, Kiyoshi stood up and declared his judgment, "We'd better check into the hotel."

It was still just a few minutes past twelve midnight. Tomoko had already found out from the Grand Hotel Web page that the hotel was open around the clock, but if they ever decided to check in, it might be the last appropriate time. Otherwise, their stay in the hotel room would be just too short to be worth the thirty-thousand-yen charge.

"We'll get a triple room so that you and the kids can check in. I don't mind staying outside and hanging around for a couple of hours." He had made many business trips and stayed at many different hotels and, from experience, knew that there might be a restriction regarding the number of people who could stay in each room. "I'll smoke a couple of cigarettes and read a sports paper under a street lamp. It'll soon be morning."

"In fact, once we've checked in, it'll be quite easy for you to sneak in, too."

"Right."

"But are you sure it's okay to spend so much money? As you said, if we wait only five hours, we can get inside the station and hop on the first train back to the city."

Kiyoshi considered the two alternatives again, but he now realized how slowly time passed for small children. He thought that the children should not be tormented for what they perceived to be a long time.

"Well, I'll go and ask at the front desk. Once you've checked in, you can sleep until the check-out hour and rest up, though I'll just have to catch the first train to head back to work."

"In fact, the children will go to school, so we'll probably leave with you." She had never let the children miss a school day except for really serious reasons.

"Yeah, you're right! But let's just get inside and let us all relax."

"Are you sure you don't mind paying thirty thousand yen?" Her repeated question brought back to him a memory of their courtship period. Before their marriage, his monthly salary was much lower, but he had always tried to take Tomoko to a plush restaurant and treat her to a full-course dinner. It had not been unusual for him to pay thirty thousand yen or more for one dinner. He had spent lavishly because he could afford it in those days when he only had to pay for himself and his girlfriend.

"Let's pay thirty thousand yen and check in. It's probably worth it." Kiyoshi stood up and headed for the hotel. He disappeared around the corner of the hotel building to reach the front gate. He was gone for a few minutes, during which time Tomoko assumed he was making a check-in procedure. However, he came back with his face flushed like a red *oni* ogre.

"Damn it!"

"What happened?"

"The front-desk guy said that the family rooms they charge per room are limited in number and have all been taken. It's a special plan for those who make reservations in advance. The regular rooms are twenty thousand yen *per head*, and there is no discount for small children."

"So, it means eighty thousand yen for four people?"

"Or sixty thousand yen for three."

"It's a lot of money, and we don't have that much money on us." Koyoshi had left his credit cards at home.

"Yes. Besides, I don't like the way they cheated us. It isn't clearly stated on the Web page. It's a rip-off!"

From his red face and the way he talked, Tomoko could see that her husband had lost his temper, had an altercation with a hotel employee, and walked out after cursing him.

"They are taking advantage of the fact that there's no other hotel available at the moment."

"They may be."

In fact, writing legal contracts was part of Kiyoshi's professional responsibilities in the insurance company. He had been trained to be a careful writer—and reader—because the written descriptions were solid evidence in case of litigation or other undesirable consequences. If a rule or regulation was publicly displayed, either on a contract or on the Web page, it served as proof that the party had clearly proclaimed their policy. When he regained his composure a few seconds later, he could understand that the hotel must have had its pricing policies officially stated somewhere, if not on the Web page he and his wife had seen.

Kiyoshi sat down on the bench, still fuming, and turned his attention to his young son and daughter. Again, five hours was not an intolerably long time for adults, but he could see that it was torture for the children. It was painful to acknowledge that the children were suffering because of his failure to bring his credit card. The plush hotel towering in front of them looked like a gigantic deity looking down derisively at the little beings who could not afford to pay for shelter.

"I'm cold," the little girl complained again, this time in a much quieter tone, afraid of his father's temper. "And I want to go to the bathroom again."

Tomoko walked her to the public bathroom near the railway station, which reminded Kiyoshi of the pavement dwellers who used the public facilities for water and sanitation.

After the two came back from the bathroom, Kohei complained of being cold again. Kiyoshi looked around the area, but of course, there was no shop open where he could buy some warm clothes, let alone an all-night coffee shop to take shelter at. The only material he could find were the old newspapers that other visitors had thrown away in front of the station. He scuttled around to collect the newspapers that were not dirtied or badly wrinkled up. He could not help associating the disposed newspapers with old cardboard boxes that the homeless used. Trying to shut the idea out of his mind for the moment, he managed to produce a primitive paper coat and covered the boy's body.

"Sorry, Kohei. But this is all we could find."

The boy nodded quietly as if understanding his father's position as a small child.

"Is it warm?"

"Yes, it's warm." He sat between his parents, leaning against his mother to relax. It appeared that the five-year-old had suddenly matured through an ordeal, which added to the young insurance man's guilty conscience.

During all this time, Kiyoshi continued to debate the idea of going back to the hotel counter. Even without a credit card, he might be able to negotiate a special arrangement with the hotel so that he could pay back afterward. With the lapse of time, however, the price of a hotel room was getting increasingly expensive in terms of the per-hour rates. It might still be possible to check in, but at one o'clock, they would be paying sixty thousand yen for four hours; at two o'clock, it would be sixty thousand yen for a three-hour stay. And of course, begging the haughty Grand Hotel employees for a favor of making a special payment arrangement would be a humiliating experience. Time dragged, and at two o'clock, he broached the issue again.

"Tomoko, I think I'll go back to the hotel and inquire . . ."

Tomoko placed her fingers vertically on her lips and hushed him. "They've fallen asleep." They were exhausted from a long day's activities, and despite the unusual circumstances in the dark, cold open space away from home, they fell asleep. With a mixed feeling, Kiyoshi appreciated the fact that small children would adapt to any harsh environment.

Then, the husband and wife started a quiet conversation, voicing their inner reflections. "Tomoko, I know you argued for giving up the last attraction and going home earlier. I should've agreed . . ."

"No, it's okay. I could understand you wanted to explore as much as possible. You paid the expensive admission fees. Besides, I insisted on coming on this particular weekend, knowing you'd been through an extremely busy and difficult week at the office."

"Well, maybe, it was a combination of different factors and incidents that brought about this misfortune."

"Live and learn, I guess."

"Right."

"I'll bet you've had enough and don't want to come back to this place again."

"No. As a matter of fact, I'd rather plan a return visit sometime soon. Next time, we'll do more careful preparation to do everything right."

"That'd be lovely."

"I'll bring my credit cards, too." They laughed quietly.

With time, the temperature lowered a few more degrees. The wooden bench behind the hotel building was their only shelter. The wall of the hotel shielded them from the chilly wind, and the warm fetid air spewing out of the ventilation hole gave them modest comfort. He could not help glancing at his wristwatch repeatedly. They still had a few more hours to go before the first train in the morning, but with the small children asleep, the hands of the watch seemed to move just a little faster.

The image that kept flashing back to his mind was the homeless man who lay on the riverfront walkway near his company. His colleague Takashi was right, he admitted painfully. In retrospect, the man had always behaved decently, had never bothered the locals or passersby, and had kept his belongings stowed away. As Takashi indicated, he might have even been a successful businessman who had taken a misstep and fallen off the social treadmill to lose his house. He might have even been married with a family, but most likely, he had not been fortunate enough to have a sensible, understanding wife like Tomoko, who shared the burden with him. He thought he would never bad-mouth any person who was not as privileged as he was, including the homeless tramps who camped out near their fancy company building.

A strong gust of wind suddenly came and blew away one of the newspaper pages that covered the five-year-old boy's body, reminding Kiyoshi as father that it was still a few hours before morning would break.

Stick it Out

The hospital was a three-story gray building with no particular characteristics, but it was easy to find it, located very close to the railway station. Taro entered the hospital, ran up two flights of stairs, and entered Room 303—a small single room where his grandfather Kamezo was accommodated. According to a woman at the information desk, he had been moved from a large room for five patients to that private room last night. The room was menacingly still and silent. Kamezo lay quietly on a metal-framed bed. Nobody else was around except the attending nurse who nodded silently to acknowledge the arrival of the patient's grandson. Just an hour before, a hospital employee had sent a message to his junior-high school teacher, who directed Taro to hurry to the hospital. So, he had a clear idea of what was happening to his grandfather. Yet the moment he stepped inside and saw his sick grandfather, he was overwhelmed by a sad and scary feeling welling up from the bottom of his stomach. His grandfather was soon going to depart—the only person in the world whom he had been able to trust and depend on. Kamezo recognized his grandson and nodded to him.

"Come closer, Taro," the old man addressed him in a weak but clear voice. It was obvious that he had been waiting for the last conversation with his eldest grandson. The junior-high boy could see that many of his neighbors had visited him at the hospital during the last few days. All the sick-visit presents, such as canned fruits, cookies, and candies, had been stacked neatly on the shelf near the washbasin. The pile of generous gifts from conscientious visitors made him feel even sadder as the recipient would never have a chance to consume them. And there were no flowers in a flower vase. His mother Akiko had always brought fresh flowers to enliven the atmosphere of a drab hospital room, but the hospital workers seemed to have disposed of them when they moved Kamezo to the present room. Even a junior-high student could understand that the flowers, at such a critical moment, would only remind people of an inevitable ceremony to be held a few days ahead. He knew that his mother had come to the hospital to pick up her father's laundry the last night, but she was not there at the moment. Grandfather's condition had suddenly worsened, and Taro had been shocked to receive the news through his schoolteacher, instead of his own mother. For Kamezo, however, it did not seem to matter in the least as long as he could talk with Taro, the eldest of his three dearest grandchildren.

"Grandpa!"

Kamezo looked him in the eyes. "You are a good boy, Taro, and the one I really wanted to talk to before I go."

"Don't say that, Grandpa. I know you'll be well."

"I wish I would, but it seems like the time has come. And I want you to understand it and listen carefully to what I have to tell you."

"Okay!" Taro bobbed his head a couple of times.

"I'm going away, and you've got to be ready for the consequences. I'm telling you this because I know you can do it."

Taro unconsciously shifted his line of sight to the nameplate clipped to the head of his grandfather's bed: Kamezo Higashi. Higashi was Taro's original and real family name. When his parents married, his father had been adopted to the Higashi family because his mother was an only child. Then, after he died, his mother married her present husband named Mishima, which made Taro and his younger brother and sister live with him and officially changed their family name to Mishima. But many of his good friends still called him Higashi; so, did Mr. Tomita, his homeroom teacher and a few other teachers who knew him well.

Except for the brief honeymoon period, the life of the Higashi children in the new home environment had been treacherous, and it eventually turned into a disaster. Kamezo, his grandfather, had been the only person who could step in and help them in emergencies. Kamezo had always doled out his savings and given Taro and his younger brother and sister allowances. He himself led a frugal life and, even after his retirement from a railway company, continued to work part-time as an apartment caretaker. In the late afternoon or on weekends, he grew crops and vegetables on a small rented agricultural field. Instead of spending his retirement and pension money on sightseeing trips or Kabuki theaters, he used all his savings to help his daughter and her children. But what Taro appreciated the most was his moral support.

When Akiko was considering marriage with Mishima, it did not take much time for Kamezo to find out that her would-be-second-husband was anything but a conscientious and dependable man who would take good care of his new wife's children. Soon, there were occasions on which he had to stick his neck out to save the small children from the vicious man's violence. Of course, during the one-month period of courtship, Mishima had pretended to be a kind and friendly man by bringing nice presents or offering loving words to his girlfriend's children. But soon after they were married, he had bared his fangs against what he regarded as unwanted dependents. Kamezo had to keep a watchful eye on his new son-in-law who emerged as a serious threat to his grandchildren. He had warned Akiko of the inevitable consequences right at the beginning, but to his regret, she had never taken his advice seriously.

A vivid image of the first violent incident came back to Taro's mind for a brief second. It was soon after Mishima moved into their small apartment. They were watching TV and eating dinner, and Jiro complained about the food that his mother had prepared. Suddenly Mishima stood up, pulled the little boy's hair, made him turn around, and slapped him in the face. Jiro was terrified and curled up in a fetal position. It was a traumatic experience, not only for Jiro, but also for Hanako, his younger sister. Jiro was seven years old, and Hanako was five. Taro soon realized that it was just the beginning of the nightmarish life, not an isolated incident. Violence was then inflicted not only on Jiro but on the other two children as well, and the situation progressively aggravated. The other apartment tenants heard the yelling and crying time and again, but they could not find a good excuse to step in and save them. Akiko always pleaded with her new husband to *pardon* her children, but the problem was that she never took any decisive measures to work out a permanent solution. She never made serious efforts to change her own attitude even in the face of a life-and-death situation.

"Taro, I'm going to go away," his grandfather said again. "And there's no helping it because I'm an old man after all."

Kamezo had a chronic liver problem, and his immunity had recently become noticeably weaker. *Stress might have shortened his life*, Taro suspected.

"I'm really sorry for you."

"Sorry for what?"

"For not being able to stay and take care of you guys. But you're the eldest sibling and you've got to look after the little guys."

Taro remained quiet as the message sank in. He knew that what lay ahead in their life would be an ordeal but acknowledged that he would have to take over his grandfather's role and protect his younger siblings. He was still thirteen years old, but his brother and sister were much younger.

"And your mother, too," the old man added with a pathetic expression. Taro understood what he meant and remained silent for a while.

"I know what you are thinking. But you just got to stick it out. I am seriously worried about the two little kids, but I'm afraid my little daughter can't handle the situation! I told her a hundred times it wasn't good, but she just couldn't kick that guy out."

Taro remembered that, ever since his mother's second marriage, Grandfather Kamezo had implied over and over again that he was unhappy with his own daughter's attitude. He was complaining about what she should have done or what she should not have done at the crucial points in her life. She should have trained and disciplined herself to deal with emergency situations, and she should not have even married her first husband because he was so weak and erratic. She should never, ever have considered marrying her second husband, who was, in Kamezo's words, the most worthless man in the world, who had no merit except for his superficial charm and shallow sexiness. And more than anything else, he was angry at her failure to take action against him after he started slapping her children around. When Kamezo vocalized his regrets on his deathbed, it really sank into the teenage boy's heart.

"She is a spoiled girl who never grew up. I hate to admit this, but it'd probably be impossible for her to change anymore. And now, Taro, you are the only one I can trust. You've got to take care of them and yourself."

Taro contemplated the issue for a full minute. "All right, Grandpa! Don't worry about it." An IV tube was attached to Kamezo's left arm, hanging from a stand. The thirteen-year-old boy held his free hand tightly with both of his own hands. He was sure that his mother, Akiko, was on her way to the hospital, but she had not arrived yet.

Kamezo smiled thinly and cocked his head to the side.

"Grandpa!" The boy choked on his words. He wanted to cry loudly at the departure of the main pillar of the family. As of that moment, the person who had protected them from the drunken savage was gone forever. His responsibility as the eldest brother would be very heavy. But instead of crying, he simply pressed his grandfather's hand to his forehead and prayed silently, relishing a few minutes of privacy before the doctor and nurses would come in. He also thought that it would not be fair to disturb the old man when he was supposed to rest peacefully, concluding his long arduous but meaningful life.

***

Mishima's first explosion occurred a week after his mother's marriage to him—that is, two weeks after he moved in—and the first victim was Jiro. There were only two rooms in the small apartment: the *tatami*-matted dining and living room and another *tatami*-matted room in the back where the children slept or sometimes did their homework. They were eating dinner at a small dining table as usual, and Mishima was dining and drinking some low-grade liquor.

Taro remembered that he had felt a little cramped after another person—a grown man—moved in to occupy one side of the small dining table. It was a strange feeling because, previously, his own father used to take his seat in the same position, but Taro had never felt so crowded. Then, for a certain period of time, it was only his mother, two younger siblings, and himself. Taro and his younger brother and sister might have grown somewhat bigger during that time, but he could not help feeling that this new man had suddenly come and unfairly taken up a large space in the small apartment.

That evening, Jiro had a little fight with his younger sister, concerning the TV program to watch, and then started complaining about the food that their mother had prepared. When tired—particularly toward the end of a long day—small children would throw a tantrum, and Taro, as a junior-high student, could understand his younger brother's bad mood as he was himself feeling rather uncomfortable in the restricted living space. But Mishima suddenly stood up and, without a warning, pulled Jiro's hair to turn him around, and slapped him very strongly.

"Damn it! I'm trying to relax and eat dinner after a long hard day's work. Why don't you just shut up and give me peace of mind?"

The impact was as strong as if all window panes had been shattered. Taro, his mother, and his younger sister stared in shocked disbelief. Jiro himself was, of course, terrified. In order to escape from further punishment, he crawled to a corner of the room and curled up. He started trembling uncontrollably, emitting feeble vocal sounds out of his constricted throat. Akiko, who had never seen her new husband's violent side before, was stunned. Almost in a reflex action, she tugged her little boy toward herself and held him tightly.

"You shouldn't have made a noise, Jiro." She tried to soothe him and help control his convulsions.

"God damn this little space, crowded with a bunch of kids! I have no breathing space at all."

Taro had a strong indignation at Mishima's remark. The four of them had been there all the time, and this big man had appeared out of nowhere and moved in to crowd their humble little dwelling. But obviously, this savage man did not share the same view.

"And I hate these stupid cartoons." He tried to switch to a baseball game, but the TV set resisted, showing a blurry image and producing a peal of squeaky sound. "Dammit, dammit!" He cursed and kicked the TV set, and all the images vanished from the screen as if the TV were permanently damaged. Mishima clammed up sulkily, allowing nobody to talk or make any movement at all. The uncomfortable silence remained until they all went to bed for the night.

Soon, it turned out that this incident was not an isolated case, and the junior-high boy realized that he and his brother and sister must be extremely careful not to offend their stepfather. But Jiro was so small that, when he was tired toward the end of a day, he just could not control himself. He tended to make noises in spite of his mother's or stepfather's warnings, clamored for candies when they were out of stock, or insisted on a TV channel when someone else needed to see a different program. Mishima had very little patience with him and began to slap him more frequently and, oftentimes, kept striking him until the small boy started bleeding out of his nose and mouth. The neighbors heard an angry man's shouting voices, Jiro's crying, and, on occasion, the sound of some object crashing against the walls or the floor. The slapping hand was targeted at the little girl as well, who was even smaller and more helpless.

Taro himself was not old enough to be exempt from punishment, either. The little errors he made on occasion or his slow response to his stepfather's order got on the latter's nerves. And when upset, Mishima never tried to solve the problem rationally. The visual image or sound that disturbed him seemed to transmit a signal directly to his fists without relaying it through his brain. In the cheap wooden apartment building, the walls that separated families were very thin and everyone in the neighborhood could hear the yelling or crying voices. About three weeks later, the police officers in uniform knocked on their door and questioned Mishima and Akiko about the loud voices and crashing sounds that some neighbors had heard and reported. The police officers returned to their apartment several times afterward but did not have enough evidence or reason to apprehend him.

***

Taro's memory of his own father, Haruo, was vague although he had lived with him for twelve years before he suddenly collapsed and died. He was in the habit of getting off to work in the morning—not very early but a little after the children left for school. When Taro was leaving for school, he was usually still in bed. Then, he spent all day in his company, came back home very late, and went to bed after consuming a few cans of beer, saying he was exhausted. On Sundays, he tended to sleep until afternoon. Of course, he occasionally spent time with the children, playing cards or watching TV together. He never tried to take them out to a theme park or the movies. They never went to the mountains, played catch, or fished together because he never liked outdoor activities. One night, he had attended a big drinking party after work. A few minutes after he arrived home, he suddenly collapsed and was taken to an emergency hospital, and died. Taro could never fully understand the cause of his death or even pronounce the difficult disease name that the doctor cited. He was simply appalled at the fact that a human being could expire so easily. As far as Taro remembered, he had not been a bad father. And as they had spent so little time together, he had rarely scolded his children.

Instead, the person who had always scolded or lectured the children for bad behavior was Kamezo, the grandfather. He would not hesitate to raise his voice when his grandchildren failed to finish their studies, showed a slovenly attitude, or neglected respect toward the older people, their teachers, or any adults in the neighborhood. He was particularly strict toward Taro.

Once, when Taro had failed to greet the next-door neighbor in the morning, Kamezo was very angry. "You neglect your courtesy, and you'll be in big trouble. You really have to keep it in mind."

Grandfather lectured him for a full hour, and the small child could not help arguing back.

"Why do you have to be so mad about such a trivial mistake?"

"You're wrong there because one mistake will lead to another, and oftentimes, it turns into a permanent bad habit. Besides, by making a slip, you are giving out an opening to whatever enemy that might be lurking behind your back."

After being scolded, however, Taro never carried any grudge against his grandfather because, young as he was, he could understand that it had been his fault and that what his grandfather said made sense. And except for occasional conflicts, Grandfather Kamezo had always been his best friend. He lived in the close vicinity, and on weekends, they often walked alone the nearby river to inspect good fishing spots. Then, they sat on the riverbank, fishing and conversing for hours, which was how the boy learned all about the family history. They chatted on frivolous matters or discussed serious moral issues. Kamezo gave him calligraphy lessons so that he could win a prize in a calligraphy contest at the school. He also taught him useful carpentry and gardening skills. And more than anything else, he served as the role model by working hard even after retirement. Taro had enormous respect for him.

They talked about everything, and his grandfather even touched on the sensitive issues that adults would not normally discuss with, or talk about in front of, children. Once, when they were sitting on the riverbank together with their fishing rods held out above the river, Kamezo complained that his son-in-law should work much harder and should not stay out until late, drinking with his colleagues.

"He should acknowledge he's the breadwinner for the family."

"But, Grandpa, Father goes to work every day and stays in his office until late. He doesn't come home early because he says he's busy working in his office. So you shouldn't speak so badly about him."

It was not a typical conversation between an elementary school child and his grandfather. But they always exchanged candid opinions because they were close to each other and trusted each other.

"You know, it's hard to explain it to you until you are a little bit older, but going to his office every day doesn't mean he's doing his best. If he's aware of his position as a father of three children, he should work extra hard to win a better position in the company, or he should, at least, come home early, instead of chatting about stupid matters and wasting money on beer."

"How do you know he's chatting about stupid matters?"

"As adults, it's not difficult to guess such things from his daily behavior."

"Is that so?"

"Yeah. He should work harder. There are many things that a grown man can do to earn extra money."

"Like what?"

"For example, he can help me grow crops and vegetables so that we can sell them for an extra income. That's what we all did when we were young."

Kamezo did not own the plot of farmland, but his rented field produced more agricultural products than the Higashi family consumed, so he sold the extra fruits and vegetables to the Agricultural Coop. His field was better tended to than any other in the same neighborhood. Of course, they lived in Tokyo; even in the area where they lived, which was away from the center of the city, the area of a farm was very small, and Kamezo never seriously encouraged his son-in-law or his grandsons to engage in agriculture. But Taro could understand that his grandfather was the person who would devote himself to whatever he could do.

"Is that why you could give us allowances?"

"Well, sort of. And of course, I don't need much money as an old man."

His mother gave him and his siblings a small amount of money in the form of a monthly allowance. But the family budget was very tight. Taro did the fast math and could understand the family's financial standing. But when his friends suddenly invited him to dine at a fast-food restaurant or when someone showed off his new video game that he could not dream of purchasing, the only person that he could turn to for extra money was his grandfather. Kamezo himself did not have any expensive hobby, except treating himself to a glass of *shochu* (low-class distilled spirits) before going to bed. He also expressed his unhappiness with his own daughter's inability to work part-time and help support the family.

Then, one night, Taro's father suddenly fell to the floor at home, blood trickling from the corner of his mouth, and was taken to a hospital. Later in the same day, he passed away, disappearing so suddenly and helplessly.

"He was a good-natured man," Kamezo repeatedly said after his son-in-law's death. "But he should've been a much stronger and more dependent father. The problem is, I had known about it before they married and warned Akiko about it. But she never listened. She only listens to what she wants to hear. It's been inherited from her mother."

"Grandpa, you shouldn't speak ill of Grandma," he argued again as a small child. Kamezo liked the fact that his grandson demonstrated his ethical sensibilities.

"Yeah, perhaps, you are right. But listen, Taro! I'd never tell these things to anybody else. I'm not a complainer but just want you to understand the problems."

Taro reflected for a second and then deeply nodded.

"I'm telling all these to you because, first, these are the facts, and, second, as the eldest child of the family, you ought to keep it in mind and never commit the same errors yourself. And you need to keep your brother and sister out of trouble." He said it in a firm voice, looking the boy in the eyes.

"When your mother was your age, I tried to discipline her more strictly, but Grandma always spoiled her, saying girls were girls and didn't have to push. But you are a boy, Taro, and there's no excuse. You've got to grow up to be a strong man. In fact, I believe girls should also be strong and patient in their own ways. I must admit I failed to educate my own daughter, and that might've been the cause of all these problems."

"Grandpa, you are so strong that *failure* just isn't the word for you."

"Everybody makes many mistakes and fails in many ways. The most important thing is to acknowledge your mistakes, learn from them, and become wiser and stronger."

***

As time passed, Taro gradually realized what his grandfather had really meant. Only a few months after his father's death, his mother started dating another man. She did not, of course, declare it loud and clear to her own children, but Taro soon started paying attention to frequent phone calls from the same man who identified himself as Mishima. His mother made up excuses to go out alone, asking a neighbor to take care of the little girl or leaving directions for the two boys to eat the food in the refrigerator and stay home until her return. Returning from school, Taro often found a note on the dining table, which said:

To Taro and Jiro,

> I have some engagements tonight, and I'll be late. Your dinner is in the refrigerator. Heat it up and eat it. And don't forget to finish your homework. I'll be back at about nine.
>
> Mother

Normally, she did not return until eleven or midnight. She dressed up nicely and wore noticeably heavy makeup on the days she had an "engagement." She looked five years younger, and Taro could even smell a perfume that she had never used before. Soon, she brought the man home, awkwardly introducing him as a member of a such-and-such voluntary organization. Taro was slightly suspicious about who he was and why he was there, whereas his younger brother and sister were pleased with the visitor who looked very friendly. Kamezo's reaction, on the other hand, was absolutely negative.

One night, when she returned home late, Kamezo, who was taking care of his three grandchildren at their apartment, exploded, which he had never done to his daughter—at least, not in the small children's presence.

"Haruo's body is hardly cold in the grave," he voiced his sympathy toward his late son-in-law whom he had never highly regarded when he was alive. "And more than that, do you really think this guy Mishima is dependable? He seems to me like a really shallow, flippant type of man. You should think more carefully about your partner."

"You always say all negative things about the man I choose, Father," she argued back in an uncharacteristically strong tone. Her face was tinged with pink. Taro noticed that his mother, who had never consumed alcohol at home, was inebriated. The way she talked was clearly different. "Ever since I was a teenager, you've always been trying to find fault with the person I'm fond of, picking minor problems that I myself think are okay."

"And see what happened to the guys you chose, including the one you actually married."

"That's none of your business, Father. And how can you be so cruel to me after I've been through the terrible experience, losing my husband?"

"You don't seem to be grieving much over your husband's death, though." There was a moment of silence before Kamezo continued, "I'm warning you because it'd be stupid to repeat the same mistake. In fact, this new guy seems to be much worse. The consequences might be disastrous. Can't you understand it?"

"Again, that's none of your business—really none of your business." She was now wailing like a preschool child. Jiro and Hanako were appalled at the sight of an adult crying like a small child. They had never thought that an adult would cry, and it was shocking to see their own mother in shambles. "Besides, I've not only lost my husband, but I've also lost my source of income. I can't raise my children on welfare."

Kamezo let out a sigh of resignation. He could not talk sense into his daughter because his late wife had spoiled her to the extent that she would never even consider the option of working herself to support her children.

"Well, if you say so, I don't care who you marry anymore."

"Why should you in the first place?"

"You'll see what happens, though, and don't say I didn't tell you. And just one last thing! You should really try to find a job and start working."

"I've never worked, and I can't suddenly start working."

"You know, Akiko, the situation has changed! You are a mother of three children, and it is your responsibility to support and protect them with your own hands. This is a crisis, and you're no longer a little princess. You've got to change your attitude and take action. The longer you put it off, the worse it'll be. You are the one who'll end up in living hell."

Kamezo recognized Mishima's flighty character at once when they met and talked for the first time. Right after an exchange of pleasantries, Mishima bragged about the fact that he had earned three million yen during a three-month period at his last job. He had been an assistant manager at a bar. Then, he told his girlfriend's father over cups of sake that he had won the championship in two prefectural field-and-track events as a junior-high student. But from his obvious exaggeration and his overly informal speech manners, Kamezo could tell at once that he was a vain, superficial type of man who would never achieve half as much as he claimed to have. He had himself worked for a railroad company for thirty-five years. Without a high school diploma, he had never held a high administrative position, but he had worked with hundreds of other people in a huge organization and had learned to recognize different people's personality traits. It might be true that Mishima had earned three million yen at the last bar where he was employed, but strangely, he never explained why he resigned his job after collecting the lump sum of money. Kamezo later learned from a reliable source that his track-and-field-events championship was a total fabrication. He was a smooth liar with no special skills or professional expertise. But to Akiko, he was a nice man with a gentle personality and someone whom she could depend on for the remainder of her life.

"You will regret it. I'm telling you you'll be terribly, terribly sorry."

"But I can't work. I have no experience or marketable skills. Marriage is practically the only alternative."

"You can't work because you never try to start doing it." Kamezo was simply devastated by the fact that he had to lecture on such a basic principle when his daughter was already thirty-four. "And you are making exactly the same mistake again, though the two men you've chosen are of different breeds. Listen, you've got to be stronger and more independent. What do you think is going to happen to your children? You've got to protect them. Again, you aren't a child anymore." Kamezo could not help voicing the major problem repeatedly. He did not want to do it when his grandchildren—or her children— were present, but he had no choice at all.

She had been a very charming girl when she was young, and now at the age of thirty-four, she was still beautiful enough, at least, to attract men in Mishima's league. But she no longer looked like what she was in her wedding photo taken fourteen years before. Her beauty was fading slowly but noticeably. The wrinkles around her eyes were getting obvious, and she could no longer wear her favorite skirts. The crisis that lay ahead in Taro and his siblings' future was now looming like dark thunderclouds.

My mother is a grown baby. It was a shocking fact that the junior-high boy was forced to acknowledge. But he had to accept it when he tried to see the situation through his grandfather's eyes.

When Taro met Mishima for the first time, he looked like any other middle-aged man—except that he was noticeably much skinnier than his late father, Haruo, who had been on the plump-to-chunky side. His mother used to complain about her first husband's gaining weight when he was alive. Her new boyfriend was not fat and looked a little like a countryside version of the soap-opera actor whom his mother admired. Except for that, in the junior-high-school boy's eyes, Mishima looked just like a plain man in his early to mid-thirties. As it turned out later, he was actually three years younger than his mother. What really surprised him was the fact that he showed up so soon after his father's death. Taro could not help being a little suspicious that his mother had been seeing him before his father died. When he implied his suspicion in a subtle way, she vehemently denied it, claiming that they had simply been business acquaintances.

When Mishima came to their home for the first time, he smiled at the three children and offered friendly words to each one of them. First, he picked up Hanako and cradled her fondly in his arms. "Hello, Hanako! Oh, you are such a cute, little princess!"

Then, he addressed Jiro, giving him a friendly pat on the shoulder. "Hi, Jiro! Have you got a hundred good friends in school?"

Jiro was delighted that this man already knew his name. "Sure I do. As a matter of fact, I have two hundred friends."

"Wow! It's great. And what do you do during recess?"

"We play dodgeball a lot, and I'm pretty good at it."

Jiro could keep on talking forever about what he did at school or after classes. Then, Mishima felt obligated to offer words to the eldest of the children. He turned to Taro and talked to him in a little more adult-like manner.

"It's great to meet you, Taro."

"Nice to meet you, sir," Taro replied in a rather formal tone.

"Your mother has told me a great deal about you."

"Has she?"

"Yes. She says you are a strong and mature boy who takes good care of his brother and sister. How are you doing at school?"

"Oh, I'm not sure if I'm doing so well."

"I hear you're in the junior-high first year."

"Yes."

"I'll bet the studies are getting more and more difficult."

"As a matter of fact, they are. I'm having trouble with math."

"Oh, looking back, I was terrible at math myself. I was rather good at history, Japanese literature, and PE, though."

"Did you play any sports?" Taro asked as Mishima looked more athletic than his late father.

"Yeah. First, I was on the school's baseball team."

"What was your position?"

"First base."

"You must have been really good."

"But then, I switched to field-and-track events. I won a ten-kilometer race in my second year."

"Is that right?"

"Uh-huh! I won the prefectural championship twice, that is, in the second and third year."

"That's amazing!"

"You said you won a big race?" Jiro broke in, anxious to retrieve his turn to talk to Mishima.

"Yeah."

"Let's go out and race! I'm a pretty fast runner myself."

"Oh, is that right?"

"Yes, yes. Let's go and run."

"Okay, let's do that." Mishima complied with the little boy's request. "Oh, I almost forgot. I've got something for you guys."

He extracted a large doll for Hanako and plastic models for the two boys. The model warship that he had bought for Taro was more difficult to assemble than the airplane for Jiro. It would present a challenge to a junior-high student, requiring more elaborate work.

"Thank you very much for your generous present," Taro said. His younger brother and sister thanked him, too, after their mother urged them to express their appreciation explicitly.

Then, Mishima and Jiro headed out to a nearby park. When they finally came back an hour later, Jiro was triumphant, claiming that he had won seven out of the ten races.

"Oh, Jiro, you can't really beat an adult. Mishima-san ran slowly on purpose," Taro said to his younger brother.

"No, I really beat him."

"Yes, he did," Mishima affirmed the ten-year-old boy's position as the winner.

***

One peculiar thing that Taro noticed during Mishima's first visit was that he was inspecting the interior of the house with unusual minuteness as if checking a piece of real estate to purchase. Looking at the rooms and furniture, he kept mumbling to himself or to Akiko: "The wallpaper needs replacement"; "This refrigerator is rather small"; "A chest of drawers of charcoal color would fit in nicely here." The comments struck the adolescent boy as rather strange because he could not see any reason why the man had to worry about *their* furniture or wallpaper.

Among the three children, Jiro—then, the second grader in elementary school—welcomed Mishima the most. He took an instant liking to the man who would eventually be their stepfather. As the second of three siblings, he was the most sociable and gregarious. And he had been the hardest hit when his father suddenly passed away because he used to spend more time with him than his elder brother and his younger sister did. He had been visibly shocked and depressed and kept waking up at night and cried, noticing his father's absence in the house. For him, this new man, who had suddenly popped out from nowhere, was the one that would fill the spot of his deceased father. For the next month, every time Mishima visited their home, he begged him to go to the park and play with him—the request that the man accommodated cordially. Of course, at this stage, Jiro did not have the slightest idea about this vicious, short-tempered man's ego hidden under the veneer of gentlemanly manners and the fact that he would be the first one to fall victim to his violence.

Taro was seriously concerned about her mother's true intention. *Father's body is still warm in the grave*, the thirteen-year-old boy wanted to repeat his grandfather's words, although he stopped short of doing it.

"Mother, are you considering a permanent relationship with him?" He broke the ice in what he believed to be polite and subtle enough a manner of speaking when the two were having tea alone.

"Well, I don't know yet, but I'm just beginning to think about various possibilities for my future." She replied hesitantly with her face tinged with a sign of slight embarrassment, which was enough to answer Taro's question.

"I understand it's only natural for you to start thinking about your future. But I want you to understand we need some time to settle into this new life without Father. You know, we need time to get over things after his death."

"Yes, of course! And I wouldn't do anything without talking to my children, first—especially to you."

Saying one thing and acting in a completely different way was what Kamezo had always lamented over as one of her weaknesses. When Taro started learning something, such as calligraphy or swimming, and failed to accomplish his declared goal, Kamezo did not hesitate to raise his voice and scold him. He ordered him to look straight into the speaker's eyes; when the small boy looked away, he punished him with a knock on his forehead and kept lecturing him for hours until he really admitted his mistake and promised to correct it. Taro would never forget his grandfather's glaring eyes and serious facial expressions. He had sometimes resented his overly strong discipline, but now, reflecting on his mother's erratic behavior, he understood why his grandfather had been so strict about his grandson's behavior. Kamezo regretted that he had not been strict enough to raise his own daughter properly.

***

About a month after his first visit, Mishima moved into their house. He did not bring his wardrobe or furniture, but he stayed the night in their apartment one day and continued to be there day after day after day. While Jiro welcomed him overwhelmingly, Taro realized that his hunch had come true, looking back on the way that this man had commented on the interior of their apartment on his first visit. Mishima must have already made up his mind, at that time, to move in permanently.

Taro could not help being resentful. When Akiko noticed his sulky mood, she spoke to him in private and defended her position, "But it's all for you three, you know. I love you and Jiro and Hanako, and I know you really need a father."

"My father is dead, and no one can replace him."

"I mean someone who can support and protect you. You'll be involved in various activities in school, and everything costs money. You want to advance to high school, and it'll cost lots of money, and I can't work because I'm always tied up, taking care of the family and doing the housework. You're already a junior-high student, and I hope you understand all such things." She began to dab at her eyes with a handkerchief when she argued for her point.

"I do, Mom."

"I want you to understand it's been really hard for me. Please don't make it harder because I just can't handle it."

"I understand, Mom, but it's just that . . ."

"Besides, Mishima-san is a really nice person, really caring about you guys."

That put an end to the conversation, leaving Taro in a state of great uncertainty. And only a week later, it would turn out that his mother's description of the man's personality was nothing other than her own optimistic imagination. His mother's second marriage was a careless, hasty move on the rebound, and there was too much risk involved in her hasty move, Taro thought in retrospect. Unfortunately, he was just a thirteen-year-old boy and her son, not her father or teacher or someone in a position to lecture her and inspire reason in her. Intuitively, he sensed that there was going to be a big surprise in store for him and his younger brother and sister.

***

A week after Mishima moved in, he and Akiko made a quick trip to the municipal government office, filled out the marriage registration form, and submitted it on the spot. They organized no reception to officially announce their marriage and treat their friends and relatives to a complimentary dinner.

"After all, this is my second marriage."

"Right. Besides, we aren't young—not in our early twenties."

"There is no reason why we should have a pretentious celebration."

Taro overheard their conversation at the dinner table and could see that Mishima and his mother had agreed on the wisdom of saving themselves time and trouble and money.

However, the way they responded to the neighbors' and acquaintances' congratulations strangely troubled the junior-high boy. Some conscientious neighbors and relatives sent them nice gifts including expensive chinaware and silverware or even gift money, and Akiko sent each of them a small package of cookies as a return gift. All the cookies were sent by parcel delivery service. She and her new husband obviously considered it as a proper arrangement to conclude their wedding procedure, but Taro had the misfortune to overhear the whispering comments by the recipients of the cookies, who did not notice him passing behind their back.

"It was a nice return gift she sent."

"You got the cookies, too."

"Uh-huh! Delivered it by parcel service. They didn't even bother to write a short message or come to see us in person!"

They were conversing in a low tone, but it rang stridently in Taro's ears. Later, he asked his grandfather what was wrong with a box of cookies sent by a newly wedded couple.

"She should've known better than that." Kamezo let out a sigh of resignation. "She should've consulted me."

"Is something the matter with cookies?"

After a moment of hesitation, Kamezo turned back to the thirteen-year-old boy with a benign smile on his face and tried to answer his question in plain and clear language.

"There's nothing terribly wrong about the cookies themselves. But in this particular context, the way they sent them was totally inappropriate, and you should perhaps remember this for your future reference, Taro."

"So what was wrong?"

"In this society when you get married and receive a gift or gift money for your wedding, it is customary to return a gift of about half the monetary value. A wedding is a once-in-a-lifetime event, and that's why people offer a generous gift. You know, nobody has a lot of extra money to spare. Some people are actually on a tight family budget and find it a huge burden when something suddenly happens to demand extra expenditure. Choosing a box of inexpensive cookies as a return gift might be, in itself, pardoned if you are poor, but you must somehow express your full gratitude. If you just send it by parcel service, instead of delivering it by hand and thanking them in person, they would feel their good intentions hadn't been appreciated."

"But you said before that, when you send somebody a gift or offer a favor, you shouldn't demand gratitude."

"Yes, I said it. And I'm proud of you for remembering it. Most conscientious and well-disciplined people wouldn't expect anything in return for the favors they offered. But as a gift recipient, you should never take it for granted that people would tolerate such breach of a social rule all the time. When such blunders pile up, your good friends would lose confidence in you, and I'm afraid that's exactly what's happening to your mother."

"But in Mother's case, it is *her* second time."

"I wouldn't blame you, Taro, for thinking that way as a junior-high student. But listen carefully. It is your—or her—point of view. Again, those who send gifts spend a large amount of money, and it doesn't matter whether it's the couple's first marriage or second marriage or third marriage. And when you are grown, thinking like a small child won't be accepted."

Taro was deeply disturbed by the revealed fact and was concerned how his mother's mistake might affect their relationships with the neighbors.

***

After Mishima officially married Akiko, he transported his belongings—packed compactly in five cardboard boxes—to the Higashis' apartment. His friend named Takeda had helped him carry the luggage in a pickup truck. Then the family and Takeda had lunch together in the small crowded apartment.

Mishima and his friend Takeda drank beer and kept on talking on topics that bore the children. A horse race was on TV, and although Jiro and Hanako wanted to watch a cartoon show, Akiko told them to be patient as a courtesy to the houseguest who had been kind enough to transport their new father's belongings. Takeda stayed until ten in the evening, chatting, watching TV, and drinking beer and whiskey. Their lunch continued on and turned into a dinner session. By the time he finally left, the small apartment was littered with empty beer and whiskey bottles and stacks of empty food containers. Mishima later complained that he had ended up paying fifty thousand yen for sushi and beverages, but when he said it, Taro was not certain whether he was lamenting over the expenditure or bragging about it.

The next morning at the breakfast table, Akiko told her children to start calling her husband Daddy. Taro felt a little uncomfortable but hesitantly did so because he did not want to be a psychological burden to his mother. He had never been happy about her quick marriage, but he could at least understand that she had been through an ordeal, losing her first husband and being left behind with children to raise single-handedly. He did not want to hurt the feelings of the man who agreed to be their new provider, either. But unless it was absolutely necessary, he tended not to call his stepfather by any address form.

Then, only a week after their parents' marriage, they witnessed their new father's first outburst. His transformation was simply shocking and unbelievable in the eyes of Taro's two younger siblings. The junior-high student was old enough to foresee, in one way or another, what the person's hidden side might turn out to be. He also remembered that his grandfather had been seriously concerned about his daughter's new partner. What disturbed Taro was the fact that it occurred much sooner than he had anticipated—that is, the man was not sensible enough to cover up his short-tempered side for a reasonably long period of time. However, it might have been a blessing in disguise in that they discovered soon enough what would have eventually come out.

***

As time passed, Mishima's violence got worse. One night about a month later, the family was watching TV and eating dinner, chatting on frivolous topics. Mishima was himself laughing at the jokes that a TV character cracked. Jiro started frolicking and romping about in the house and, then, leaned on his stepfather's shoulders.

"Daddy, will you lift me up and swing me like an airplane? Will you? Will you?" he begged persistently. Mishima had done it for Jiro many times in the past, but obviously, the new stepfather was not in a mood to play with a little kid at the moment.

"Not now! Just watch TV. Okay?" he abruptly declined.

Jiro became sulky because his new father turned down his request. Then, he started complaining about the baked mackerel that Akiko had prepared for dinner.

"I don't like this fish. I'm not going to eat it. I'm definitely not going to eat it."

Taro was a little sympathetic toward his younger brother who threw a tantrum because he was himself a little stressed, suffering a feeling of spatial discomfort.

"But that's all we've got today. Just eat it. Okay?" Akiko insisted.

"Then, I want Dad to lift me up like an airplane." He moved up to Mishima again and leaned more heavily on his shoulders, which made Mishima wince.

"Airplane, airplane, airplane! I want to play airplane."

Mishima suddenly twisted his own body and knocked Jiro down violently on his back. The boy was sent flying backward, and the back of his head crashed against the wall. Jiro had a concussion on impact and was dizzy for a second. When he came around, he started wailing like a fire truck as if to inform the entire neighborhood of the incident, which, in turn, made Mishima furious. He reached out toward the small boy and repeatedly slapped him across the face. "Shut up, snotty boy!"

Now, it became clear to Taro how his stepfather regarded the children sired by another man that he had nothing to do with. He had no genuine affection toward them at all.

"Damn it! I'm goddamn tired after a long day's work. Can't you see it, idiot?" Everybody froze. Jiro started sobbing with his body convulsing, covering his face with his hands to protect himself from more slaps or punches that might come.

Akiko pulled her second son closer and hugged him protectively. "You don't have to hit him!" she protested, her face pale as a sheet.

"Then, you just shut him up. I just can't tolerate the little kids making all the noise." Taro could see that their honeymoon had not lasted long.

Akiko looked into Jiro's face and exclaimed in shock, "He's bleeding out of his nose. I must take him to a doctor."

"Give me a break. It's just nose bleeding and nothing serious, and you don't have to make a fuss about it."

Jiro was sobbing and shuddering. Akiko had not realized before her marriage that her new husband had such a violent temper. She had dated him twenty times, but they had always been alone in restaurants or bars, having pleasant private conversations. Now, the same man revealed his obvious hatred for her children, which shocked her.

"Come on, Jiro." She held Jiro tightly. "You shouldn't have made such a noise in the first place. Okay?"

"I . . . I . . . I didn't mean to." Jiro tried to say something but just could not enunciate his words as his convulsions continued.

"It's okay. Your mamma is here. Just try to be a good boy! Then, there won't be any more trouble. Okay?"

Jiro continued to sob, although his convulsion gradually subsided. Then, in a few minutes, he began to sleep in his mother's arms.

"Goddamn it!" Mishima himself was still fuming. "Damn this little space, crowded with a bunch of people! I really can't put up with it."

***

Jiro woke up at midnight, reliving the terrifying experience.

"It's okay, Jiro." Taro tucked his younger brother into a *futon* blanket again. Jiro had his nose stuffed with a piece of gauze. His lips were swollen. "You've got to be careful, though, or you'll be in bigger trouble."

Jiro nodded quietly at his elder brother's advice. When Jiro was out of hand, it was difficult to comfort or control him. He would throw a tantrum, screaming and crawling on the floor. But normally, he was a good obedient boy and by no means a rebellious type.

"I told you to behave yourself. Besides, life has now changed much, you know. Mom has married another man, and you can no longer behave as you used to. He's not our own father, Jiro," Taro explained in a whispering voice. "We've got to accept this reality. Understand?"

"Yeah." He nodded again.

"He works and provides for us, and we must appreciate his efforts. Also, he chose to marry Mother, and we were just additional dependents that he hadn't even asked for. You've always got to keep it in mind and be careful about what you do."

"I will." Jiro soon fell asleep again, physically and emotionally drained. Taro gritted his teeth, staring up at the ceiling, and cursed to himself, "Bastard!"

***

Mishima woke up at six at the sound of his wife's cooking knife chopping vegetables on a chopping board. They slept in the dining and living room at night, and the small kitchen was right behind a thin partition. She was preparing ingredients for *miso* soup. He usually slept until much later, but he crawled out of his *futon* and made his way to the kitchen. He approached her from behind and put his hands on her shoulders. She just kept chopping leeks without responding to it.

"How are you doing?" he said and tried to turn her around. Akiko jerked away from him. "Hey, what's the matter?"

She still did not speak, but now Mishima could see that her eyes were filled up with tears.

"Hey, what is it? Tell me."

"You know what it is, don't you? Why did you have to do it?"

"I . . . I was just so tired and couldn't control myself, you know. You should understand my feelings and position."

"But why did you hit him so hard? You really hurt him. He was bleeding out of his nose. And he was really shaken up."

"Oh, I'm sorry! I really didn't mean to do it. But you know, till recently, I'd been living all by myself and was used to quiet evenings, and then, suddenly, small children were around me all the time."

"You said you loved small children. You said you'd wanted a merry and cheerful home, instead of living a lonely life by yourself."

"I did, and I do care for them, but it's just that I haven't had a chance to get used to it. I was still trying to adapt to the new environment, and then, he made a lot of noise. Sorry that I lost my temper, and I'll never hit him, or the other kids, again. I promise. Just give me a chance to adapt to the new life."

***

Kamezo was a patient and disciplined man who knew better than making a scene with anyone in public. Although he sometimes raised his voice and scolded his grandchildren for the purpose of discipline, he was sensible enough not to explode at another adult. But when he learned that Mishima had raised his hand for the third time and hit Jiro and Hanako, he was more furious than a raging Godzilla monster. Jiro was an easy target of Mishima's violence because of his restless nature, but this time, Hanako, who was romping in the room together, was also victimized. The seventy-year-old man, who stood only 158 centimeters, confronted his new son-in-law and threatened to report it to the police the next time he inflicted physical violence on his grandchildren. Mishima flinched at the sight of an angry old man who growled like a raging animal. But as weeks went by, his attitude became increasingly arrogant and defiant, and soon he learned to tower above his father-in-law and glare down at him in an obvious gesture of intimidation. Kamezo, of course, did not flinch or yield on his principles.

"You rough up any of my grandchildren again, and I'll call the police at once and make sure to have them lock you up. You got that? If you don't like this family, just get out of this house and leave."

"Hey, don't forget that this is now my house, too. And I'm the one who works and pays the rent."

"So what? You get out, and we'll manage."

"No! I'm the master of the house, and I'll do what I want."

"You will do that over my dead body! You got that?" Grandpa declared an all-out war against the invader.

***

When Mishima was off to work, Kamezo talked with his daughter face-to-face. His face was flushed crimson like a red *tengu* ogre.

"Just slam a divorce paper in his face and throw him out."

"But I can't."

"Why not?"

"I can't work, and I have no work experience."

"Listen, Akiko! You're no longer a little princess. You've got three children to protect and can't go on like this forever. You've got to learn to be strong and mature."

"Don't torture me like that! You know I've already got enough problems on my hands."

"I always told you to be more independent, but you'd never listened. When you dropped out of a swimming class, I said you shouldn't give up so easily. When you quit your piano lessons after only a few months, I said you got to stick it out. But now, I'm really telling you, Akiko, you've really got to reflect upon your past failures and grow out of it."

"Don't call me a failure. You make me sound like I'm totally useless and a permanent loser."

"I'm not calling you a loser, but you failed in many things, and unless you pull yourself together, you *will* be a loser. And that'll be a disaster."

"Oh, Mother said it was okay for girls not to be so aggressive."

"I know she did. Your late mother always spoiled you, saying things that contradicted my words. And you always listened to her because it was easier. You always chose an easy way out. When you didn't get into your favorite high school, I told you to study harder to get in a good college. You said you didn't want to push yourself because most girls wouldn't. Let's say, for the sake of argument, I could somehow close my eyes to your poor performance in the past. But in the face of this crisis, you've got to change. As a mother of three children, you ought to be tough and have a strong sense of responsibility."

"Then, what do you want me to do now?"

"You know, there is a rather nice food market around the corner, and I just happen to know the manager. It's not like a big, bustling supermarket, and they deal in branded food products and other nice things. The shop attendants wear nice uniforms, and it's a popular place for young housewives to work part-time. I hear that one of the workers is a former flight attendant."

"They keep standing for hours, don't they?"

"Yes, they do," Kamezo answered firmly. "But you can do it if you put your mind to it. You'll soon get used to it."

Akiko remained silent for a while, casting her head down.

"I know what you are thinking. You don't want to be suddenly exposed to the neighbors as a shop attendant. But you have to change now, or a couple of years later, life would be ten times harder for you and your children. I hate to say this, but I'm already beginning to see an ominous sign around here. You know, I won't be here forever. I'm sure the day will come that I'm gone. And you should take a measure against it before it's too late."

She began to sob, dabbing at her eyes with her handkerchief, but Kamezo did not relent.

"You want me to work at a market, is that it?"

"Yes, unless you can find a different job for yourself," the old man answered firmly, again. "Again, this market isn't such a bad place, and of course, you can later find something more to your liking. But you've got to get started at once in order to cope with the situation."

"I have three kids, and taking care of them is a big full-time job."

"Yes, I know that. But when you have to do it, you just have to do it. Take a risk, and enlarge your horizons. You see, you always had opportunities to find nice jobs when you were younger, but you missed them all. Now, it isn't a bad idea to start with a humble position in order to break the pattern and make up for past mistakes."

"How about the kids?"

"When I'm off duty as an apartment caretaker, you can leave them to me, of course. But it's also a good chance for you to learn to establish a close rapport with your neighbors. You may have to ask them for help in emergencies. You must help them in return, though, whenever you can." After a little hesitation, Kamezo added, "You need to learn about the social customs and rules as well."

"I . . . I don't know."

"You don't know what?"

"I don't know if it's good to leave the children alone and work outside."

"The small children would get used to their mother's absence during the day. They'll stay somewhere with some other people while you're not home. And at least, it's much better than exposing them to that jerk's violent temper day and night."

"Don't call him a jerk."

"I will because that's exactly what he is."

"You insult me by denying everything I did or chose. But after all, it's my marriage, not yours."

"Yes, and your marriage is now causing a lot of trouble. Don't say I didn't warn you."

***

But after all, Akiko never filled out the application form for a job at the market. Neither did she apply for any other job, using one weak excuse after another.

Mishima handed her only a small portion of his salary as he spent a lot of money on drinking and gambling. Whenever the children needed a new pair of shoes or shirt, Kamezo secretly gave them money out of his savings. He still had a small source of income as he worked as an apartment caretaker and sold vegetables and fruits to the Agricultural Cooperative. At the same time, however, he repeatedly warned his daughter that he would not be alive forever, urging her to be independent and establish her own financial position.

During the couple of months after marriage, Mishima repeatedly lost his temper and battered the children and, then, tried to make up for it afterward. Living with three children, he came to understand that he must tolerate a lot of noises in the house. After exploding, he often admitted his mistake to Akiko and promised to control himself as best he could. On weekends, he played with Jiro in the park and walked Hanako back and forth to her friends' houses, holding her hand and escorting her across dangerous intersections. Occasionally, he even taught Taro how to pitch a fastball. When in a good mood, he took them all to a local candy shop and bought them chocolates and candies.

"You want to buy a soccer ball and play soccer, Jiro?" Mishima asked one day.

"Yeah, but you said the other day we couldn't buy it because it's expensive."

"No, I didn't say that. I just said to wait until next week because I was short on cash."

"And can we buy it now?"

"Sure! Do you want to do it?"

"Yeah!" Jiro beamed with happiness.

"Come on! Let's go." He patted the little boy's head affectionately.

"Can I ride my bike to the shop?"

"Of course."

However, Mishima's psychological stress was building up progressively in the new life environment. He had never been disciplined to withstand strong psychological pressures in the first place and was, after all, not the type to learn through experiences.

Three or four months later, Akiko and her children rarely saw his smiling face at any time of the day. Trips to the candy shop became infrequent, and he raised his voice over every minor mistake that the children made. When his mood was foul, he relentlessly slapped them around and took out his frustration on both the children and Akiko.

"You never try hard to discipline your own kids, and they behave like idiots. That's why I get so stressed," he started yelling at his wife mercilessly in front of her children.

The sight of their own mother being yelled at and insulted by a big man who had moved into their house a few months before terrified the three children. Young children are ten times more sensitive than adults to human expressions. Traumatized, Hanako started wetting her *futon* bed at night, and for this, Mishima punished her by forcing her to stand naked outside their apartment, exposing her to other tenants who passed through the hallway. As far as Jiro and Hanako were concerned, they cried when they were punished but, then, behaved obediently because they just accepted their positions. However, Taro began to harbor more deep-seated resentment with time, reminded of the fact that it was their home in the first place and Mishima later came to occupy it like an invader. He could see that his mother's new husband did not care for those who were not his own flesh and blood, but if so, he should have chosen to marry a woman who had never married or given birth to a child. He was the one who came uninvited and, from Taro's perspective, invaded *their* small living space.

This is not an animal world where a lion mates with a lioness with kids and kills all the cubs sired by her earlier mate. This is human society, he thought.

Jiro was still an elementary school boy, and although he was basically a good, obedient child, when tired, he tended to throw a tantrum even after being beaten up by his stepfather several times. Anyone who had learned the rudiments of child psychology—either from their own experience or from reading—would understand and accept children's erratic behavior. But Mishima was neither sensible nor educated enough to share the same concept. He could not tolerate the children who kept him from having enough privacy with his new wife, and the small, crowded apartment was a cause of constant stress and frustration. After all, they were the children that Akiko had had by her earlier marriage. Now that he was the lord of the house, he expected more respect and affection. Another cause of his stress was that, when he asked Akiko to quiet the children, her reaction was always slow and inefficient. Then, he knew no other way to express his frustration than yelling at her or slapping her children.

For Akiko, being humiliated in front of her children was the last thing that she had expected from her second husband whom she had assumed to be the kindest and dearest man. However, it was one thing that she felt humiliated, depressed, or shocked; it was quite another for her to take measures to prevent further aggravation. She suffered a great deal but just did not come up with any idea to solve the problem.

***

Kamezo came to their apartment again when Mishima was absent. Through Taro, Kamezo had learned that his son-in-law would not be home that night; he was staying at his friend's house, drinking *shochu* all night. Hanako and Jiro had already gone to sleep, and Taro pretended to be asleep, tucking himself under his *futon*. At two in the morning, the father and daughter had a conference under a dimmed light. Kamezo offered to hire a lawyer on their behalf.

"Look at the bruises on Jiro's face. This is clearly a criminal case."

"What are you suggesting we do, then?"

"My old friend's son runs a law firm in Asahi Township, and I've already talked to him about this situation."

"Are you saying you are going to sue your son-in-law?"

"Legally, he might be my son-in-law, but I've never really regarded him as such. And more importantly, he's really hurting my own grandchildren. I won't put up with this anymore."

Lawsuits were still rare in Japanese society. Akiko was lost for words at her father's bold suggestion to hire a lawyer and kick him out or have him locked behind bars. Mishima was still her husband after all, and more than that, she was not sure if she could handle all the complicated legal procedures. "Besides, it costs a huge amount of money..."

"We'll worry about that later, but now, we really have to take a measure before it's too late. Soon, we'd have no choice at all."

Overhearing his grandfather's words, Taro sadly realized how serious the ultimate consequences were likely to be. But he really hoped that his mother and grandfather would take decisive measures before it was too late.

It was approximately five months after his mother remarried that Taro was taken to a gray concrete building in the compound of the municipal government, a half-hour drive away from his home. The people who came to pick him up neither carried guns nor were in police uniform; they were in dark-blue business suits. But Taro had an impression that they were somehow related to the prefecture's law-enforcement department. When he arrived at the building, a man in his late thirties or early forties and a woman of about the same age ushered him into one of the small conference rooms, which resembled a counseling room at the junior high school that Taro attended. There was only one table and three chairs in the middle of the room—no other furniture or equipment. Both the man and the woman had a gentle, friendly expression and started asking questions in a soft tone. They looked like schoolteachers with years of experience in student-life guidance, reminding him, particularly, of Mr. Tomita, his homeroom teacher. Their precise identity was beyond the scope of the junior-high student's understanding, but at least, he could tell that they intended to help him. He was sometimes lectured by schoolteachers for missing classes or failing to finish homework assignments. But his intuition suggested that the man and the woman were trying to help him, instead of reprimanding him.

"First, let me tell you, Mishima-kun, that we're here to help you," the man declared. "Whatever you say to us will never be repeated to anyone in the way it could hurt or inconvenience you and your brother and sister. Do you understand?"

"Yes."

"Good. And whenever you are in doubt about any particular aspect of our questions, just stop us and ask. Okay?"

"Yes, sir."

However, because it was his first interview with police-related investigators, Taro was not sure how much of each episode he was supposed to voluntarily relate to. It was partly because he was afraid of his stepfather's retaliation but mainly because he thought he must figure out the best way to protect his younger brother and sister. Through his harsh experiences, he was maturing in his own way and had his own ideas of appropriate interaction with adults. His grandfather had always been his guardian and mentor but had just been admitted to the hospital a few days before, having contracted the flu. According to his mother, Akiko, the doctors were also examining Grandfather's liver condition as well. At the moment, he just tried to think independently and make the best judgments he could.

"Has there been an occasion that your stepfather got angry at you?" The male investigator started with a broad question.

"Yes."

"Can you tell us how often it has happened?"

He thought for a while, trying not to be inaccurate. "I . . . I don't remember."

"Okay, don't feel pressured to answer any question at once. Let's take one at a time. Okay?"

Taro nodded quietly.

"Is it like once or twice?"

"No, it's more than that!" His response was immediate.

"Like ten times?"

"Well, yes. Or, maybe, a little more."

"If I say anywhere between ten and twenty, is it closer?

"It's probably more than that."

"Like thirty?"

He answered after a little hesitation. "Yes, I think it's something like that, but I . . . I'm not sure."

He had never tried to keep count of how often his stepfather yelled at him and his siblings, but it should be a safe underestimate. For about two weeks after he moved in, Mishima had been quiet and gentle, acting like a caring new father. But after his first explosion, he had been irritable all the time, betraying the fact that he did not like the presence of the noisy children sired by his wife's previous husband. He soon started yelling at, and intimidated, them on a daily basis, and several times a week, he slapped or punched him or his brother either for punishment or just in a fit of anger—especially after a bad day at his work. And as it had already been five months since their mother married the man, thirty times was a very conservative underestimate.

"Okay! And on any of those occasions, did he ever touch you—like thrusting at you or twisting your arm?"

"Yes."

"Did he ever inflict an injury on you or your brother or sister?" the male examiner asked, glancing at the junior-high student's bruised right eye.

"Yes," Taro answered in a firm tone.

"Can you describe any of the incidents in detail? Just try as best you can, and don't be afraid of making little mistakes in your description. We have ways to verify the facts, and you won't be blamed for any possible discrepancies because we requested you to provide the information voluntarily."

"I'll try." He started to recount some of the major incidents. It was not difficult to remember the details because every experience was so painful and traumatic that he could not easily forget it even if he tried; every scene had been seared into his memory. He recounted each case of battery as accurately as possible, trying not to let his subjective feelings affect his description. He knew that exaggerations would ruin his precious chance to report on the savage man's nefarious conduct. He started with an incident in which his mother's husband had lost his temper at his refusal to go to the local liquor shop and buy a bottle of sake. The stepfather had ordered him to buy liquor on credit, and he, as a junior high-school student, knew that the shop owner would refuse it not only because he was under age but also because his father had not paid for the previous month's purchases. Mishima punched him repeatedly in the face; his face was swollen so badly that he was too embarrassed to go to school the next day.

"Then, were you taken to a hospital after sustaining the injury?"

"No, I wasn't allowed to go to see a doctor."

"Why was that?"

"He got angrier when I mentioned a doctor."

"Can you tell us why he got angry at your mentioning a doctor?"

"He said it'd cost money, and the family couldn't easily afford it. He said my mother and I were overacting over a tiny injury and trying to burden him with extra expenditure when he was working hard to support the family."

"Did you agree not to go to a hospital?"

"I didn't have any choice. And I suspect he had another reason not to let me go see a doctor."

"What was that?"

"The doctor would ask how I got injured."

The two inspectors exchanged glances, although not making any comment. The female examiner was running her pencil on the writing pad, trying to take down every point.

"How about your brother and sister?"

Taro bit his lips with a painful expression, recalling one occasion on which Jiro had been really brutalized. He was almost sure that the inspectors had already learned about it from a different source and he was just being requested to tell the story with his own words. "My younger brother Jiro was taken to a hospital when he got his nose broken and had his front tooth knocked out. He was bleeding badly out of his nose and mouth. My stepfather said it was okay, ordering Mother to stuff something into his nose, but Mother insisted that it was very serious. She usually accepts his decisions and follows his orders, but on that particular occasion, she insisted on taking Jiro to the hospital because he kept crying uncontrollably."

"Was your brother treated, okay?"

"Yes, he got a few stitches on his lips, and the doctor fixed his nose, too. He's still missing a front tooth, though."

"Do you remember when it happened? You know, it doesn't have to be exact. Just tell us when you *think* it was. It's important for you to describe it in your own language. Again, even if you are wrong, nobody will have it against you. Okay?"

"Actually, I remember it exactly because it happened to be the day when . . ." He tried to determine the date and the time of day based on what kind of activity he had engaged in at school earlier in the day and what show was on TV when it happened.

The horrible scene that he witnessed was just so vivid in his memory that he just could not shake it out of his mind. His little brother was terrified and in uncontrollable pain. He kept wailing as if it were the end of the world; his face was crimson, and tears were flooding out of his eyes. Soon, the next-door neighbor came over to their apartment and provided the injured boy with first aid. Mishima, feeling sore and insulted by an outsider's intervention, spat out some abusive words and then retreated to the back room to drink more liquor. Taro could determine the time of this happening to the minute.

"Now, Mishima-kun," the female examiner said toward the end of the interview, "your brother and sister will be accommodated in the general hospital for a couple days. That's for a general medical checkup, and I want you to take the same examination, too. Okay?"

"Yes, ma'am."

"Then, we will discuss what you want to do from now on. Do you understand?"

He nodded deeply. "Yes, ma'am."

***

Then, two weeks later, what Taro had been most afraid of took place: Grandpa died. He had been first hospitalized because of the flu he contracted but developed pneumonia and had other complications. The doctor explained that, because of his chronic liver ailment, his immunity had weakened tremendously. The grandfather who had always protected and supported Taro and his younger siblings departed and was no longer with them.

After dinner one evening, Mishima ordered the children to turn off the TV as he was trying to discuss some home economy problems with his wife.

"We really need a new rice cooker," Akiko said hesitantly, aware that the extra expenditure was likely to bother her husband.

"I'd better take a look and see if I can fix it."

"Please do that, but I'm almost sure it's really broken."

"Jesus! We just bought Hanako's jacket and paid a lot of money to have that stupid washing machine repaired, and now this." He did not bother to hide his foul mood. Jiro was at the time watching a cartoon show on TV, which was loud enough to disrupt their conversation.

"Hey, Jiro, turn that down. We are discussing something important."

Absorbed in the TV show, he did not seem to hear his command. Mishima barked his order again, "Hey, turn that stupid TV off, or you'll be sorry."

"Okay." This time, Jiro replied but did not make an immediate move.

"Jiro, did you hear what your daddy said?" Akiko repeated the same warning. "Jiro, I said, 'Did you hear it?' Did you or didn't you?" Akiko herself could not hide her irritation. With or without her new husband, taking care of three children was a taxing job, and it was not rare for her to be irritated.

"I will, but just a minute!"

As the second child, Jiro was so accustomed to the *noises* in the family. He took for granted that parents would shout at their children and that his siblings would always scream and yell at him over daily conflicts. But at the moment, he was so preoccupied with his favorite TV show that he was completely oblivious to his father's short temper—and the fact that the man was not his real father. Mishima suddenly stood up, made his way to the little boy, and delivered his clenched fist to the boy's temple with all his might. Jiro screamed in pain and drew back to a little corner of the room.

"Please don't hurt my brother!" Taro protested.

"Damn it!" Mishima turned around to Taro and yelled at him. "As the elder brother, you should behave better to be a good example. You don't do that, and the little guy acts like an idiot."

Taro was angry at Mishima's taking his irrational anger out on the third person. But he knew enough about the man's temper and tried hard to contain his own resentment.

"Hey, did you hear me?"

Taro chose not to reply.

"Goddamn it! What's wrong with you?" Mishima stood up, grabbed his lapel, and punched him in the face. Taro staggered on impact and flinched in pain for a moment, but he did not apologize. Then, at that same moment, Hanako suddenly started crying, terrified by all the yelling and grappling. She started wailing like a fire engine.

"What's wrong with all these stupid kids?" Mishima released his grasp on Taro's lapel and stomped his way back to Jiro who he thought had not been punished enough. "You started all this. You'd never learn till you're really sorry."

There was no longer a shred of sensibility in the mad man's head, and all hell broke loose.

Mishima lunged at Jiro and tried to hit him again with his fists, but the little boy somehow dodged him, guided by the instincts of a cornered little animal. The angry stepfather's punch missed its target, which made him angrier and out of control. He grabbed the boy's arm, pinned him against the wall, and bashed his head with a barrage of karate chops. "Dammit! Dammit! Dammit!"

The little boy had no way to escape from this execution-style punishment. His face began to swell, and his twisted arm dangled from the shoulder at an unusual angle.

Recognizing the serious physical damage to her son, Akiko jumped up to her feet and darted forward. "Stop it! Please stop it!" She clung to her husband's elbow, desperately trying to prevent further battery.

Mishima slapped Akiko in the face, but she did not yield her grasp on his elbow. So he finally stopped hitting Jiro, who slid down to the floor lifelessly, clearly having lost his consciousness. She held his limp body in her arms, picked him up, and stormed out of the apartment, screaming for help.

"Help me! Somebody, help me, please!"

A few neighbors popped out of their apartments, sensing that something was terribly wrong. In fact, they had heard shouting voices many times in the past and had gossiped about the family's problems. Someone had even uncovered the backgrounds of the dubious man who had recently married Akiko and moved into her apartment. They had been ready for the inevitable consequences, if not looking forward to it.

"What is it?"

"Jiro is badly hurt. He's unconscious!"

"I'll call an ambulance," one neighbor said.

"He's bleeding badly out of his mouth and nose. Let me get gauze and disinfectant," another neighbor offered.

Practically all apartment tenants' attention was drawn to the site of pandemonium, although their reactions differed from person to person. Timid neighbors just peeked through their cracked doors while the conscientious or brave ones, regardless of whether or not they had been close to Akiko, came out and gathered around her and her wounded son to offer a helping hand. One of those who arrived first quickly retreated to her apartment and requested an ambulance to be dispatched; she also dialed 110 to inform the police department of the situation.

Soon, the ambulance and the police arrived, and Jiro was laid on a stretcher and carried into the emergency vehicle. Akiko boarded the ambulance with her son while the neighbors watched it pull out of the alley and disappear around the corner, heading off to a nearby emergency hospital. The police officers entered the Higashis' apartment, and the next-door neighbor invited Taro and Hanako to wait in their apartment, instead of going back to their own. The other neighbors retreated to their home in twos and threes, looking askance at the door behind which the savage man holed up.

Jiro was examined and treated at an emergency hospital and accommodated in the intensive care unit. He suffered brain contusions, but thanks to the doctors' quick and proper treatment, there was no permanent damage to his brain. His elbow and shoulder were put in a plaster cast. Mishima was taken to the police station and questioned. This time, there was clear evidence of his brutal battery, and Taro did not doubt that they would lock him up behind bars for whatever length of time he deserved.

"I was just trying to discipline him for his own good." Born a smooth liar, Mishima blatantly tried to make up stories to defend himself. "I know I didn't hit very hard, but it seems that he hit his head when he fell on the floor, and it was a 100-percent accident."

When the investigators rejected his self-justification on the basis of Jiro's serious injuries and Taro's accounts, he suddenly switched to the story that he had lost his temper as he was exhausted and stressed, having been under insurmountable psychological pressures at the work. He profusely apologized that he had lost control of himself.

Of course, the doctors and detectives were not fooled. Mishima was not smart enough to conjure up a credible story to convince the seasoned police investigators.

***

The next day, Taro was taken to the municipal government again and interviewed. The welfare officers said that they had made an arrangement to have his siblings accommodated in a foster home for children whose parents could not raise them. There was an injunction dictating that Jiro and Hanako, as elementary-school children, be separated from their stepfather at once.

"It's a little far from your present residence, and your brother and sister will start attending a new elementary school."

"Okay." Taro was relieved that his younger siblings would be in a safe place away from their stepfather.

"But you are a junior-high student, and we want you to tell us what you exactly want to do. You can live in the facility with your brother and sister and transfer to a local school yourself, or you can choose to stay with your parents and finish junior-high studies at the same school."

The word *parents*—in the plural form—bothered him, but Taro was old enough to understand that his stepfather was likely to be released sooner or later. He took a minute, debating the issue in his mind. It would be much safer and more comfortable to live in the foster home, removed from the violent man. He would also be able to take care of his brother and sister every day. But on the other hand, he preferred to attend the same school with his good friends. The strong bondage with his friends and teachers had always provided him with great moral support.

"We understand your teachers are quite supportive," one of the officers added as if reading his mind.

"Yes."

"And we know Mr. Tomita very well, too."

Even if he continued to live at the same place, he would be able to bike to the foster home and meet his brother and sister every weekend. And there was another reason why he was reluctant to move out of the present apartment. From his perspective, the small rented apartment was still his home, not Mishima's. When his stepfather was released from prison, Taro wanted to be there as the original resident along with his mother, not giving the man an impression that he had abandoned it.

"As far as I'm concerned," he steeled himself to say, "I'd rather stay at the present place for the time being. It's hard to explain, but there are reasons I want to stay there for a while longer."

"Are you sure you can handle it?"

"Yes. I'm already a junior-high student. I can, at last, stick it out for a while longer."

"All right. If you say so, we respect your idea and will see what we can do. Just stay in touch with us, though."

"I will, sir. And thank you very much for your support."

Later, in retrospect, Taro regretted that he had not moved into the foster home with his siblings.

***

Everybody thought that Mishima would be imprisoned for the hideous domestic violence for the time being. He might be bailed out before serving his term in prison, but he would, at least, be locked up for a while. But there was a totally unexpected turn of events. When the state lawyers were ready to prosecute him with all the hard evidence for child abuse, he was released after only a few days in jail because of his wife's statements in his defense. Akiko pleaded with the police to release him, claiming that he had not meant to do any serious harm to the children. The junior-high boy could see that it was partly because she was afraid of her husband's retaliation and partly because she did not want to work at a supermarket. He could not blame his mother because he and his brother and sister would inevitably be in trouble if the family had no income. The police placed Mishima on a one-year probation and allowed him to return home.

The welfare department officers visited with Taro and tried to confirm his intention. "Are you sure you want to stay with your parents or would you rather move to the home where your brother and sister are accommodated?"

"Thank you very much for asking me again, but I'd rather stay at the same place at least a while longer. I appreciate your protecting my little brother and sister, sir. They are so small that they really need to be taken care of at a safe place away from our stepfather. But I'm already a junior-high student and know how to take care of myself. Besides, I want to keep an eye on Mother, too."

Akiko had been in serious depression after Jiro's hospitalization and was taking medicines that her doctor prescribed. The series of interviews with police investigators after her husband's arrest seemed to have taken its toll on her mental and physical condition. Her skin was chapped, and she had streaks of gray in her hair, looking five years older than the time she remarried.

The officers from the welfare department and the police respected Taro's decision and decided to let him live with his mother and stepfather. Naturally, they made arrangements for him to be able to seek advice and help from the schoolteachers and the welfare department staff whenever he thought it was necessary.

***

After his younger brother and sister were accommodated in the foster home, Taro was the only child left in the home. He tried to be very careful not to provoke his stepfather, and Mishima himself was behaving somewhat decently after being jailed for several days.

But the junior-high boy's feeling of hatred and disgust against his stepfather became increasingly stronger. He pretended that he had learned to be obedient, but the rebelliousness and animosity deep inside was growing intense with each passing day. When Mishima was at the job and absent from home, he broached the crucial issue with his mother.

"Mom, this just isn't right. We can't go on living like this forever. It's just a matter of time that he'd bare his fangs and start slapping us around again."

"But he's been rather nice lately."

Mishima had been acting carefully not to be caught by the police again, but the junior-high student knew that the savage, uneducated man with no common sense would soon revert to his innate behavioral pattern. It was difficult even for a strong disciplinarian to rid himself of old habits, and the man was anything but a disciplinarian.

"I know he's rather quiet now, but soon, he'll start doing it again. I'm 100 percent sure about that."

"But what do you want me to do?"

"Divorce him! We've got to legally separate ourselves from him."

"Oh, come on, Taro. What does a junior-high student know about marriage and divorce? You shouldn't even think about telling your mother what to do about her marriage."

He completely disagreed with her. His grandfather had brought up this issue with him many times when he was alive, and he knew it was *his* position to debate this problem with his mother. But for the moment, he refrained from making any comment on her personal perspective. He was more concerned about the crucial problem.

"Mom, we just can't go on like this."

"Why can't we? Besides, if we collaborate behind his back and he finds out about it . . ."

"We'll talk to the police, then. They'll help us. They said they'd even help us find a lawyer."

"Let's say we get separated just for the sake of argument, but then, what are we going to do? How are we going to support ourselves? I have no work experience, and you are still a junior-high student."

Taro could see that his mother was, at least, aware of the problem with her marriage.

"I can deliver newspapers in the morning before I go to school. You will work just part-time so that you'll have time to do the housework."

"Well, I don't know. But let me just think about it for a while."

She always terminated their conversation by saying that she would consider the broached issue, but her "for a while" could be an eternity. She never seemed to take action soon enough, making up one lame excuse after another, which always frustrated Taro. He was scared of another incident, which might really get him or his mother killed.

"Damn that dirty-minded creature!" he kept cursing to himself when he was alone. There was not much that he could do as a fourteen-year-old boy, while his anger deep inside was shimmering and building up like a volcano threatening to erupt any minute.

***

For the few months after Jiro and Hanako were taken away, Mishima restrained himself from violent or irrational behavior. Also, when two of the children were gone, the house was suddenly more spacious, and there was much less noise in his surroundings. Mishima finally had some *breathing space* and was not disturbed by small children. From time to time, he even initiated a friendly conversation with Taro.

"How's everything, Taro?"

"Okay."

"You tend to get home rather late."

"Uh, there are things to do after classes."

"What do you do? Hang around with your buddies?"

Taro did not participate in any extracurricular activities. The judo club, which he had wanted to join, had been dissolved before he entered junior high school because very few boys were interested in the event. He had no intention of playing any other sport that would cost him a great deal of money. Yet he never returned home immediately after school after his mother married Mishima.

"Well, we get together and try to finish part of the homework in a reading room."

"Is studying all you do?"

"Well, I don't know. Sometimes, we play catch in a little corner of the playground."

"I played baseball all the time when I was in junior high." He went on boasting about the games he had won. Taro just kept responding with nods and formulaic phrases of admiration in order not to ruin his good humor.

When Mishima came home drunk, however, Taro always made a point of staying away from him, claiming that he had a load of homework to finish. It was partly because he was wary of his violence or arrogant behavior, but at the same time, he was afraid that his own anger might eventually burst at his stepfather's inane remarks or haughty attitude.

By then, his frustration had built up almost to the breaking point. Mishima had lost his job after he was jailed and, then, found employment with an office-building maintenance company. Ironically, the company offered him a position because of his father-in-law Kamezo, who had worked at an affiliated company and had a great reputation. However, his monthly wage was minimal, and he frittered away a major portion of it on liquor. Akiko had to make ends meet with an extremely small amount of money every month, and Taro had a number of miserable experiences in his school life. As he attended a public junior high school, lunch was served at school, but there was a minimal charge for it. Mr. Tomita, his homeroom teacher, summoned him to the faculty room every month and explained that the money had not been deposited in the school account. The same teacher telephoned Akiko and asked her to pay the bill. She always agreed to do so over the phone but never paid soon enough, piling up unpaid bills month after month. Taro was just old enough to understand the situation and was extremely embarrassed at the teacher's repeated notification. It was torture for an adolescent boy who was sensitive to the issue but was not old enough to make money and support himself. His grandfather who would have slipped an allowance in his hand was no longer alive. He intentionally missed his field trips because he could not even mention the travel expenses to his stepfather. One great consolation was that he had good friends who always offered him moral support and covered for him when he missed classes or school events. He talked to them about his problems with his stepfather as well, but being junior-high students themselves, they could not help him solve his real-life problems.

Mr. Tomita was a history teacher of twenty years' experience and had been paying particularly close attention to Taro after he learned about what happened to his younger brother. Tomita made special efforts to investigate Taro's family backgrounds and had personally uncovered a number of secrets concerning Mishima's background. His findings included, for example, the existence of two women whom he had previously married, his miserable scholastic achievements in elementary school and junior high school, and the arrest records of his father. His parents had been ostracized by their own relatives, and Mishima himself had been hired and fired by seven different employers at short intervals, the period of employment ranging from one week to nine months. The chronological data about his irregular and erratic professional career led the history teacher to the hypothesis that this man's present employer might dismiss him any time soon.

Tomita was seriously concerned, and scared, about what might happen to Taro and decided that it was his mission to detect any early sign of further trouble and to deal with it at once. He was not a particularly inquisitive type of man who might probe into everybody's private life, but he kept his ears perked up and watched out for potential problems. In fact, when the news ran that Taro's stepfather had seriously injured his younger brother and had been taken to the police, he was the only person in school who was not surprised at the news. He was certainly shocked, but not surprised.

Tomita occasionally telephoned Taro's parents, for example, to notify them of the backlog of unpaid lunch money. The school had contingency plans for students whose parents were too poor to pay lunch money, but it was more an excuse for the homeroom teacher to talk to the parents and find out the family's characteristics through conversations. Before placing the phone call, he made it a rule to talk to Taro first, explaining the situation in a way it did not hurt him. When he called Taro's home and asked for Mr. Mishima, the latter was always evasive and pretended to be absent. Sometimes, he just hung up when a male voice on the phone sounded like a schoolteacher. Tomita continued to call Mishima because it was an effective way to fathom the parent-child relationship and subtly remind the father of the consequences of another case of parental negligence. At the same time, he made a point of talking to Taro himself on a daily basis.

"Hey, Higashi! Is everything okay at home?" The students were exiting the history classroom, heading for the playground for next-period physical education.

"Yes, sir. I think everything is okay."

"How is your brother?"

That was one of the formulaic questions he used to initiate a conversation; sometimes, it was a question about his sister, instead of his brother.

"He's okay. I went to the foster home to visit him and Hanako. It seems that they're settling nicely in their new home. Jiro says the people there are very kind and friendly."

"Kinder and friendlier than his new daddy?" he asked jocularly, looking into his student's eyes.

"It seems like they are."

It might be a crude joke, referring to his student's stepfather. Whether Taro was on friendly terms with him or not, the man in question was still his family. Schoolteachers might refrain from touching on ethically sensitive issues, but Tomita did it on purpose because it was important to share honest feelings with students who needed help. He knew that junior-high students appreciated honest and frank opinions, instead of social niceties; it was his strategy to win his students' trust and continue to communicate with them.

"And how are you doing yourself?"

"I think I'm doing fine. Sometimes, things he says or does bother me a little, but I just ignore it."

"That's good. Leave him alone. Okay? If he gets nasty, pretend you don't mind his behavior and make sure to talk to me. Okay?"

"Thank you, Mr. Tomita. I surely will."

***

Three months later, however, there was a totally unexpected change in Taro's life. Mishima decided to live and work in a remote city in Hokkaido—nine hundred kilometers away from their present home in the suburbs of Tokyo. If Taro moved to Hokkaido with his parents, as a junior-high student, he would not be able to freely travel back to his hometown. He might learn about the geographical route back to Tokyo but certainly would not be able to afford the train fares. He probably could not even afford to call his friends long distance. He considered the option of moving into the foster home with his brother and sister once again. However, he was, at the time, more concerned about his mother. He knew that his younger brother and sister were in the most competent and conscientious people's hands; in reality, there was not much he could do for them. Instead, his instincts dictated that he stick with his mother who tended to be depressed.

When he looked back, his mother and stepfather had been frequently engaged in hushed conversations in the past month. He had only picked out words like *train fares*, *wages*, and *apartment*. Then, one day, Taro was suddenly told that they would move to Hokkaido the next month. Mishima explained that it would be easier to find a good job there because he had some contact. It was true that, after his arrest, he had been stigmatized and was experiencing tremendous difficulties in finding new jobs. Although he had somehow found a couple of jobs after the incident, his new employers were always watching his performance and behavior very carefully. And as Mishima was lazy by nature, they soon found an excuse to discharge him. Aside from the lack of job opportunities in Tokyo, though, Taro was suspicious that the vicious, crooked man might have decided to move to the remote land partly to separate his stepson from his friends, neighbors, and homeroom teacher.

"Let's stay here, Mother!" He tried to talk her out of it when Mishima was absent. He argued fervently because he felt that it was a real turning point in his own life. "We'd better stay. If we go, something is going to go terribly wrong, and we'll be in big trouble and be sorry for good."

"We can't. If he decides to go, we'll go. Remember he is the one who works and supports us. After all, we just can't survive without him having a decent job."

"You and I can work and support ourselves."

"No, you don't know anything about society and real life. Things won't work out the way you think, and attempting to break up with him is no solution."

"Then, what is your idea of a solution?"

"Oh, Taro! You're already a junior-high student, and I want you to understand it."

"I understand what is happening, and this isn't going to be alright."

"No, no, you should try to think and act more like an adult." She started sobbing.

You are the one who never grows up! He felt like crying, although he could not bear to hurt her any further. Besides, when he had a more serious enemy, he knew he should not fight with his mother and turn her into another enemy. It was most important to have his mother on his side. Nonetheless, he could not help attributing the entire family problem to her naïveté and childlike stubbornness. He now seriously regretted that he had not chosen to be accommodated in the foster home in the first place. But on the other hand, if he parted with his childlike mother, she might disappear completely into an unknown, faraway place, abandoning him and his younger siblings and probably turning into the sole target of the savage man's violence.

Grandpa! Please protect us, Grandpa! He grasped his hands and prayed to his grandfather in the heavens.

***

Taro found himself in Hokkaido five months after his grandfather's departure, that is, about ten months after his mother remarried. When they arrived in the faraway town, Mishima found employment at a *ryokan* hotel. His duties were transporting customers back and forth between the nearby railway station and the hotel, cleaning up the rooms after guests left, and doing the inventory check in the linen storage rooms. It was not exactly what he had expected before his arrival. He had assumed that his position would be more administrative, interpreting the job descriptions in his optimistic way. He was soon discharged for a reason that he never fully explained to his family. Then, he worked at a textile factory for a while and, after that, waited on customers at a local restaurant. But he did not last long at any of the work places in spite of the fact that he was away from the community where he was stigmatized for his arrest record. Every time he had trouble at his work—and was eventually fired—he drank like a fish. The period of his employment at a new job became progressively shorter, whereas the amount of alcohol that he consumed increased. The vicious cycle started again: he was expelled from a new workplace, consumed a huge amount of alcohol, and took out his frustration and anger on his wife and stepson. In the remote town, far away from their relatives and old neighbors, there was no longer anyone who might intervene in the family affairs. Even though Taro did not openly rebel against him, his stepfather became increasingly mean and hostile, yelling at, or beating, him over trivial matters. Mishima did not like Taro's subtly rebellious expressions, and the hostility was building up steadily on both sides. He knew that his adolescent stepson was, deep inside, contemptuous of him for his failure to hold a steady job. The angry stepfather cursed him all the time, and when there was a sign of resistance on Taro's side, he did not hesitate to slap him in the face.

Mishima's hatred aggravated partly because of the boy's physical changes, which Taro himself was not unaware of. Junior-high boys would grow noticeably taller and bigger with each passing month, and the idea that he would soon be big and strong enough to overpower him—or to be, at least, on an equal footing—made him feel uneasy and indignant. Additionally, the boy was maturing intelligently as well and beginning to recognize his stepfather's weaknesses more objectively. One evening, he returned from school three hours late, which was past the family's dinnertime.

"What were you doing till this time? You know we eat at six."

"I had things to do at school."

"What things?"

"Oh, just the usual things."

"I said you were late, and I'm telling you to explain," Mishima shouted. He had already drained several cups of *sake*.

"There are things we must do after class. Why do I have to explain everything to you?"

That day, Taro had failed to submit his Japanese literature homework, and his teacher had scolded and ordered him to stay and finish some extra work. It had been his fault not to finish and submit his homework, but living in an adverse home environment, he could not help feeling that he had a clear disadvantage in finishing his schoolwork. He was so depressed and sore after his bitter experience at school that he abruptly turned his back to his stepfather and tried to retreat to the back room.

"Hey, I'm talking to you. How dare you turn your back and walk out?"

Taro ignored him, defiantly proceeded to the back room, and opened his history textbook. Mishima's face flushed like a red *oni* ogre, and Akiko who noticed it stepped in.

"Taro, you must come and eat your dinner." The saved food, covered with a plastic sheet, was placed on the dining table. "And why don't you explain what happened to your father? Maybe, he can even help you."

"I'm not hungry."

"Damn it!" Mishima barked again. "You don't realize someone is working hard to earn money and feed the thankless brat."

"I'm not hungry," Taro was now openly defiant, knowing that his attitude would be sure to cause more trouble.

"All right. Then, you'll never eat dinner again." Mishima turned to his wife and barked his angry order. "You'll never, ever feed him any food for dinner again. You got that?"

Mishima stood up and followed Taro into the back room. He raised his hand as if he were going to punch him the next moment. But of course, he was aware that the power relationship between him and his stepson was subtly changing. The teenage boy stood up, and the two men were face-to-face, glaring at each other. Taro did not flinch anymore, and the standstill lasted for a full minute.

"Please stop! Both of you," Akiko screamed.

"Huh! I got no time to waste on the stupid kid." Mishima turned around and sat back at the dining table to pick up his *sake* bottle.

The older man failed to punish his stepson for the first time, which was evidence of his acknowledgment that he could no longer behave like the lion king. Taro himself realized that the stepfather-stepson relationship was now a powder keg waiting to explode.

Mishima executed his declared policy of not providing full meals to his stepson: a meager breakfast but no dinner. On school days, he had lunch at school, which was supplied regardless of the fact that his parents did not pay the fees. But on weekends, he was fed only a bowl of rice and a few pieces of pickled radish for brunch. Taro could see that it was partly meant to keep the rebellious stepson from gaining physical strength. He was skinny and short for his age, yet he was growing taller every month, putting psychological pressures on his stepfather, who was a timid man by nature, and made him feel frustrated and wary and angry.

***

At his new school in Hokkaido, Taro felt a little isolated and lonely at first but soon started striking up friendly conversations with his classmates.

"How do you like this town, Taro?" asked a friendly boy named Tsutomo, who could not help offering words or a helping hand to a transfer student who was always sitting by himself.

Taro hesitated, remembering that he had been forced to move to Hokkaido against his will.

"I know there isn't as much excitement in this small town as in Tokyo," Tsutomo added when the transfer student did not respond at once.

"Well, it's not that. I miss my friends back there, but I think this is a beautiful place."

"You think so?"

"Yes, I do."

The next weekend, they were sitting on a riverbank, Taro teaching Tsutomu the fishing techniques that he had learned from his late grandfather.

"It's amazing that you came from the big city and know so much about fishing."

"Well, it's a long story, but my grandfather taught me all the tricks," Taro told his new friend a little about his grandfather.

"Do you play any sports other than fishing?"

"No. At first, I wanted to join the judo club at my former junior high school, but the club had been dissolved the year I advanced to junior high."

"Yeah, the same thing is happening all over. Boys tend to join soccer and baseball clubs. It's been several years since our school lost its judo club, too."

"How about yourself? Do you play baseball or soccer?"

"No, I'm not into those ball games. Like you, I'm more interested in Japanese martial arts."

"What do you do?"

"Karate!"

"Oh, does the school have a karate club?"

"No, but I practice at a downtown karate dojo."

"Is that right?"

"Yeah, our instructor is really good. I really wanted to learn self-defense techniques to protect myself, and he teaches us a lot of excellent techniques." Tsutomu was of average height and as skinny as Taro.

"How often do you practice?"

"Three times a week. Each practice session lasts one and a half hours."

"That sounds great."

"You want to come and see our practice?"

"I'd love to."

"And if you want, you can start taking karate lessons with me."

Taro considered his friend's suggestion for a second. He could probably make up a good excuse and stay out until a little late three times a week.

"Oh, I don't know." His face clouded over, and his new friend detected a sign of embarrassment.

"Is anything the matter? Are your parents against that kind of thing?"

"Oh, I don't know." In fact, he was sure that his stepfather would not approve of any athletic event, which he regarded as a cause of unnecessary expenditure. The stepfather would not like the idea of his stepson being stronger, either. The second problem was the lesson fees to pay. "How much do you have to pay?"

Tsutomu sensed that Taro's parents were not supportive but could see that he was interested himself. "Four thousand yen per month. I know it's not very cheap, but it's much cheaper than at most of the other schools."

"Right. I knew someone who was learning karate back in Tokyo, and he said he was paying eight thousand yen."

"Our teacher has a different job in the daytime, and he teaches karate more like a volunteer job."

"But how about the robe, pants, and belt? How much does a practice suit cost?"

"The cheaper version is about seven or eight thousand yen. But I have an extra one. You can borrow it till you get enough money to buy a new one."

When Taro was contemplating the issue with a serious expression, Tsutomu offered his idea to help solve the problem.

"You know, I'm telling you what I do on the days I don't practice karate."

"What is it?"

"I work part-time at a *dango* dumpling shop near my house."

"Is it okay for junior-high students to work?"

"At that particular shop, yes. My family and I have known the shop owner for a long time. The work at the shop is very easy. You just have to knead millet dough, chop them into small pieces, roll them into balls, and stick five onto each bamboo skewer. Actually, the shop owner or his wife usually does the cutting part, and even six-year-old children can do the rest of the work. In fact, Kumoi-san—that's the owner's name—hires a couple of elementary school kids. He is very friendly, takes good care of the young children, and gives money as allowances in return for their help. He says there is no legal problem as long as he ensures the safety of young workers."

"You think he'll let me do that, too."

"I'll ask, but I'm almost sure he will," Tsutomu said firmly. "I've known him since I was very small, and I'll tell him you are a very good friend of mine."

Taro went over to the karate school that afternoon to observe the practice. The instructor, a former Hokkaido champion and kind, friendly man, assured him that he would be more than welcome. The next day, he was introduced to Mr. Kumoi who ran a *dango* shop in the downtown area, which happened to be rather close to the karate dojo and to the junior high school that they attended. So it was easy for him to bike back and forth between the three places. Most fortunately, both Mr. Kumoi and his wife turned out to be the most thoughtful and conscientious people.

Kumoi paid the young workers in cash at the end of each day, and Taro could soon start taking karate lessons. His studies suffered to some extent because he spent three to four hours at the *dango* shop two days a week and practiced karate three times a week, but he somehow managed to keep it a secret from his stepfather. And as he picked up two or three thousand yen on each work day, he could save some money after paying the karate lesson fees.

***

One late afternoon, however, when Mishima was home and Taro was off to karate practice, Kumoi called their home.

"Hello! May I speak to Taro, please?" Mishima was puzzled at the middle-aged man who referred to his stepson by first name as if he were his own child. Taro's biological father was in the grave.

"He's not here. Who's this?"

Mishima was suspicious that the man at the other end of the line might be an inspector from the welfare department or Taro's former homeroom teacher named Tomita—a sneaky, persistent guy who played Colombo around his home. But the caller spoke in a much higher-pitched voice, and he resented the fact that yet another man was lurking around his family, obviously trying to play a nasty trick on him.

"Oh, pardon me! My name is Kumoi, and I'm the owner of a *dango* shop in Yokotecho."

"What does the *dango* shop have to do with my son?"

"Is this Taro's father?"

"Yeah."

"Oh, how do you do?"

"Hey, I don't remember sending my kid out to pick up any dumplings at a *dango* shop. You got to be mixed up somewhere," Mishima could not help flinging a few hostile words at the stranger on the phone. In reply, the *dango* shop owner politely started explaining that he was calling Taro to ask him if he could cover for another boy who called in sick. Taro had never told Kumoi that he had kept his job a secret from his stepfather.

Mishima remembered that there had been a phone call the last night and that Taro had picked up the receiver himself and started talking in a strangely hushed tone. When he asked what it was about, the boy had just said without meeting his eyes that it was from one of his classmates and retreated to the other room at once. The strangely evasive attitude had bothered him.

Kumoi, who was taking care of small children all the time, was quite sensitive to other people's verbal reactions. He immediately realized that Taro had probably never told his stepfather about his small job. He was fully aware that adolescent boys had their own worries and secrets and that, when they had to keep something a secret, they had good reasons for it, which must be respected. He decided to terminate the phone conversation before it became more complicated; he would, of course, apologize to Taro afterward for his inadvertent phone call.

"Well, never mind, sir. We can somehow manage here, and I will talk to him later and explain why I called." In fact, he could easily make up for the boy who was absent that day. The real reason why he had called for Taro's help was to offer him a chance to earn some extra money.

"Hey, wait a minute! You called up here and then say 'never mind'? What the hell is that?"

"Pardon me, Mr. Mishima." Kumoi remembered Taro's stepfather's family name. "I've been asking him to help me here at the shop, doing simple work, but if you are worried about his well-being, I assure you that . . ."

"Cut that bullshit out! Is he working at the *dango* shop for money?"

Kumoi debated his next response for a second, but taking note of Mishima's crude and mean personality, he decided that he had no choice but to tell the truth in explicit language. Again, he would talk to Taro later and apologize to him for betraying his secret. He would then think of some follow-up measures to protect the boy's position. For the moment, however, the only way to deal with the mad man was to explain the fact as it was in order to prevent complications. It would also be troublesome if he were legally or ethically challenged afterward. From a brief interaction on the phone, Kumoi could clearly see that Taro's stepfather was a dangerous man.

"Well, yes, he helps us at our *dango* shop, and I give him some money in return as a sort of gratuity. And I was wondering if he would put in a few extra hours covering for another junior-high boy who cannot come today. You know, since the work at our shop is very simple and mechanical, we employ young children as helping hands."

"I'm not sure if it's legal to employ children and pay them wages, not even notifying their parents."

In fact, when Kumoi interviewed Taro, the boy said that his mother had approved it. But he decided not to refer to it, afraid that it might put Taro in a more difficult position.

"Sir, the kind of work at our place poses no danger to their health or safety, and at least, I can assure you that I'm not overstepping the legal or moral bounds."

Understanding what kind of person his telephone interlocutor was, Komoi, a mild, soft-spoken person, decided that it would be best not to be involved any further. "I'm sorry to have disturbed you, sir." He gently replaced the receiver in the cradle, overhearing Mishima's yelling voice on the other end of the line. "Hey, we're not finished . . ."

***

Mishima was infuriated at his stepson's sneaky conduct and the way a stranger had abruptly called him and hung up. The moment Taro returned home and crossed the threshold, he blasted at him, demanding explanations for his working for money without his permission. The fact that his son was holding a job insulted him because, by doing so, he was virtually broadcasting his father's inability to provide for the family.

"What the hell is this all about? Just explain it to me."

"My friends are doing it, and I just thought it'd be okay," he said meekly.

"I'm not asking whether your friends are doing it or not. I'm asking how you dared to do such a thing without my permission."

"I'm sorry."

"You should be. And what were you trying to get extra money for?"

Taro hesitated to answer the question. While Mishima was chewing him out, Akiko, who had tacitly approved his plan, just remained silent and stayed away from the argument. Taro could understand her position but was disappointed at her failure to intervene and defend him.

"I . . . I don't know. I just needed some money to do things."

"What things?"

"Like snack food," Taro answered. In fact, he had just started buying a lot of bread and cookies with the money he had earned at the *dango* shop. After paying the karate lesson fees, he had some money left, and he was always hungry because he was given only one frugal meal a day at home.

"So you work at a *dango* shop as if your father isn't feeding you properly."

In fact, that was more or less what Mishima was doing to his stepson. "It's not that, but . . ."

"Damn it! You think it's right to go ahead to find yourself a job and get everything you want. You don't appreciate how hard I work to provide you with everything for your daily life, school, and all the other things."

As an uneducated, chauvinistic man, Mishima was not capable of logical reasoning. After spitting out angry words, he called Kumoi himself and declared one-sidedly that Taro would stop working there as of that day. He also made a point of harassing the dumpling shop owner with a barrage of cursing and yelling. As a punishment against Taro, he reaffirmed his policy to give him only one meal a day—only a simple meal in the morning and no dinner, let alone any kind of snack.

"You got that, Akiko? Don't give him any food or snack to him behind my back, or you'll be sorry yourself," he barked his order to his wife.

After losing his job, Taro had to give up his karate lessons, which had lasted only one month. His indignation and hatred rekindled. Mishima had inflicted violence—or corporal punishment—on Jiro repeatedly and ended up hurting him seriously. But when he slapped Jiro, it had been mainly due to the stress that the three children had brought on him. Jiro had always been the noisiest among the three and tended to provoke him with his careless behavior. The constant noise and crowd, when combined, had stressed Mishima to an intolerable level and made him beat up Jiro to vent his spleen. The little boy had acknowledged his own problems and had never carried any grudge against his stepfather afterward. However, the animosity between the big intruder and the teenage boy was far more deep-seated and complex. The conflicts between them were not accidental. Taro had come to hate the guts of the selfish man and despise him. Mishima was conscious of his stepson's rebellious attitude and felt he needed to nip it in the bud. His problem was that he was not intelligent enough to find a rational solution. His simple logic dictated that the junior-high kid's ego must be crushed. Strong animosity was building up over time like a volcano, threatening to erupt any minute. Then, one night during the dinnertime, the ruler and the ruled finally came to have their final confrontation.

"Hey, son, will you run to the convenience store at the corner and get me a copy of a sports paper?" Mishima asked Taro. He was in good humor that night after consuming a couple of beers. As Taro happened to know, he had won a derby earlier in the day and had a lump sum of cash in his pocket. Detecting a sign of hesitation on his stepson's face, he offered a small incentive. "You can pick up some snack food for yourself. How's that?"

The drunken man's smiling face disgusted the adolescent boy. Obviously, his stepfather took it for granted that he could always send him on an errand like a servant or underling. In fact, when Jiro and

Hanako were still living with them, Jiro had always volunteered to do it, accepting a little award appreciatively. Those were the chores that small children tended to compete for in order to prove their ability to perform household jobs. But Taro was a junior-high student, not an elementary school pupil, and he also had a different personality. The crude man was triumphant over his stroke of luck in gambling and, at the moment, indulging in his other favorite sport—drinking. Intoxicated, he was oblivious to the progressive change in their power relationship. He could only view the world from his narrow, biased perspective while his stepson had, by then, been fed up with his arrogance. In addition, Taro had his own problems and worries and causes of psychological stress. Earlier in the day at school, he had been scolded by his mathematics teacher for not turning in his homework. He was depressed and sulky. When Mishima ordered him to run like an errand boy, his hatred against him flared up; the heinous man's self-complacent smiling face added insult to injury.

"Did you hear what I said?" Mishima raised his voice when Taro did not respond; his euphoric mood at the moment was gone. He tended to have trouble with his colleagues at the present job, and some of his fellow workers at the present job always ignored him when he invited them to a drink after work. When his stepson ignored his words, the image of his hostile coworkers flashed back to his mind and sparked his anger. "Damn it! When I ask something, answer it."

Without turning to his stepfather, Taro said in a mumbling voice, "Why don't you go to the shop yourself if you want a newspaper?"

"I'm telling you to do it."

"But why should I take such an order from you?"

"Taro, don't you ever talk to your father like that?" his mother said in defense of her husband.

"Another thing I want to make clear is," Taro turned to his mother, "he isn't my father in the first place. My father is dead. And why should I call your husband Daddy?"

The next moment, Mishima leaped to his feet without another word. He made his way to where Taro was, grabbed his shoulder with his left hand, and slammed the clenched right fist into his face. Receiving the strong punch, Taro staggered backward. Without releasing his grasp on the boy's shoulder, Mishima slapped him two more times. Taro managed to break free from his strong grip; by then, he was profusely bleeding out of his nose. There was also a gaping cut above his eyes.

Damned that I had to give up my karate lessons! Taro cursed to himself. Then he thrust his stepfather with all his might and sent him flying backward to hit his head against a pillar. Mishima obviously had a slight concussion and took a full minute to stand up, during which time the junior-high boy dashed out the door and fled into the night.

"Bastard! Don't you ever cross the threshold and enter this house again!" Mishima yelled through the open door.

Unfortunately, it was raining that night and started pouring a few minutes later.

***

Taro knew that he had crossed the Rubicon. He could not return to the house again. It was not a tentative escape; his relationship with his family had been permanently severed as of that moment. Mishima was a stranger after all—not his flesh and blood. If his own child ran away, he might launch a desperate search, scouring the entire city to find and protect him even after an ugly domestic fight, but he would never bother to do that. At the moment, Mishima must be angry enough to find and kill his stepson, but he would soon be happy to be rid of the unwanted teenage boy. Had Taro been patient for another year, his chances of overpowering his stepfather might have been much greater. But the odds were still against him if they ever had a deadly fist fight. He had jumped the gun, and there was no way to make up for it. He just kept running in the pouring rain until he was so far away that his enemy could not follow and catch him. He was drenched to the skin when he finally found his shelter under a bridge. A few homeless men were seen sleeping in cardboard boxes, which were, at the moment, placed on elevated areas in order not to be inundated. Taro despaired at the fact that he had been degraded to the same level as the tramps.

The only consolation was that the homeless did not threaten to harm him, so he remained there for a few hours, crouching by the river. He had no other place to go, and his grandfather was gone to the heavens and no longer able to come and help him. In his hometown, he might have sought shelter at his distant relatives' home in cases of an emergency. But in the small town in Hokkaido, nearly a thousand kilometers away, he had no one to turn for help in the crisis. It was still raining very heavily. As he was drenched like a rat that had crawled out of a sewer, he would be ashamed to walk down the street the next morning. Now, he literally belonged to the homeless clan. His jacket was stained with blood because of nose bleeding. Even as a fatherless boy who had been degraded to the bottom of social strata, he had a vestige of vanity and could not bear to expose himself in public places. It was nine o'clock at night, and he only had three one-hundred-yen coins in his pockets, with which he would probably buy bread and milk the next morning.

"Grandpa, I have no home to go back to. I have no future to look to." He looked up into the dark sky. By then, he was frozen to the marrow, both physically and mentally. When he stood by the river and looked down, the stream of water—increased in volume after the heavy rainfall—was fast enough to mesmerize him. He became dizzy and disoriented for a moment and felt he was going to be swallowed into the current.

"I think I'm going to go to where you are." When he vocalized his inner thoughts, he felt that he really wanted to throw himself into the river and terminate his miserable life at once. There was a metal guard fence along the river, but lifting his body up by half a meter and shifting his weight forward by a few centimeters, he could cross over from the world of misery to the heavens where his grandfather was waiting. The fact that he had been born was an unfortunate accident, he thought. His younger brother and sister were in the good hands at a solid welfare institution for children. At the moment, there was nothing he could do for them as their elder brother, and there would probably be nothing he could do to help them at any point in the future. Jiro and Hanako might not be provided for most affluently, but they were now much better off than when they had been with the savage, loathsome stepfather.

"I just hope they got a trait of Grandpa's toughness in their genes and would adapt to the new environment on their own. They might even revenge themselves on the scumbag someday. I made the wrong decision and ended up as a loser. I really should have chosen to go to the foster home myself, flinging out my attachment to Mother. I was stupid, and I am going to pay the price."

As the elder brother, he had thought that he should keep on fighting, eventually resolve all the problems, and take care of his younger siblings in the future. He would study hard, enroll in a university on a scholarship, find a good job, and provide for the entire family. But tired, hungry, and wet, he was quickly losing his mental and physical strength to continue his fight. What could a junior-high boy with no money, no relatives, and no resources do after all?

Yes, dive into the strong current. It would wipe out all your misery and solve all your problems at once, a devil whispered in his ears.

When he was gone, society would not miss anything at all. In the land far removed from his hometown, nobody would even notice that he was missing—dead or alive. One jump, a gulp of water, and a few painful coughs under the water—then, everything would be over. Everything would cease to exist, and he would no longer have to worry about, or be troubled by, anything in his life. He could even forget about his mother who had never stood up and tried hard to protect her children. All thoughts whirling in his head, he remained frozen under the bridge for what might be either a brief moment or an eternity.

***

The next day, the sky cleared up, and he found himself sitting alone on a bench in the park in front of a railway station. His clothes were still wet and soggy, and he was numb and disoriented. His major concern was to dry his clothes, so he took off his shirt and draped it on the back of a bench. His shoes were placed upside down on the bench beside him. Then, he stretched his limbs and exposed himself fully to sunshine, hoping to get the rest of his clothes dry.

He vacantly regarded the entire structure of the railway station. As at any countryside train station, it would be easy for him to climb over the fence near either end of the long platform and sneak into the station without buying a ticket. Stealing a free ride on a local line, reaching a big city, and changing trains to head back to Tokyo—it was the first escape plan that he had come up with. But he was not sure how far he could travel. Not only that, but something in his mind—a nagging feeling that he could not clearly define—urged him to stop running farther away from that point.

"Tonight, I will hide in the back of the Shofukuji Temple." He remembered a large temple that he had visited with his friends after a fishing expedition. The temple was built on a hill—a fifteen-minute walk from where he was at the moment, and he happened to know that the owner and his family lived in a different house in a downtown area when they were not serving visitors at the temple. There was a little attached building behind the main hall, which he had found to his liking on his last visit; it was the place where he would sneak into and sleep. On his previous trip, he had thought that it was a spooky place, but now, it seemed like an ideal hiding place because no one was there at night. Even if he could not get inside the building, he could at least sleep under an awning, not exposed to rain or morning dew. He would also appreciate the presence of the Buddha for his peace of mind, rather than the tramps. What a wonderful issue for a junior-high student to dwell on when his classmates were studying subjects in school, preparing for high school entrance examinations, and dreaming about their future professions! He was sad and depressed at his deprived position. When talking with his classmates back in Tokyo, he had always complained about long class hours and tedious events and meetings to attend. But now, he really appreciated the school programs prepared for the benefits of young people.

When he could no longer tolerate his hunger, he decided to buy some food with his three hundred yen. He put on his shirt, which was still wet and soggy, and headed out. There was a small supermarket and a convenient store near the station, so he stepped into both places first and compared the pricing. Eventually, he ended up buying his milk and bread at one shop in the supermarket, but visiting the two places, he obtained two important pieces of information for his survival. First, the convenience store was a remarkably convenient place to kill time at. He could pick up a magazine from the racks and read without actually buying it. There were shop attendants on duty, but they hardly seemed to notice it. Different customers kept coming in and leaving continually, and the workers tended to tolerate browsing and loitering, preoccupied with their tasks of dealing with customers at cash registers, checking the inventory, or replenishing the products on the shelves. It was a perfect place to kill time. The second discovery, which was even more important, was that, at the supermarket, he could help himself to free sampling foods. In fact, he soon found another supermarket within walking distance, so he could keep feeding himself alternately at the two places. After all, he had been fed only one meal a day in the past month and could survive on sampling food. What would he do when the shop attendants finally noticed his loitering and ordered him to leave or threatened to report it to the police? He might have to consider a follow-up plan, but at the moment, he just could not think so much ahead as he literally lived from hand to mouth.

He reflected upon various things because he had plenty of time: his late grandfather who had always supported and protected him, his classmates to whom he could confide his problems and secrets, and his mother who might be actually concerned about his safety at the time but would never take any concrete measures to save him. He thought about his younger brother and sister who lived in a foster home. Then, he missed his old friends back in Tokyo and hoped that they remembered him. But they were probably busy with more important matters including their studies and exams and had no space for worrying about the one who had transferred to a faraway city. Even if Taro successfully stole a series of free rides to return to his hometown, could they, as junior-high students, actually save him from his predicament? He was not confident, either, that he could seek shelter at his distant relatives' homes that he had never been invited to visit. There was a strong possibility that they would turn him away because of the box of cheap cookies that his mother had sent to them after her second wedding.

The idea of going to the police flashed across his mind time and again. They might arrange to have him accommodated in the same facility with his brother and sister. But he would be so ashamed of exposing his miserable figure to his younger siblings by returning as a loser. And of course, after being protected by the police, he would have to meet the savage man who destroyed his family again. He needed some more time to organize his thoughts in order to prepare himself for all the consequences.

The mixed feelings tormented him, but his immediate concern was, how many days could he actually survive by eating small portions of sampling food at the supermarkets? Should he try to find a job? If so, where and how could he apply for employment? His grandfather had said that, in his days, people started working without going to high school. So he must be capable of working, perhaps, delivering newspapers or washing dishes at a restaurant. Or in a small town in the rural area where he was at present, he might be employed as a field hand on the farms. With no physical disabilities, he would certainly be able to work as a manual laborer. But who could he ever talk to without a proper referral?

He did not even have fresh clothes to wear for an interview. Am I going to have to steal? An idea flashed into his mind. Stealing would really be the last resort, but his list of alternatives was getting extremely short. Fleeing from his home was not actually a crime. It might be regarded as a delinquent act, but he was not a criminal at least until he stole things, destroyed someone's property, or physically injured another person. He had just fled from his home because his physical well-being was in danger. But it might be a matter of time before he was forced to snatch a sandwich or an *onigiri* rice ball from the market shelves. On the other hand, to give up, accept his position as a loser, and steal was something that his grandfather would never have approved of.

***

His life of loitering started, and he located three convenience stores around the railway station. He spent an hour or so at each place every day. The sandwiches and cakes displayed on the shelves made his stomach growl, and the chocolate pudding—his favorite dessert—glared each time he entered the shops. He did not buy anything because he had no money; he just lingered, shuffling magazines on the racks. One of the convenience stores named Yokomachi Convenience had his favorite magazines, and he tended to be there longer than at the other two places. Unlike the other two stores, which were nationwide chain stores, Yokomachi Convenience seemed to be owned and operated by a local entrepreneur, but it had a wide floor area and a huge selection of goods in each aisle. The shop attendants were quite friendly and treated each customer like their own neighbor. But as he kept going back to the same convenience store, the middle-aged manager, whose name tag identified him as Kumatani, started looking askance at him.

He was very tall for a Japanese man—about 185 centimeters—and of a solid build, suggesting the possibility that he had played basketball or volleyball as a student. He appeared to be in his early thirties. At first, he was smiling all the time, but soon his expression turned into a mixture of slight suspicion and weariness. Taro was there every day—often at odd hours when boys and girls of his age were supposed to be in school—and hung around for a long time without purchasing any food or consumer products. Besides, his clothes were soiled, and the cut and bruises in his head were still visible, not having been properly treated. After being struck by his stepfather, he had chilled the injured parts with a damped handkerchief, which he later had to throw away because it was soaked in blood, but his crude first-aid treatment was obviously not sufficient and appropriate. The lump on his forehead was prominent and a sign of internal bleeding.

Taro instantly noticed the manager's suspicious expressions. Anyone who had worked at a convenience shop for several years should have encountered a few cases of shoplifting or other customer-related incidents. He looked toward the teenage boy from time to time as if sending him warnings. His glaring eyes seemed to evidence his strong—if not belligerent—personality. Taro could understand that the only feeling that the man could entertain for a junior-high student loitering in the store at that time of day was disgust, contempt, or hatred. But deep inside, he was beginning to think that this convenience store was the place where he would have to *take action* eventually.

Toward the end of his third day as a homeless man, Taro was starved. For the last three days, he had visited one of the two supermarkets at either lunchtime or dinnertime and then moved on to the other place at the next mealtime, hiding his identity in the crowd of people. He had taken a piece of ham in one store, a piece of bread in another section, and a miniature plastic cup of milk in yet another section. But the free food was not substantial even if he picked it up at several different shops and stores within a supermarket. At the end of the third day, he was really starved and went to all the stores in the two supermarkets and scoured for all available food. Then, he decided that it was time to take action.

At around nine in the evening, the small portions of food that he had eaten at the supermarkets had been completely digested, so he went to the Yokomachi Convenience store. As usual, Taro shuffled a magazine from the racks and, then, slowly made his way to the sandwich aisle and laid his hand on a ham-and-egg sandwich on a food-display shelf. He grabbed and shoved it into his pocket quickly and started walking toward the exit. He moved with noticeably quick paces, although not dashing out. A young female attendant noticed his move and called out toward the manager who was, at the time, engaged in an inventory check in a back aisle.

"The cash register number 5, please," she said in a loud voice. It was an in-house code to signal that shoplifting was being committed. Kumatani emerged from the back aisle and dashed after Taro. He grasped the situation immediately when he saw the teenage boy walking toward the exit with his hand stuck in his pocket. It was the same boy who had been lingering in the store for the last several days without buying anything. Taro's eyes met his, and then, as if on cue, he started walking faster toward the exit. Manager Kumatani had an expression of a tough, seasoned policeman. If he had a mean trait that matched his expression, the shoplifting suspect would receive a strong blow in the head the next moment or have his arm twisted to a breaking point. But deep down inside, Taro was secretly hoping that Kumatani would deal with the situation, not any of the other younger workers.

"Hey, you! Hold it right there!"

Taro ignored his warning and kept moving toward the exit. The manager ran down the aisle after him and caught up just outside the exit. At once, all the shop attendants' heads—and those of most customers in the store—turned to the two persons at the exit and soon converged around them. The manager clutched at the boy's right elbow with his strong big hands. He did not twist his arms, but he deftly blocked his way so that the shoplifter could not slip away and escape.

"Will you just come with me?"

Ignoring the curious customers' stares, Kumatani swiftly led him toward the back of the shop and showed him into what looked like a staff room where various charts and schedules were pinned on the walls. He released his grasp on Taro's elbow and motioned for him to sit on one side of the table. Kumatani and the girl who had witnessed the shoplifting had a quick conference, exchanging whispering words to confirm certain facts. Then, the manager sent the female employee away and took his seat across from Taro. Thus far, the treatment had not been as brutal as the junior-high student anticipated from the tough-looking guy. He had even been ready for an attack by the entire staff who might pile up on him and pin him on the ground. Manager Kumatani maintained a stern and unyielding expression like a sumo wrestler on the ring, but he did not raise his voice. In his authoritative yet calm voice, he started asking broad questions.

"Are you a junior-high student?"

"Yes," Taro answered with his eyes cast down.

"And you live in this area?"

When Taro hesitated, the manager paraphrased his question.

"You know, I'd never seen you till a few days ago, so I just assumed you might be visiting your relatives or friends here."

"No, I'm not from this town, and I don't have any relatives or friends in this area, either."

"Where are you from?"

"Minami-machi," he answered meekly.

Kita-mashi, to which he had fled empty-handed, was about five kilometers away from his home. It was far enough to evade his parents' and neighbors' eyes, and at the same time, he was somewhat familiar with the geography, having previously biked around there. For a brief moment, he felt extremely ashamed that he had not traveled farther away.

What he anticipated as the next question for a juvenile delinquent was, *Why aren't you at school in the daytime?* But it did not come.

"Is your head okay?"

"What?" *Do I really look crazy?* He blushed at the thought.

"You've got a big lump on your forehead, and the cut near the temple is quite visible. I think it requires treatment."

"I . . . I think it's okay."

"You want to tell me what happened?"

"It's nothing. It's just that . . ."

"All right. We will talk more about it later, but we'd definitely need to do something to prevent infection."

Taro had been preoccupied with his attempt to pull off a stunt until a few minutes before, and now, he is a captured shoplifter. Therefore, he had been completely oblivious to his own injury.

"You've got to disinfect it. Okay?"

He nodded and then slowly extracted the stolen sandwich out of his pocket. It had been partially crushed and flattened. "I'm sorry." He felt like crying like a small child but somehow held back his tears.

The manager simply nodded his acknowledgement. Then, after instructing a female employee to bring the first-aid kit, he stood up, took out a paper cup, and poured hot tea into it.

"You are hungry, aren't you?"

Taro was ashamed to admit it, but now that the manager's intention was clear, he honestly answered in the affirmative, "Yes."

"You eat the sandwich first," he said, offering the hot cup of tea. "Then, you tell me a couple of things. Okay?"

Taro did not react at once, not sure what he really should do.

"Go ahead, and eat it. It's on the house."

He was famished, so he unwrapped the sandwich and started eating it. Then, he gulped down his tea as if he had reached an oasis after trekking fifty kilometers through the desert. The manager filled up the empty cup, while the female employee sterilized the cut on the boy's forehead and bandaged it.

"I've seen you a couple of times in the past several days, and I had an impression you are in some kind of trouble. You don't attend Kita Junior High, do you?"

Taro remained silent, which he thought was enough to affirm the manager's inference.

"Do your parents know you are here?"

Taro shook his head.

"I'm sure you've got a reason to be here. Want to tell me what it is?"

It was a difficult question to answer. First of all, he had no legitimate reason to be in the convenience store, not even to be in that town. But he had been starving, and in that sense, he certainly had a motive to be where food products were displayed. He could not determine whether the store manager was referring to such an immediate motivation or whether he was asking about his motive for being away from his hometown. The manager noticed that he was hesitating.

"You know, I'm in charge of this store, and I have a responsibility to ask the right person to come and pick you up. When I say the *right* person, I'm talking about someone who can take you home and take care of you. Do you understand?"

"Yes, sir."

"Now, tell me who you want me to contact first. Do you want me to call your parents or do you want someone else to come and meet you here?"

He could understand that, by the latter, the manager was referring to his relatives or a schoolteacher. Now that his grandfather was gone, he had no family or close relatives to rely on—especially in a remote city in Hokkaido.

"I . . . I don't know. But I just don't want to see my stepfather except in the presence of the police. At the moment, I don't really want to see my mother, either." If they contacted his mother, his stepfather would be sure to know it.

"All right! Just tell me what you really want me to do. Okay?"

"Yes."

"How about your school teacher? Do you want me to contact your homeroom teacher?"

After debating the issue for a few seconds, he answered in the affirmative, "Yes."

"Do you want to tell me his name?" He thought of Mr. Tomita, his former homeroom teacher back in Tokyo, but knew it would be impossible for him to come to where he was now.

"My homeroom teacher is Mr. Yamada."

"Do you want me to call Mr. Yamada?"

"Yes."

"Then, we can all go to the police if we decide it's necessary."

Taro nodded.

The manager called his school, talked to a teacher who still remained at the school, and explained the situation. The same teacher immediately relayed the message to Yamada, who rushed from his home to the convenience store by bicycle. After a quick discussion, he and the shop manager called 110 and requested law enforcement officers' attention.

"I've been so worried about you, Taro," Yamada said on arrival. "And now, I'm so relieved to find you."

"Thank you for coming, Mr. Yamada."

"No problem at all." Then, while waiting for the police officers to arrive, he gave surprising news to Taro. "And you know, I quickly called Mr. Tomita before I left home. Your old homeroom teacher will fly in tomorrow morning and help us."

"All the way from Tokyo?"

"Yes. When you transferred to our school, he specifically requested me to notify him at once when something happened to you."

"And he said he would come here tomorrow?"

"Yes. He says he's got a reservation for an early-morning flight. He seems to be a really dedicated and conscientious teacher. He and I just had a quick conversation, and he sounded like a really nice guy."

***

The next day, Mishima was taken to the local police station. The police officers were professional enough to make a special arrangement so that the junior-high student would not have to meet his stepfather face-to-face, although Taro actually did not mind confronting him if it was in the presence of police officers. He just needed to make sure that the police would lock him up behind bars for a long enough time.

In fact, when Taro met his stepfather at the jail several weeks later, Mishima, beaten and haggard, looked straight into his face and winked at him in a subtle way, hinting that he should say something in his defense. By doing so, he implied that Taro would, otherwise, have to face the consequences. However, the convenience store manager helped Taro explain the situation to the investigators in a precise and straightforward way, adding how terrible the injuries looked in his eyes even a few days after the violent incident. He stated that the teenager's physical condition evidenced a case of serious physical abuse. Tomita and Yamada collaborated in describing the history of the family problems in chronological order. Mishima was arrested and indicted on charges of battery and parental negligence—this time, without his wife's testimony either for or against him. Reporters for newspapers and magazines competed to disclose Mishima's hideous conduct and doomed him as an outcast for the rest of his life. The man who had taken advantage of a helpless widow and physically and mentally abused her innocent children was now branded as an incorrigible criminal, broadcast across the country. Akiko was also charged with being an accessory to his domestic violence but was placed on probation. Taro hoped that his mother would never have to go to prison but, at the same time, believed it was time for her to learn and change. It is always better than never.

***

After he settled into his life at the foster home with his younger brother and sister, he paid homage to his grandfather's grave.

"Grandpa, I stuck it out and got him locked behind bars. You were always the main pillar of the house, and you are still here with us."

The Owner of a Castle

It was almost twelve noon; the bright sunshine filtered through the white curtains and woke up the occupant of Room 709. He groggily rose to his feet, trying to shake off his hangover, and made his way to the water closet. The man was a professional singer. The Oyama Grand Hotel, where he was staying, was larger and ranked higher than the other hotels and *ryokans* in the neighborhood, but it was by no means comparable to the topnotch hotels where he used to stay ten years earlier. His room was a three-to-ten-meter single room, and the cubicle that contained a shower, a toilet, and a washbasin threatened to close in on him. Then, when he looked into the mirror, the image of a pathetic middle-aged man's face, wrinkled and chapped, looked back at him with a sad expression. His hair had become noticeably grayer and thinner in the past few years, and without his stage makeup, he looked much older than he was. Up until three or four years before, he had been able to hide the traces of aging by using expensive male cosmetics and made himself look ten years younger. Now, such camouflage no longer works. He just had to accept his position as an old, forgotten *idol*, who could never retrieve his past fame and glory.

Masumi Takeshita, fifty-five, publicly known as Ken Togo, was a former star singer. Soon after his debut at age eighteen, he started appearing on major TV shows every day and, in a few months, rose to stardom like a legendary dragon soaring up to the heavens. He had a resonant, characteristic voice and an extremely handsome face that attracted young women. From the very beginning, TV-show producers and theatrical agents had predicted that he would be a billion-dollar idol, and he did. Before debuting, he had never trained as an opera singer or received formal music training at a music university but was endowed with a combination of particular qualities required of a *TV singer*. Handsome and perfectly fit for the latest fashion, he imparted an image of what Japanese girls dreamed of as an ideal boyfriend or future husband. His manager invested a billion yen and hired gifted composers and songwriters to write perfect songs for him. As a result, each song he sang turned into a million-seller product, and he won one big award after another. At the prime of his career, Ken Togo was literally a household name, whether or not they found his singing to their taste.

Soon after his debut as a singer, Ken started acting as well. TV companies offered him a major part in one weekly drama after another because the audience rating was sure to rise when women knew Ken Togo appeared in it. After all, the producers were not working for an Academy Award; they just needed to produce episodes on a weekly basis to meet the deadlines. Gifts and techniques of a Dustin Hoffman were not required. Then, when Togo traveled to different locations, he was hounded by reporters, and young female fans flocked to the hotel where he was staying or the airport where he arrived, hoping for an autograph or a glimpse.

As is the case with many TV singers and actors, Masumi's, or Ken Togo's, private life was not sound and stable. He married and divorced two actresses and one singer and had a total of three children by two of his marriages. All the children now lived with their respective mothers.

He sent alimony and maintenance to raise and educate the children, but he had never been in regular contact with them. He had a certain attachment to his children, but after all, he had no enthusiasm for raising his biological successors with his own hands. Recently, he had hardly kept track of each child's age, preoccupied with his pursuit of a new girlfriend.

Now that this former superstar was way past the prime of his career, his engagements with TV companies or major theaters were scarce, and in order to support himself, he needed to travel to remote prefectures and hold dinner shows at local hotel restaurants. The audience was mostly middle-aged people. He would sing old popular tunes, flash big smiles, and shake hands with people who attended the restaurant recitals either because they were his old-time fans or because there were no major entertainment shows in rural areas. Truly gifted singers would coach younger singers or write songs for others. However, Masumi, who could not read music notes, had no such responsibilities.

Masumi noticed a few specks of rouge on his face—evidence of his flirting with hostesses at a local bar. He took a quick shower and shampooed and dyed his hair. When he stepped out of the claustrophobia-inducing bathroom and turned on TV, a big breaking news was on the screen: Taki, a Major League baseball player, had decided to retire at age thirty-nine. He had been the number-one home-run hitter for the Yomiuri Giants and later transferred to the New York Yankees in the United States. He had then played for several American teams and set a number of national and international baseball records during his twenty-year career. He was truly a national hero for all

Japanese: young and old, men and women, athletes and non-athletes. At the press conference, Taki, with a little moisture in his eyes, proclaimed that he had reached his limits as an active baseball player and was no longer offered a position by any major baseball team. A newscaster on the TV screen praised his past accomplishments over and over again and expressed his regrets at his "early retirement." Masumi was not sorry for the retiring baseball star, though; instead, he was just envious. A man like Taki, who had left an indelible mark on the Japanese and American baseball histories, would be remembered forever and would have a number of job offers as a baseball-team head coach or a TV commentator after his retirement as an athlete.

Masumi's dinner show was scheduled for 6:00 p.m. at the main restaurant of the Oyama Grand Hotel. A quick rehearsal with the staff and the restaurant owner would be held at 5:00 p.m. When he was a star, a "rehearsal" took hours—or days or weeks—but now, he only needed to talk with the manager and the restaurant owner and decide where on the small stage he would sit or stand and how many songs he would sing. He did not bother to practice singing before his performance as he did not need to aim for perfection. The task of singing in front of a small audience of eighty people was easy and relaxing. On the other hand, it was not a thrilling engagement for a professional singer, either.

The singer rode an elevator down to the first floor and went to the hotel's main restaurant for his lunch. He handed his meal ticket to one of the waitresses at the entrance.

"Are you by yourself, sir, or are you expecting some people to join you?" the waitress asked in a polite but businesslike tone.

"Just me." His manager, who had accompanied him to the bar the last night, had a different engagement in the morning and was out of the hotel at the time.

"Follow me, please." She showed him to a table by the window and seated him, but during that time, she never showed any special interest in his presence. Her reaction was quite different from the bar hostesses who had offered flattering words to him. But after all, while hostesses earned money by entertaining customers, waitresses were just required to serve meals and drinks. Later in the day, the same restaurant would be the venue for his recital, but the young waitress did not even seem to recognize him as the singer. In her eyes, he was just a middle-aged guest staying at the hotel. The absence of recognition hurt, disappointed, and depressed the former star. Another possibility—which would be more depressing—was that she recognized him but pitied him as a *former* TV singer who had been degraded to his present position as a traveling performer. She might have considered it impolite to recognize him and, therefore, pretended not to be aware of his identity.

The meal was soon delivered to his table by another waitress who did not recognize him as a singer, either. Masumi finished the tasteless hamburger steak—a special lunch provided for the meal ticket—gulped down his coffee, and stepped out of the restaurant. He had hardly been in the restaurant for fifteen minutes when he fled from the hotel and headed out for an aimless walk outside. With almost five hours to kill before his engagement, he started wandering in the neighborhood.

As it happened, the hotel, or the venue for his show, was in his home prefecture, which was why his manager could easily set up the event for him. But Masumi's memory of that particular neighborhood was somewhat vague. It was five kilometers away from where he had been born and raised, and a number of new buildings had been built after he moved to Tokyo thirty-seven years before. But he clearly remembered his first visit to the area on an elementary school excursion and the Oyama Castle that he had first seen then. The five-tier castle, which had been built by a feudal lord three hundred years before, served as a major landmark in the area, but elementary pupils who lived in towns and villages several kilometers away could not go there by themselves. Unconsciously, Masumi was walking toward the castle, and after a few minutes of walk from the hotel, he found it looming in the distance.

"Oh, there it is!" His mood was brightened for the first time since morning, and he trotted toward the magnificent historical monument.

However, when the singer reached the park in which the castle stood, a sign at the gate indicated that the castle was closed that day for repair work. As he had been hoping to go up to the observation deck on the top floor, it was a big disappointment. He could not even enter the inner compound surrounded by the fence, so he walked along the moat around the castle and appreciated the castle tower from outside. After walking around the entire compound, he found a spot where he had a magnificent view of the castle. There was even a nice observation platform that jutted out above the moat.

The short flight of stone steps led to the platform situated at a level about a meter lower than the pavement. There was a bench on that platform, and visitors could sit on it, facing the castle across the moat with their back turned against the face of the cliff side. When Masumi descended to the deck and sat down, he had an almost perfect view of the castle tower except that he could not see the frontal part of the fifth, or top, floor because of the angle at which he was looking up. Although not perfect, it seemed to be the best place to sit and appreciate his favorite castle from outside.

Masumi looked back on his first visit to the castle as an elementary school pupil. Small Masumi had been fascinated by its beauty and air of authority. The teacher, who had chaperoned him and his classmates, took them to the top floor, which commanded a magnificent view of the entire neighborhood. Masumi had never been keen on studies, but he listened intently to his teacher's explanations about the history of the castle and the feudal lord's family. During that field trip, he dreamed of becoming a person who would occupy the top floor of the towering castle, overlooking all the scenery and activities in his territory. It was then that young Masumi had first held an ambition of conquering the world. In fact, he later found himself on top of the world by becoming a star singer but, in retrospect, could not help admitting that his professional accomplishment was quite ephemeral. The status that he had attained as a young singer now seemed like an imaginary castle, compared to the solid five-tier castle that had lasted for centuries.

As a small boy, he had really been fascinated by the castle. When he grew a little older and entered junior high school, he found every opportunity to bike to the castle, which did not charge any admission in those days, and climbed up to the top floor. "I'll just run to the castle," young Masumi would say to his mother, mount his bike, and head out for his favorite place for pastime.

His mother saw him off with a smile, saying, "You are really obsessed, Masumi." Now, both she and his father are gone. He was an only child, and he had hardly been in touch with the relatives. At age fifty-five, he could not help feeling that the castle was the only link between him and his homeland.

The singer took out a cigarette and noticed that he had not brought his Dunhill lighter. When he was wondering what to do, a middle-aged man with a bamboo broom in his hand walked past the observation platform. Masum's peripheral vision caught the man when looking right and left for help; the man noticed him when he was a few steps past the observation deck. Although the deck was on the outer side of the moat, it was still part of the castle park. The man who wore a gray work suit seemed like a maintenance or janitorial worker for the park and was probably responsible for that area, too. Their eyes met. At first, the man regarded the unfamiliar visitor with a mixture of curiosity and slight suspicion, but he soon recognized Masumi's problem, came down to the platform, and offered to light his cigarette, using a one-hundred-yen disposable lighter. He labored to light it, pressing the button several times. Obviously, there was not much kerosene left in his plastic lighter, but a thin flame burst after several clicks.

"Thank you. I appreciate it," Masumi said and inhaled deeply on his cigarette.

The man was of an average height and had no characteristic physical features. The name Oyama was stitched on the breast pocket of his jacket. Without being invited, he put down his bamboo broom and sat next to the visitor on the bench. "Are you from out of town?"

"Yes," Masumi answered with a crisp Tokyo accent. Although the man's expression was rather stern, compared to show-business people who were in the habit of flashing a broad smile at everybody, the singer could see at once that he was a kind and friendly person who would go out of his way to help others. His good-natured and unsophisticated expression suggested that he was not the type to expect any return favor.

"From Tokyo?"

"Y-yes. But when I was small, I lived in Heiwamachi and visited this castle on a school excursion."

"Hmm. Our paths might have crossed somewhere. It's only twenty or thirty minutes by bike."

"Right."

"I guess the school districts were different, though. You went to Heiwamachi Elementary School, didn't you?"

"Yes."

"I went to Oyama Elementary School."

"Have you been living and working in this neighborhood all the time?"

"Yes, I'm a maintenance worker for the municipal government, which has jurisdiction over the castle."

Masumi realized that he and the man were about the same age. At first, he had thought the man was much older than him partly because of his work clothes and dark skin. The uniform work suit designed for gardeners and repairmen imparted the image of an old man who volunteered to do gardening or repair work after retirement. But looking closely, he was obviously in his mid-fifties. His face was tanned and freckled obviously because of hours of exposure to sunshine that his outdoor work entailed, but his hair was much darker than Masumi's, that is, on the assumption that it was not dyed.

In front of the bench was a metal ashtray in the form of a cylinder—a piece of common equipment in public places. The maintenance man dragged it a little closer toward the visitor.

"Please use this."

"I will, and thanks." The singer flicked the cigarette ash into the metal ashtray. "I know you've cleaned up around here, and I won't scatter ashes around."

The maintenance man smiled. He took out a cigarette himself from his breast pocket and lit it with his disposable lighter.

"You like this castle?"

"Oh, I adore it. It really fascinated me when I first saw it as a small child. The castle tower looked like a symbol of power and glory. Looking at it, I couldn't help thinking of myself as the *daimyo* who ruled the entire county." The next moment, Masumi was a little afraid how his slightly exaggerated expression might have been accepted. As a showbusiness man, he admitted that his habit of using rhetorical phrases was hard to kick.

"I like it very much myself." The maintenance man concurred with his comment, his face beaming with pride. "Not a bad thing for a small city of this size, is it?"

"Right!" The singer was a little amused because the maintenance man talked as if a compliment had been given to his own real estate.

"It's a five-tier castle built by Lord Mitsutoshi Oyama in June 1710. Before that, the older castle was located about three kilometers to the south—just beyond the Kappa Bridge, but they decided to build a larger and taller one in this area."

"Hmm."

"There were no mountains or hills around, and it kept enemy warriors from launching a sneak attack. Naturally, the master of the castle had a moat dug around the castle to deter the enemy infantry's intrusion. The construction cost about a billion yen in today's money, but Lord Oyama could afford it because he'd been promoted to a million-*koku* daimyo the previous year."

Masumi was impressed with his fluent delivery of information. He sounded like a professional guide, not a janitor or maintenance man. Masumi's primary school teacher had not provided such detailed information. But after all, it was not surprising for a man who had been born and raised in the area to be versed in the history of his own township and its historic attractions regardless of his educational or professional backgrounds.

"The Oyamas and their relatives owned approximately one hundred acres of land around the castle. He let his relatives and high-ranking subordinates live there."

"That makes sense. A wise arrangement for defense purposes!"

"Exactly. Hey, did you see this?" He twisted his body, leaned backward, and pointed to a square cement cover on part of the cliff side right behind the bench.

"Oh," Masumi had never noticed it when he sat on the bench.

"Do you know what it is?"

"I have no idea."

The man stood and moved around to the small space behind the bench. Then, he extended his hands, twisted the cement plate off, and revealed a ring made of cement-like material. It looked like the end of a large concrete pipe, about one and a half meters in diameter.

"What is that?"

"Lord Oyama made three secret escape tunnels just in case the castle was surrounded by the enemy. This is one of them."

"Hmm."

"The tunnel has been filled in with concrete, but in those days, there was a trap door here, hidden by plants and grass. This platform looks like an ordinary observation deck so that nobody suspects there's a secret exit here."

"Uh-huh! I'm familiar with the attrition strategy that an invading army uses! And an escape tunnel is an effective countermeasure against the enemy's attempt to starve the castle residents into surrendering." Masumi remembered some samurai stories.

"Yes. But your elementary school teacher didn't tell you about the tunnels, did he?"

"No, he didn't."

"As a matter of fact, very few locals know about it."

"What was the tunnel made of?"

"The exit part was made of powered rock mixed with special clay. The rest of the long tunnel was shored up with wood."

"Wow! It must have been a lot of work for tunnel diggers."

"I'll bet it was. It's a shame that the city government filled in the tunnels."

"Why did they do that?"

"Well, the tunnels tended to cave in here and there as it was neglected for a long time. It was eroded by the underground water and pressure from above. And the city found no reason to spend money to restore it."

"It's too bad that you lost such a great part of historical heritage."

"And of course, they were afraid that small children might play inside and get caved in."

"Yeah, I can understand that. Hey, it looks like you know a lot about the castle. I'm impressed."

He nodded with a smile of satisfaction at the visitor's compliment.

"And you still live in this area?"

"Yes, my apartment is right around the corner. Our family has been here for generations."

"Is that so?"

"Yes." The maintenance man paused for a second, hesitating to add some information about his residence, but he shifted the focus of conversation to the visitor's concern. "What brings you to this town?"

"I have a small business engagement in this town tonight. I arrived last night, and I just thought I wanted to visit my favorite castle again using my free time."

The man's expression did not change at once, but a few seconds later, his face registered a sign of recognition.

"So you are Ken Togo—the star singer?"

"A former star singer, at the best," Masumi corrected it, giving a wry smile.

"Well, your debut made a big sensation. Everybody in this town was talking about you. They proudly said to their friends and acquaintances, 'Ken Togo is from Heiwamachi, which is pretty close to my home,' you know?"

The past tense that the man used bothered the former star singer a little, but he was happy to know that someone still remembered him. "Thank you for your kind words, but I wonder if they still remember someone like me."

"Of course, they do. My cousin—she is two years younger—is a great fan of you. She's still listening to your songs all the time. And now, she says there's going to be a dinner show at the Grand Hotel."

"That's what I'm going to do tonight."

"She said she was going to be there. She'd been looking forward to the show for months."

"I'm delighted that someone still likes my songs."

"She has a complete selection of your CDs."

"I'm flattered. Uh, are you coming yourself?" Masumi asked half jocularly, aware that the addressee clearly was not planning to do so.

"I wish I could, but I just cannot afford it."

"Sorry about the expensive tickets."

"Don't apologize about the pricing. It's just my problem. I know the show is good and worth a lot of money, but as a park maintenance man, I just don't have enough money to dine at a hotel restaurant or attend a recital."

There was a brief silence as Masumi did not come up with an apt response at once. Then, the maintenance man brought up a new topic. "You know something?"

"What?"

"We used to live there."

"Where?"

"On the inner side of the moat," he pointed his finger at the castle.

"What?"

"My great, great, great, great, great-grandfather was Mitsutoshi Oyama himself. He built this castle." Masumi was stunned speechless.

"Is that right?"

"Yes, but in the course of time, the family lost its power and riches, and a few generations down, the castle was taken over. And look where I am now. I don't even own a small house. I rent a small apartment, struggling to pay the rent out of my small salary."

Suddenly, Oyama, the name stitched on his breast pocket, glared. It was common for many people in the same area to share the same family name. Masumi had never suspected that the maintenance man who offered to light his cigarette was related, in any remote way, to the daimyo who had built the castle towering in front of him. He was astonished by the revealed fact. On the other hand, being in the cutthroat world of show business, he understood better than anybody else that successful people could easily encounter an unexpected obstacle in life and lose everything or let their conceit or lack of self-discipline drive them to self-destruction. He knew many popular singers and actors who had had a sad ending. His own status had been downgraded considerably, but some of his former colleagues had really perished. It could happen within an individual person's life and career, and it was more likely to occur to a family or group of people over generations. For a brief second, the former star tried to imagine what the glory and decline of a daimyo family might have been like, looking at the castle with a different frame of mind.

"I'm sorry that your family has lost the castle."

"Well, there's no helping it. It's just the law of the universe, I guess. Properties are to change hands in the course of time, and old tough soldiers' rationale tends to be lost over generations."

"Were the Oyama samurais strong?"

"Yes, Mitsutoshi Oyama was an expert swordsman himself—and a great commander—and he encouraged his followers to engage in regular martial arts training. The army was strong, and he had financial resources, too. With the fertile soil, they produced high-quality rice. And as water was clean, breweries became the second industry. Citizens in general were all disciplined and high-spirited, and the central commercial center, right here, was extremely prosperous. Visitors and traders from remote areas kept coming."

"So I have heard. Well, even if you no longer own the castle, you must be really proud of the legacy that your ancestors left."

The maintenance man cast his head down for a second but soon looked up and turned back to the singer. "Yes, I'm proud of my ancestors," he said with a smile. "The stories of those prosperous days have been handed down through generations, and yes, I've always been proud of my family history. And at least, we know where we are from."

But, of course, no one can sit on his laurel and be on top of the world for a long time, Masumi thought. Likewise, it was difficult for anybody in modern society to keep a reasonably good social or economic position, whether he was a businessman or a professional entertainer. He could not help comparing his own downfall to the story of a daimyo family.

"Mitsutoshi reigned for twenty years," Oyama continued, "but when his son Matayoshi succeeded, the economy went bad, and he had no expertise or wisdom to restructure the governmental system. As they say, the second generations didn't have the ability or determination to keep up what their fathers had left. Matayoshi was no exception. He lacked a perspective, too, and never learned to cope with difficult situations. He hired sons of his father's followers who kept flattering him. He shouldn't have done that, you know. He should've gathered information for his own army and business projects and recruited really capable people. Then, Katsuyoshi, the third generation, ruined the entire heritage. He indulged in heavy drinking and frittered money away on concubines. The morale of soldiers declined, and the army was no longer strong. When an enemy from the east was encroaching on the territory, he didn't take appropriate measures in time to deter the advancement. And when a war was declared, he ended up yielding the castle without having an all-out war. It was the most humiliating defeat for a feudal lord, but Katsuyoshi probably didn't even care. He just didn't have the guts to fight."

"I see." Masumi had played the role of a young daimyo in a samurai drama when he was young and popular. "All in the universe continues to change. Objects are to be broken, and the living ceases to breathe."

"Here you go!" Oyama appreciated the rhetorical expressions, not offended. "Now, here I am, several generations down. I don't even have a decent house or apartment of my own. And my job is to clean up the park around the castle, picking up the trash and cigarette butts that visitors leave." He looked a little sad for a brief moment but, then, laughed it away. "But there's no use crying over the spilt milk or clinging to the past glory."

"I . . . I was just wondering, Mr. Oyama. If the way I put it is inappropriate, please pardon me. But I wonder if you ever wish you'd been born several generations earlier, when your family was at its pinnacle. Do you ever imagine that you own and live in the castle yourself, looking down at the rest of Oyama City from the top of the castle tower?"

"I used to when I was a small boy. But seeing it from a different perspective, I might have been the good-for-nothing Katsuyoshi myself in my earlier lifetime—the prodigal third-generation daimyo who lost all the inherited wealth and real estate."

"Do you believe in reincarnation?"

"In fact, I do, but let's not go into the debate now. The issue is a bit too complicated. One solid fact, though, is that the genes of those daimyos have been passed down to me, though attenuated by a series of intermarriages. One would have to leap what he'd sown—or his ancestors had sown."

"Right," Masumi replied hesitantly. "I guess you're right."

Then, Oyama switched the conversation to his interlocutor's concern again. "If I remember it correctly, your real family name is Takeshita, isn't it?"

"Yes."

"I've heard of the name. My mother told me that a Takeshita family had been here for a long time. They'd first come from a faraway prefecture with a group of traveling performers. After traveling across the country, the troupe came to this town and staged their theatrical events—dancing, singing, and dramas. They were pretty popular with the locals and were asked to stay here long term. Lord Oyama himself invited the troupe to the castle several times and appreciated their performance. A half year later, the troupe finally left town, but your great, great, great, great, great-grandfather married a local girl and settled down. I heard that he started working for a local government or something. But whenever there was a chance, he and his children volunteered to sing and dance at local festivals and entertained people."

Masumi had no way of verifying the authenticity of Oyama's narrative at once, but his story made sense in many ways. Although his position as a star singer was a thing of the past, he admitted that he had been extremely lucky to become rich and famous at one point in his life. His success was indubitably attributable to a combination of certain qualities and conditions, and it was probably not a farfetched speculation that his ancestors' ability to capture audiences' attention had been passed down to him.

"Hmm. I didn't know that."

"Why don't you talk to your parents or grandparents? They might know more about that."

"I will." Although his parents had passed away, his grandfather on his father's side was still alive, living with one of his daughters, not far away from the castle. He had not intended to visit him during the current short trip, but he was beginning to consider a quick stop-by.

"Your ancestors were really gifted. Maybe that's why you made it to the top in show business."

"Perhaps, and I must say, your ancestors who built this magnificent castle were really great, too. And I'm particularly impressed with the idea of escape tunnels."

Their attention turned back to the remains of a tunnel exit behind their back.

"The major and longest tunnel connected the secret basement room to where we are sitting. In cases of emergency, they let women and small children escape through the tunnel."

"A clever tactic!"

"They used the tunnel on the offensive, too. The moat is about ten meters deep—that is, five or six meters below the surface of the water. And the tunnel was quite long, dug at a deep level. But the soldiers were trained to crawl through the tunnel very quickly. While enemy ninjas were trying to swim across the moat and scale the base of the castle made of heavy rocks, Oyama's soldiers got outside and shot arrows at the intruders from behind. The tunnel was fully utilized for defensive and offensive, and that was why this castle was called an impenetrable fort in those days."

"That was in Lord Mitsutoshi's days, wasn't it?"

"Right."

Neither man touched on what might have happened during his sons' and grandsons' periods.

"And this small observation deck had already existed in those days."

"Did it?"

"Yes, the Oyamas' security guards sat on this deck, dressed as common citizens and pretending to be fishing."

"Hmm. That's interesting."

"Different people in different clothes took turns sitting and fishing here."

Masumi tried to imagine how the fishermen might have felt sitting three hundred years before.

"Now, I sometimes fish to kill time myself."

"You do?"

"Yes. You want to try fishing?"

"Y-y-yes, if the gear is available."

Oyama smiled and fetched two fishing poles from a hiding place in the bush.

"Here! How much time do you have before your dinner show?"

It was still two. "About two hours."

"You have enough time. Let's try."

"Okay."

"Do you fish a lot?"

"No. As a matter of fact, I've done it only twice, and I wasn't good at all."

"I'll show you how to catch a fish."

Each of the fishing poles that Oyama had fetched was already fixed with a fishing line, a hook, and a sinker, and he took out a piece of dried squid out of his breast pocket and attached a tiny piece to each hook as bait. The two men cast the fishing lines and waited for the fish to take the bait. Masumi had never caught a fish in his life, but he strangely felt calm and relaxed.

A minute later, something tugged at Oyama's line, and he pulled up a large carp. He showed it to Masumi as a trophy and then tossed it back into the water. He swished the fishing line again and soon caught another large carp. He handled the fishing rod and line like a magician shuffling a deck of cards to perform a card magic. Not surprisingly, Masumi was not so successful, but Oyama taught him a little trick, and the singer soon caught a large carp himself. The first big catch in his life really thrilled him and made him feel as triumphant as when he had won his first major award as a young singer.

Time flew as they enjoyed each other's company, and it was almost time for Masumi to return to the hotel and be ready for the dinner show. The singer could see that the duties of the maintenance man were very flexible. He was allowed to sit and talk or fish with a visitor for hours; he could perhaps catch up on his cleaning and maintenance work afterward. His daily work was uneventful—and not stressful—which was contrasted with the former media idol who had burned out after years of brutal and stressful life in show business.

"Thank you very much for everything, Oyama-san. But I guess I've got to go now."

"Show time, isn't it?"

"Yes. Uh, I think I need to use the bath before heading back to the hotel."

"There's a bathroom right behind us, but I'll show you to the best bathroom of the castle park," Oyama offered. "It's around the next corner, but you'd like it."

They made their way to the place that Oyama had referred to, and there was a two-storied building in the shape of a castle, which Masumi had not noticed when he first arrived and walked around the castle. Closely looked, it turned out to be a scaled-down replica of the Oyama

Castle.

"Hmm! That's interesting."

"It's a crude replica, but it looks like the castle, doesn't it?"

"It certainly does, and I like it."

The first floor was a bathroom, which was spotlessly clean and spacious. After Masumi finished his business, Oyama guided him upstairs to the second floor. The stairs were uniquely made of dark-colored oak, reminiscent of a solid ancient castle. Then, up on the elevated floor, Masumi was astonished at the interior. It was an exact replication of the top floor of Oyama Castle.

"Wow!" The monosyllabic exclamation popped out of the visitor's mouth, expressing his deep impression.

As a great fan of the castle, Masumi accurately remembered the inside of the castle that he had seen as a small child. From rafters supporting the roof to straw mats on the floor to the *tokonoma* alcove, everything seemed like an exact copy of what was inside the top-floor room of the castle. Then, the best part was its observation deck outside the windows, which provided a perfect view of the Oyama Castle itself.

Standing on the deck, he could see the real castle to the west like a mirror image. It was in the late afternoon, and the sun was about to set behind the castle, illuminating the castle in the most aesthetic orange and pink colors. The sight was breathtaking.

"You hit the right time!" Oyama said, reading the visitor's mind.

"This is spectacular! Did the city make this structure for visitors?"

"Yes. This was supposed to be a side attraction."

"Everybody needs to use the bathroom, and I can see that quite a few people would come here and appreciate this structure."

"That's what it's meant for."

"Gee, it's great! I wonder who decorated the interior. He must be a real professional."

"I did."

"Oh, is that right?"

"Yes, the interior is my handmade work. They hired local contractors to put up the pillars and walls very quickly, but it took me an entire year to reconstruct the second-floor interior. The task kind of turned into my hobby."

Masumi was speechless, deeply impressed by the man's abilities and assiduity. What he referred to as his hobby must have required him of a great deal of concentration. Obviously, no expensive timber and materials had been provided; he must have substituted them with plaster and plastic. But every tiny detail was reproduced perfectly. The observation deck alone was made of solid wood, which he seemed to have procured somewhere. Masumi felt quite safe standing on the deck to appreciate the outside scenery. "This is a state-of-the-art bathroom!"

Of course, the creator would never be rewarded or publicly recognized. He had completed the task just for the sake of perfecting his own skills and techniques as a craftsman. Before coming to the park, the former star singer had been quite depressed at his present position as a traveling performer: having to sing at local hotels for money was humiliating. But now, he felt that there was still a lot of room for polishing his own techniques as a singer independently from his status or the limited opportunities.

Oyama guided Masumi down the stairs and saw him off.

"Well, it was great to meet you, Mr. Togo. I hope your recital will be a big success."

"Thank you. It was great talking to you."

"Come back and visit your favorite castle again."

"I definitely will." Masumi meant it. He was also going to rehearse his singing before the dinner show, utilizing the hour that he would normally waste by smoking and chatting with the recital staff.

www.ingramcontent.com/pod-product-compliance
Lightning Source LLC
LaVergne TN
LVHW021232080526
838199LV00088B/4317